DEEP MADNESS

SHATTERED SEAS

By

Byron Leavitt

DIEMENSION GAMES

Inquiries may be addressed to:
Byron Leavitt
byron@diemensiongames.com

Seriously, we'd love to hear from you!

Published by Diemension Games, Inc. To learn more about Diemension Games, visit us at https://diemensiongames.com, or on Facebook at https://www.facebook.com/diemensiongames.

ISBN 13 (Hardcover - English edition): 978-1-953161-00-0
ISBN 13 (Paperback - English edition): 978-1-953161-02-4
ISBN 13 (eBook - English edition): 978-1-953161-01-7

SEQUENCE

This book is dedicated to Roger, Cherry, Chauncey, and Yichuan. Thank you for allowing me to play in your world, and for embracing my madness. I couldn't ask for better colleagues or to be part of a better team.

And this book is also dedicated to you, our backers, believers, fans, and friends. You are the reason we are able to live our dream (even if it is a nightmare) and do the things we love. Thank you for believing in Deep Madness and Diemension Games. I am incredibly grateful for you, and I hope you enjoy this book even half as much as I enjoyed writing it.

INTRO

BRIEFING ALPHA

For Golden Dawn-approved eyes only.

It is with a heavy heart we must report that the Kadath deep-sea mining facility has been destroyed under decidedly suspect circumstances. Following the discovery and retrieval of a singular artifact from a nearby fissure on the ocean floor, communications with Kadath were mysteriously severed. An investigation unit was dispatched to ascertain the cause of the station's silence. Shortly after their arrival, however, the facility was annihilated – presumably taking the team and their findings with it.

However, it has now become evident that the Kadath story did not end with the structure itself. A spatial anomaly has recently been discovered at ground zero, which seems to have begun emitting strange particle waves into the surrounding ocean. All available Leng Corporation and Golden Dawn resources are now being redirected to the study of this singular phenomenon. We appreciate your understanding during this unique situation and expect your complete cooperation as we fully explore this matter. May we all yet bask in the Golden Dawn's glow.

SEETHING WATERS

"Initial scans following the incident at the Kadath facility have proven bewildering, fascinating, and exhilarating. I am convinced we have catalyzed something extraordinary. We are detecting particle waves surging from the anomaly at an unprecedented rate, with no immediate sign of dissipation. If I had to stake an opinion, I would say we may begin to see manifestations from these waves within a matter of weeks."

Phillip Reed – Leng Corp. Specialist

TOWER WORLD

In the depths of the seething sea, pummeled and tossed by blind, capricious currents, the drowning man felt his mind shatter. Or was it the other way around?

The man burst through the ocean surf with a gasp. Saltwater stung his eyes and assaulted his cuts as he flailed in the brine, his hair and clothes adhering like papier mâché to his skin. The man jerked his head from side to side, trying to orient himself as his thoughts slid like chunks of ice amidst angry waves. How was he here? What was happening to him? And where was land?

The man's pupils were dilating and contracting at random, bringing the world in and out of focus. During a lucid moment, though, he thought he could make out a white sand beach in the distance. Forcing his body to move, to comply, he started paddling toward where he hoped the shore would be. His limbs moved spastically, his muscles jittering with spasms. His stomach lurched and rolled within him, but he tried not to focus on it. Or on the streaks of fire arcing through his muscles. Or on the feeling that everything was horribly, monstrously wrong.

It was only a few seconds later that his ears popped, and it was after this that he began to notice the sounds. He heard the waves, of course, as they beat one upon another. But he also perceived something else. It sounded like moans – or maybe wails. And then he heard the roar.

Panic welling within him, the man began to swim as fast as his malfunctioning limbs would take him, desperately willing his body to obey. He so hoped he had seen the shore. The world was still reeling in and out of focus like a punch-drunk wrestler.

Something splashed in the water to his left. It was close. The man forced himself to move faster, kicking his feet as hard as he could.

The water grew warmer, and then the man felt seaweed and anemones brushing against his toes. A smooth, fleshy mass slid across his shin.

The world burst into focus as sand enveloped his fingertips. The man scrambled up onto the shore and whirled around to see what was behind him, falling on the wet beach with a thump. His heart stopped in his chest.

Other people were crawling out of the surf. Or at least they had likely *been* people at one point. A ten-foot-tall man stumbled as he stood up, his arms and legs unnaturally long like taffy that had lost its shape. As he gained his feet, though, his torso bent backward, his hands splashing down into the waves as his body became an inverted human "U." Then his head drooped downward, his mouth elongating further and further until his hair drug in the sand. A guttural sound emerged from the thing's cavernous gash of a mouth that was far from human.

A woman, meanwhile, rose from the waves. As she did, however, her legs dissolved, her shins ripping off at the kneecaps before her thighs disengaged from their sockets. Her waist was the next to go, leaving ropes of intestines trailing out behind her. Even still, she advanced, pulling herself forward on arms that cracked and shifted. Then the crab legs slid out from the depths of her guts, and as she looked back at her new appendages, she screamed.

The man felt his whole body threatening to seize up on him. His mind couldn't process the horrors he was seeing. Perhaps that was why it was some time before he saw the… *thing* rising from the water.

The crown of the creature's head formed a wake on either side as it advanced, its scales slick and gleaming. More of it arose from the ocean as the water grew shallower, and soon its bouquet of black fish eyes could be seen gleaming like clusters of caviar in the sun. Next, its mandibles emerged, churning as they dripped. Then the spines. Then the whipping tendrils.

The man howled. Scrambling to his feet, he forced his limbs to obey him as he ran up the beach for the forest in the distance. His mind had frozen with numbing shock, his heart hammering in abject terror. Behind him, he still heard the shuffling, scuffling, slithering procession of the damned as they made way for the monstrosity that followed.

Scruffy brush first greeted the man, followed by rugged, squat vegetation that clung stubbornly to the ground. Next came long, waving grasses that whipped against his skin as he raced through them, followed by the first thin stragglers of trees that slowly clustered tighter together to form a sparse forest. The man didn't pay heed to any of them. He just ran as if all of hell was seething at his heels.

The forest broke, and the man saw a towering black skyscraper piercing the heavens in the distance. Clouds seemed to be swirling around its apex, but of course, that was impossible. Behind him, the man heard the forest *actually* break.

The man's limbs were obeying him better now than they had been, but the burning stitch in his side and the pulsing fire in his lungs informed him he wouldn't be able to keep his current pace up for much longer. But then the bellowing screech shook the ground below him and rattled his eardrums, and he stopped caring about the discomfort in his body.

The road leading up to the skyscraper was made of red cobblestones rather than pavement. Part of the man recognized that as odd (as were the radial roads that fanned out from the building like spokes on a wheel), but he pushed that observation aside. There wasn't time for anything now but survival.

At last, the man reached the glass front doors of the building and jerked one open. Tumbling inside, he landed on the hard marble tiles within before turning to look for some way to lock or bar the door. Alarmingly, there was nothing at hand but a second set of glass doors. Pulling one of those open, he entered a pristine, elegantly decorated lobby that seemed to span across a big chunk of the skyscraper's width. A waterfall chuckled off to his left, concealing the base of a towering glass elevator shaft. Tables and chairs were carefully arranged around the space to the right before the lobby opened into an even wider walking space. Along the walls were several small closed, dark shops, which might have been cafés or bars. Glancing upward, he saw that the broad central shaft of the skyscraper seemed to rise nearly forever.

"Hello?" the man called, his voice cracking. "Is anyone here?"

There was no reply.

Hurriedly he turned to better scrutinize the doors. There had to be a way to lock them down. No one would design a skyscraper like this without a way to secure it –

"Who are you, priest?"

Something sharp was jabbing into the man's side. He slowly raised his hands.

"There's… something out there," the man said. "Something *monstrous*. We need to lock these doors right now, or we're all going to die. Please, you must believe me!"

"You did not answer my question," the woman said, her voice like cold steel. "So, I will ask you one more time, priest. Who are you?"

The man blinked his eyes. Once. Twice. The question set his mind reeling like a tipsy merry-go-round. *Who was he?* "My name is Connor Durham," he said slowly, the words bobbing to the surface of his consciousness syllable by syllable. "I'm a preacher from Ireland. Do – do you happen to know where we are?"

"You awoke in the ocean?" the woman said.

"Yes," Connor said. "Yes! I bloody well woke up in the ocean!" He found that words were flowing easier now. More like they belonged to him, and he knew how they functioned. "Now, can we *please* get this door sealed before we both die!"

The blade retracted from Connor's back. "The door is

immaterial. Follow me. Quickly."

Turning around, Connor saw a lean Asian woman darting away from him, hugging the lobby's wall. With one more tense, uncertain glance back at the doors, Connor followed her.

The woman wound through the shadows and then darted behind a counter. There was a door there, which she now opened after a final quick scan of the lobby. Connor followed her through the doorway, mimicking her look uneasily before closing the entry behind him.

They were in a corridor now with cherry wood walls and warm ambient lighting. Connor noticed soft jazzy music playing through what he assumed were carefully concealed speakers. He frowned. Something about this hallway seemed off.

"Shouldn't this be a staff room?" he said. "It feels like this is a guest hall."

The woman stole a look back at him. "The ways change from time to time. This one is here now." Then she stopped in front of a door with a room number on it. Looking back and forth, she opened it and stepped through. Connor followed her – and found himself in another hallway.

"What in the bloody hell?" he said.

"This way, priest," she said. "Before it changes again."

They moved deeper into the labyrinthine hotel until, at last, the lady stopped again. Opening another door, they entered the room beyond. It was a dimly lit space, probably a little larger than a typical suite. There were candles arrayed on various surfaces, and an Asian man sitting cross-legged on the floor.

The Asian man's face was round, his physique not quite as fit as the woman's but also not overweight. His head was shaved, and it almost seemed he had the robes of a Buddhist monk on underneath the black tactical gear which covered most of his body.

Connor thought he might have been Chinese. There was a stillness to him that the woman lacked, and maybe a warmness, too.

"You're just in time, Mitsuko," the man said, looking up at them. "The ways were about to change again. Who is our guest?"

"His name is Connor," the woman, Mitsuko, said. "He was about to get himself killed." Connor took a second to look her over now, too. She was taller than many Asian women, her black hair pulled back into a ponytail, and she was clothed in tactical gear similar to the man's outfit. Over her back was slung a sheathed sword, and mounted to her hip was a machete. Her attractive, thin face made him think she could be Japanese.

"Ah," the man said, rising. He bowed to Connor, then extended his hand. "Welcome, Connor. I am Wang Min. Or, in your Western cultures, I suppose it would be Min Wang."

Connor stared at the hand, momentarily confused. Then he reached out and clasped it. "Connor Durham," Connor replied, shaking Min's hand. He turned to Mitsuko. "Thank you for not letting me get myself killed then," he said to her.

The woman nodded. "You're welcome," she said.

"This is Mitsuko Takenaka," Min said. "She's not always the most talkative soul. Or the most trusting, at least to start."

Connor tried a smile, remembering that was something people did. But then he recalled the monsters, and his smile faded. "There are creatures outside," he said. "We're not safe here. We need to do something."

"You are quite right, we're not safe here," Min said. "Quite right. But the beasts you saw are not our only threat."

"Where on earth *are* we?" Connor asked. "What the *hell* is going on?"

"I fear you have them reversed," Min said. "We have somehow been brought to and trapped in this place, Connor. I have not ascertained where 'here' is yet, but whatever happened has undoubtedly eviscerated the standard laws of nature. Biology, physics, life, death, all that we know has been turned on its head."

A cold, unwelcome tingle shivered down Connor's back. He remembered the abominations changing as they rose from the surf and how his body had felt elastic in the ocean. Could he have become like them? "That's madness," Connor murmured.

"Precisely so," Min said. "Welcome, Mr. Durham, to the very depths of madness."

TWO

INTO THE DEEP

"We are pursuing a new avenue of experimentation. Harnessing energy patterns from the anomaly, we have started integration directly with the bodies of human hosts. While naturally occurring mutations have been recorded even at great distances, the effects on the hosts when in immediate, unprotected proximity to the waves have proven staggering."
Dr. Jayce Norton

KADATH FACILITY

There are flames. Everywhere.

A siren screams outside along with the shriek of steel clashing on steel and the tremor of a collision. The building buckles around you like it's been kicked in the shins. You strain toward her, fingers groping – why can't you reach her?

With a deep inhalation of breath, Lucas Kane wrenched awake.

Sitting straight up in bed, he snapped his gaze back and forth. The room was cold. Sterile. No flames anywhere.

Wiping the sweat from his thin, chiseled face and tousling his matted black hair, Lucas swung his feet off the bed and onto the floor. He wouldn't be getting any more sleep tonight. Might as well do something productive.

Lucas got dressed, his fingers shaking as he buttoned his shirt and pulled on a pair of pants. Shuffling into the spartan bathroom, he tried to make himself look slightly less like a half–dead vagrant in the mirror. No matter what he did to his hair or how much water he splashed on his pale skin, though, nothing could lessen the haggard, haunted look in his sea-blue eyes. Finally, Lucas gave up. Slapping on his wrist unit and inserting his node, he tapped the hatch control and stepped out into the corridor beyond.

During the day, there was barely a skeleton crew roaming Kadath's corridors, so at night the station was practically the underwater equivalent of a ghost town. Lucas walked alone through the silence, trying to suppress the chatter of his thoughts. Perhaps it was fate that led him to the observation gallery. Maybe it was luck or a tug on his subconscious. Regardless, he found himself sinking into a seat dead-center in front of the room's sweeping viewport.

The gallery wasn't very deep or exceptionally tall, but it was certainly long. Benches lined its front while tables and chairs dotted its back, a low, muted illumination rising from the floor to provide just enough light for you to see where you were stepping. The viewport itself ran the entire length of the room, offering what felt like a nearly panoramic view of the abyss beyond it.

Lucas stared out at the limitless ocean depths. Floodlights bathed the deep in a muddled glow, the murky illumination sifting through the currents and fending off the near-consuming dark.

Some could find the constant gloom oppressive, like living in a sunless bubble. But Lucas found it comforting. Soothing. Out there lived the greatest wonders in the world. Beyond the reinforced composite mere feet from his face sprawled a landscape as alien as any foreign planet, teeming with the most incredible lifeforms on Earth. Perhaps he would see some of them if he sat here long enough. He had noticed several creatures flit by in the past, attracted by the light from the lamps. Amazing things sometimes happened if you waited.

"Couldn't sleep either, huh?" a voice said behind Lucas.

Lucas looked back to see a gaunt, hollow-eyed man standing in the hatchway, his lean, unkempt body casting a stick-figure shadow across the gallery's floor. Lucas tried to smile politely at the man, but looking at him was just too eerily like staring in a mirror. "Not tonight, I guess," Lucas said. "Lucas Kane. Marine biologist."

"Marine biologist?" the man said. "I thought you scientist types would be coming later. When the facility was officially open."

Lucas shrugged. "I'm here early to cover the requirements for the Ocean Conservation and Endangerment Act. Even on a secretive project like this one, they wanted to make sure they had someone to blame if something hits the fan."

The man chuckled. "In that case, I'm surprised we haven't met each other sooner, fall guy. I'm Edgar Kayce, lead engineer for Kadath. My team built this place."

"Nice to meet you, Edgar," Lucas said, extending his hand as he stood. Edgar shook it. "Want to sit for a while?"

"Might as well," Edgar said. "What *else* am I going to do tonight?"

Lucas laughed humorlessly. Edgar sat down beside him, and together they stared into the sea. "I have to commend you," Lucas said after a while. "This station is truly extraordinary. I've never seen anything quite like it."

"It came with a great deal of blood, sweat, and tears." Edgar shrugged, then looked down at his hands. "So. What're *your* demons?"

Lucas frowned. "What do you mean?"

"What's keeping you awake at night?" Edgar asked. "Is it this place?"

"No. No, not that," Lucas said. "Just… nightmares, I guess. How about you?"

"I suppose I've been down here too long," Edgar replied. Then something caught his eye, and he jerked in his seat. "Whoa! What was *that!* Did you *see* it?"

"See what?" Lucas asked. And that's when he did.

The creature swept past the window, its massive body streaking through the tepid beams of the exterior lights. Lucas sat bolt upright in his seat, his breath freezing in his chest. It was… *gargantuan.* The beast looked a bit like a giant or even a colossal squid, but it couldn't be. It was too different. Too… *scary.*

Lucas bolted from his chair and pressed himself against the observation window. He strained his eyes to peer into the dark water, hoping for another glimpse of the creature.

"What *was* that thing?" Edgar exclaimed.

"Beautiful," Lucas replied. He kept staring out, trying to will the lithe predator to come back. It didn't. At last, Lucas looked back at Edgar. "Did any of your teams ever report seeing something like that during construction?"

"No," Edgar said. "We saw some strange stuff, sure. But never anything like *that.*"

"Have you heard if the surveillance monitoring is up and running yet?" Lucas asked.

"I think they just got the bugs worked out of it a few days ago,"

Edgar said. "It should be operational now."

Lucas nodded. "I've got to check this out. Maybe my night won't be a complete waste, after all. It was great to meet you, Edgar."

"Same to you, Lucas," Edgar said. "Hope your dreams improve."

Lucas smiled. This time it was genuine. "You, too."

Lucas stepped into Kadath's control center and looked around. The place was eerily quiet. Many of the rounded room's screens and consoles lounged dark and dormant, its various stations abandoned. Only a few operators still labored at their posts, their hands swiping across controls as they scanned through the facility's feeds.

Lucas advanced toward the nearest person. "Hi there," he said. "I'm Lucas Kane, the marine biologist overseeing the OCEA requirements. Can you tell me if we have surveillance up on the outer perimeter yet?"

"Let me check," the woman said. As she worked, Lucas couldn't help noticing how she lit up the drab control center. She seemed effervescent, with blonde hair that didn't quite reach her shoulders and eyes that sparked with green fire even in the middle of the night. "I think it initialized yesterday… Yes. It looks like I have access to several channels. What are you looking for?"

Lucas's lip quirked upward. "A sea monster," he said.

Lucas sat in his spacious laboratory and ran the holographic images through his fingers. The renders of the beast were good, even if they lacked some details. But there was enough to show him what he had thought upon first seeing the creature: while it had similarities to the giant and colossal squids, this was something that no one had seen before. It looked nasty. Vicious. This thing was unquestionably an apex predator par excellence.

Spinning the render in the air, Lucas expanded it to examine the thing's thick talons, barbs, and what almost appeared to be a chitinous substance. Its eyes were different from a typical squid's, too. The pupils weren't circular, but more like a ragged 'w' made by a dull knife. Perhaps this was closer to a cuttlefish than a giant squid? But even *that* wouldn't explain everything. It was almost more like a mythological beast than any known species. *A kraken.*

Regardless, there was no doubt in Lucas's mind that he had just discovered a new species. This find was *huge*: the sort of thing that scientists dreamed about at night. This creature could put his name in the history books.

A whisper tickled the backs of Lucas's ears, the words an unintelligible murmur. Lucas jerked with a yelp and spun around. What the hell?

The hairs on his body were standing on end as Lucas stood, surveying the laboratory. He had felt the voice's breath on his neck. It had been *right there.* "Hello?" he said. "Is someone here?"

But, of course, no one was. Lucas was utterly alone.

Shaking his head, Lucas swiveled back around. It had to be the lack of sleep catching up to him. There was no other explanation.

Lucas returned his focus to the renders of the kraken. What if he could find it again? Get up close to it and see what made it tick? Would he dare?

Lucas nearly laughed. What a ridiculous question. *Of course,* he would.

More people were arriving in Kadath every week. With their advent came a new flood of excitement as the hustle and bustle increased, and the corridors began to fill with throngs of enthusiastic personnel. There were times when Lucas missed the relative quiet of his early days in the facility, but there was also something energizing about the influx. It was like things were genuinely about to get moving.

The day had finally come for Kadath to be declared fully operational. A grand ceremony had been in the works for some time, and now Lucas found himself milling with the other new residents of Kadath in Dome Two's second level. The place served as the facility's recreational area, and it was a work of art in nearly every sense of the word. It had been explicitly designed to relieve people's homesickness, offer visual and artistic flourishes, and provide a locale both for people to mingle and to spend their pay. It had quickly become one of Lucas's favorite places in Kadath, apart from the observation galleries and his lab. They called it the promenade.

A stage had been erected in the middle of the promenade, bedecked in broad, colorful swaths of banners and ribbons. It had a decidedly old-fashioned aesthetic, as did its surroundings. A band made up of fresh Kadath residents was playing passably enough on it, and, when their set finished, they exited the stage to make way for a trim, sharp blonde woman whose hair was wrapped fastidiously into a bun.

The woman unleashed a dazzling smile. "Welcome, residents of Kadath! Some of you have just arrived, and some of you are responsible for bringing this wonder of human ingenuity into existence – to whom we all owe our deepest gratitude and admiration. Yes, that's right, let's give them a round of applause!

"My name is Judy Blake. Many of you have likely met me already, but just in case you haven't, I am the station liaison for Kadath. I could ramble on for ages about the glorious future in store for this place, for us, and humanity in general. But today, I'm just here to introduce the man who will guide us into this bold new tomorrow. He is a person of strength, integrity, and nearly limitless vision. I am lucky enough to call him both my friend and mentor. Will you please put your hands together for Station Commander Terrence Wade!"

The residents applauded as Judy stepped aside, and Terrence Wade ascended the stage to the antique-styled microphone. His movements were like his uniform: sharp and precise. His black hair, similarly, was immaculately kempt, his face and gaze both a bit like a hawk's. Clearing his throat, he offered a measured smile to the gathered masses.

"Once in a great while, a person genuinely gets a chance to make a difference in the world," Wade said. "To leave a mark in his or her generation, and to tangibly impact humanity's course. Many on the surface wouldn't understand why a mining facility of *any* kind – even a cutting-edge one at the bottom of the ocean – could conceivably aspire to make such strides into the future. Perhaps you might even feel that yourself, to one degree or another. But this facility will not just be a mining operation: It will serve as a hotbed of scientific progress. It will offer a bold new model for oceanic colonization. It will even point toward advancements in interplanetary exploration. And, perhaps, it could ultimately lead to improvements for the entire human condition."

"He certainly has a healthy ego," the woman standing beside Lucas whispered to him. Chuckling, Lucas glanced over at her.

"So, you're saying you *don't* think we'll change the world overnight?" Lucas murmured back.

The woman shrugged. "One can hope, I suppose." She glanced up at Lucas. "I've seen you around before," she said. "You're the scientist chasing monsters."

Lucas looked harder at the woman. "Oh, you're the control operator I keep harassing for security renders!"

"When you agreed to come to Kadath, you didn't just sign up

for money and exploits," Wade continued. "You came to be part of one of the grandest experiments in human history. And the success of this endeavor will rise or fall on our efforts. Our determination. Our perseverance."

"Guilty," the woman said. "I'm Rachel Wilkins."

"Lucas Kane," Lucas replied. "It's a pleasure to officially meet you, Rachel."

"Likewise." Rachel smiled, her eyes once again sparking with the emerald heat Lucas had noticed before.

"Today is a day of celebration," Wade declared. "Today is a day of new beginnings. Today, it is my supreme pleasure to announce that the Kadath deep-sea mining facility is fully operational. Humanity's shining dawn begins here, my friends. With us."

That night, Lucas returned to his quarters with a smile and a slight alcoholic buzz. The speeches had been a bit much but, overall, the event was the best time he'd had in Kadath. He actually thought Rachel might *like* him. He was undoubtedly attracted to *her*. Maybe they had honestly made a connection.

Collapsing on the bed, Lucas blacked out almost as soon as his head hit the pillow. He slept deeply all night long, not waking until the morning. And, when he finally dreamed, he dreamt of a massive metallic green sphere. It was waiting, drifting in its dark cradle of silt. And it was calling.

THREE

THE SHIPWRECKED

"Worldwide reports seem to suggest that the number of receptors has increased dramatically over recent weeks. Furthermore, the incidents do not seem to be isolated to any one geographical region. To match this flurry of activity, we have begun to see the numbers of confirmed apparitions rising in the wild. We do not know yet if these two phenomena are intrinsically linked, but one could hazard a guess they are."

Regular Activity Update – For Authorized Eyes Only

TOWER WORLD

Connor awoke with a yelp, sweat streaming down his pale face and soaking his black suit. The white collar beneath his shirt's lapels felt unusually constricting. Reaching up, he pulled it out and unbuttoned the top few buttons of his shirt so he could breathe.

Min stood and approached him, while Mitsuko just glanced

at him before returning to watching the door. Connor noticed her sword was resting on her lap. She seemed to be listening carefully for something.

"The nightmares are normal," Min said, trying to calm Connor. "You will grow used to them in time. At least, more so."

"It… It felt so *real*," Connor muttered, running his hand through his brownish-red hair.

Min nodded. "The thought has crossed my mind that our subconscious experiences here are not, in fact, dreams at all, but rather memories. That is a most unpleasant notion, of course."

Shaking his head, Connor sat up and swung his legs over the edge of the bed.

"Here," Min said, handing Connor a protein bar.

Connor took the bar and examined it, grimacing slightly.

"I realize you will not want to eat," Min said. "But you must. You will require the energy."

Mitsuko shot to her feet. "Quiet," she hissed. "I hear movement." Mitsuko stalked toward the door like a leopard on the prowl. Pressing her ear to the wood, she listened intently. Min and Connor froze, barely breathing. Mitsuko stayed like that for some time before finally relaxing. "They're gone," she said. Retracing her steps, she moved toward Min and knelt beside him. "How long before we have to move?"

"I think we have twenty minutes," Min replied.

"Twenty minutes before what?" Connor asked.

Min's smile was grimmer this time. "Before this room disappears."

Connor blinked. He nodded. "Of course," he said dryly. "That makes perfectly logical sense."

Min's cheery demeanor roused. "Finally, someone with a sense of humor!" he exclaimed. "Mitsuko is a deep soul, but her jokes…"

That nearly earned a smirk from the woman. Min looked at Connor, his eyes twinkling, and shrugged.

"Where will we go?" Connor asked.

"We are running low on supplies," Min said. "We must refresh them. And then we will see what options are open to us."

Connor shook his head. "Shouldn't we try to escape? We need to warn people about what we've seen! Find the military or the police or something."

"For whatever reason, the aberrations will not come in here," Min said. "We've watched them. They will gather *outside* the lobby doors, but they do not step inside. I don't know why. As to leaving, I don't know that we're prepared for that yet."

"Why worry about *preparedness?*" Connor asked. "We just need to get to the nearest town and tell them –"

"How do you know this outbreak hasn't impacted *them* as well?" Min asked.

Connor paused. "Bollocks," he cursed.

"Besides," Mitsuko finally added. "Without some protection and something to defend yourself with, you'd be skewered in minutes."

Connor looked down at his tattered suit. "I take your point," he said.

"Well," Min said. "Our time draws short, so let's gather what we need."

"How do you know when and what is going to change?" Connor asked as they collected the few things in the room they could carry.

"It is a sense I receive," Min said with a shrug. "To begin with, it mainly occurred during meditation. But recently, it's been happening even when I am focused on other things. It's like a whisper behind my ear, or a hand brushing my skin. Perhaps to call it a premonition would be more accurate."

"How long have you two been here?" Connor inquired, buttoning his shirt again and sliding his white collar back into place. Lastly, he donned his thin black coat once more and slipped on his mud-caked black shoes.

"It's difficult to say, exactly," Min replied, tightening the straps on his chest. "I have had a difficult time keeping track of it recently. But if I had to estimate, I would say between two and three weeks for myself. Probably a week and a half for Mitsuko."

"Enough talking," Mitsuko said. "We need to move."

Quietly Mitsuko stepped to the door and cracked it open. She peered out at the hallway beyond, then, looking back, she nodded at Min and Connor. They all hurried through the doorway.

"Why are we avoiding other people?" Connor whispered. "Don't we want their help?"

"People here are not necessarily our friends," Min replied. "We learned that early on."

A groaning arose behind them like the moans of old timber. Mitsuko glanced back. "You were off, Min," she said.

Connor followed Mitsuko's gaze and gasped. Another corridor was cutting through the one they were walking down, barreling toward them as it swung around in a wide arc. It seemed the two hallways were sliding through each other like oil and water, barely impacting one another, but Connor didn't doubt that it would not be so kind to them.

The moving corridor twisted and spun, its chandeliers dipping to one side before disappearing from view as the hallway banked and rotated. Now Connor could briefly see some of the rooms still clinging to the passage's exterior as it twirled around, cutting through the original hall. It was surreal viewing the unfinished beams, boards, and metal behind the spinning hallway's polished interior. But it was even stranger to watch some of the corridor's rooms break free from their adjoining doors to plunge up, down, or sideways through the stationary passageway's walls, vanishing from sight.

"What in God's name –" Connor cried.

"RUN!" Mitsuko roared.

The three vaulted down the first corridor as quickly as their feet would take them while the other passageway hurtled onward. Alarmingly, Connor felt like their hallway was beginning to pivot, too, as if it were turning on an axis. He smacked into a door, which swung open. Darting a glance to his left, he saw the room beyond pop off and drift away, leaving only an empty void where it had been. Connor let out a strangled cry and stumbled past the opening to oblivion.

"Min!" Mitsuko snapped. "Where?"

Min shook his head. He closed his eyes briefly and took a deep breath. "Right!" he ordered. "Three doors ahead!"

The floor was tilting significantly now. Mitsuko sprinted up the incline toward the third door while Min and Connor stumbled after her. The other corridor was almost upon them.

Mitsuko cracked open the cherry wood entry and peered through. Nodding, she leaped inside and swung around, offering her hand. Min grabbed it, and she hauled him into the space beyond. Then she turned back for Connor. The other hallway was almost upon him, its opening once more yawning in his direction –

"Connor, jump!" Mitsuko cried. Connor did, his fingers reaching for Mitsuko's hand. She jerked it back.

The other corridor swallowed Connor whole. Connor came down on its ceiling and then tumbled end over end as the thing spun like a barrel down a hill. Connor tried to grab onto something. *Anything.* Finally, his hands wrapped around a chandelier, which he clung to with all his might.

The new corridor righted itself and stabilized, forcing Connor to drop to the floor again as the chandelier gave way. Shaking his head, he looked up to see that the end of the original hallway was swiftly approaching. Connor looked back for some means of escape, but quickly realized it was hopeless. He couldn't outrun this. He was going to die in here.

The first hallway's wall adhered to the end of Connor's, breaking free of its original passage. Connor's corridor continued onward, spinning around once more. The friction created by the two carpets passing through each other gave him a rugburn on his palms. Connor looked up as other rooms and places slid through his passageway, but finally, everything seemed to slow and settle. Looking up, Connor watched the chandeliers from the two corridors pass through one another before both halls finally came to a halt, their open ends sealing together. Connor collapsed to the ground in a heap and blacked out.

Connor opened his eyes with a groan. There was a bright light in his face. Immediately he squeezed his eyelids shut again, trying to block out the glare.

"Doctor, he's waking up," someone said nearby.

"Ah, very good," a woman replied. Then she spoke again, right above him now. "Hello there."

Connor felt the light move off his face and opened his eyes. A tall, stately black woman was hovering over him. Her hair was pulled back into a tidy bun, her milk chocolate skin offset by the brilliant snow-white of her lab coat.

"My name is Dr. Sephora Jenkins," she said. "How do you feel?"

"Like I've been kicked by a mule," Connor said, looking down at his medical gown and inclined hospital bed. "And then it kept kicking me while I was down."

Dr. Jenkins chuckled. "Well, you've certainly had a nasty accident. A couple of men found you and brought you to me. Do you remember what happened?"

Connor blinked his eyes. The madness that assaulted his memory was impossible. He shook his head. "I'm afraid I don't, Doctor. Only some very vivid nightmares. Was it… Was it something to do with my church? Is everyone okay?"

"I wish I had answers to your questions, but unfortunately, I don't," Dr. Jenkins said. "I was hoping *you'd* be able to tell *me*."

Connor smiled. "I hate to disappoint a lady. My apologies, Dr. Jenkins."

Dr. Jenkins laughed, the sound lilting and musical. Her smile was dazzling. "Please, call me Sephora," she said. "Perhaps you can ease my disappointment by telling me your name?"

"*That* I remember, at least," Connor said. "It's Connor. Connor Durham."

"Well, Connor, it's nice to meet you," Sephora said. "Now, why don't you rest. I'll have someone bring in some food for you and some pain medication to help you sleep. We'll continue our discussion later."

"It's a date," Connor said. Sephora winked and then left the room.

Connor winced as he sat up. Whatever he had done, it had been a doozy. His whole body felt like a bruise. An unwelcome image of the revolving corridor assaulted his mind, and he thrust it away. It had just been a dream. He was safe now.

An orderly came in with a tray of food and a cup with a few pills rattling inside it. The man set both items on a rolling cart near Connor's bed.

"Where is this place?" Connor asked the man. "Are we near

Limerick?"

The man didn't speak. Turning, he headed back out the door. Connor frowned. Strange.

Turning to the food, Connor tried to eat. His stomach was twisting inside him, but at least he managed to get some down. He took the pills, too, and the pain started to recede slightly. When he had eaten all he could handle, Connor found himself drifting off again. He absentmindedly hoped that he wouldn't dream.

Connor awoke to find Sephora smiling down at him again. Two orderlies were flanking her, hovering near the entrance. Connor realized something about their stances made him vaguely uneasy.

"I hope you had a good rest, Connor," Sephora said.

"It was just fine, thanks," Connor mumbled in reply. Why was he feeling more and more uncomfortable?

"On a scale of one to ten, how would you rate your current pain level?"

"Oh, not bad. Maybe a three." Connor cleared his throat.

"Well, that's a definite improvement," Sephora said, flashing another stunning smile.

"I couldn't help but notice your American accent," Connor said. "How long have you been practicing medicine in Ireland?"

Sephora's smile thinned. Wheeling over a chair, she sat down on it, leaning in toward Connor like a conspirator about to divulge a shattering secret. "There's something we need to discuss, Connor, and it's something you may find a little alarming. But please, bear with me. Any sane and ordered society needs to run on a certain agreed-upon set of rules for peace to prevail, don't you think?"

"Of course," Connor said, perplexed by the sudden shift. "Otherwise, there would be anarchy."

Sephora's smile grew wider again. "Yes, *precisely*. And those who break these rules must be reprimanded and brought into conformity so the system may function optimally. When a body has a pathogen, the body will not function properly until the hostile organism has been eradicated. This fact applies to our physical bodies, but also in a broader sense to our communities, states, nations, etcetera. Yes?"

"Yes, I follow."

"Good." Sephora leaned in even closer. "Now. Here's the alarming part. You and I, Connor, find ourselves in a place that, at first blush, can seem frightening, hostile, and isolated. However, this is really all just a matter of perspective. Where some see horror, others might see opportunity. Even *hope*. But hope, like society, can be a fragile thing. It must be fostered. Nurtured. Allowed to thrive, grow, and flourish. But for *that* to happen, the rules of the society which sustains the hope must be upheld."

Connor's heart was hammering in his chest, his stomach clenching around the boulder that had taken up residence inside it. He kept trying to swallow. "We're not in Ireland, are we?" he managed.

"No, dear," Sephora said. "I'm sorry to say that we certainly are not."

"So, all of my nightmares…"

"They weren't nightmares." Sephora put a comforting hand on Connor's arm. "We found you unconscious in a hallway right after it shifted. It was a miracle you survived. Perhaps there is a… *greater purpose* for you."

Connor nodded slowly. He felt faint.

"Now, there are two ways to look at this place," Sephora continued. "One is as a world of terrors trying to consume us. Another is as an opportunity to build something fresh and new.

Perhaps *both* are true, but the question is, where will we choose to focus? What narrative will we choose to perpetuate? There is safety both in numbers and order. That's why it's so important to embrace both."

"Why… why are you telling me this?" Connor asked.

"Because we have all been shipwrecked on this proverbial island together, and these early formative days will determine what the future of our little hamlet will be. It could be a place of redemption, where we can be 'born again,' if you'll pardon the saying. Or it could be a place that becomes a charnel house for every one of us. The choice is up to us."

"Why haven't you tried to contact the outside world?" Connor said, his voice rising. "Why haven't you attempted to escape?"

Sephora's smile was sadder now. "It's not that simple, I'm afraid."

"What's so effin' *difficult* about it?" Connor said, sitting up. "Why is everyone so bloody soft that they won't even *try?*"

"Connor, calm down," Sephora said, rising off her chair to apply pressure to Connor's arm and force him back. "We have sent out groups to ascertain the lay of the land. Thus far, none have returned. That is *not* to say that we shouldn't try again. Maybe we will be able to discuss an expedition outside if we can find a way past the mutations. But first, there's another matter to consider."

"And what's that?" Connor asked.

"There are two aggressors in our midst as we speak," Sephora said. "Perhaps they don't know any better. I have no doubts they are scared. Regardless, I can't put their minds at ease until they allow me to talk to them. We have had… *disagreements* between our parties, and, surely, they received the wrong message from these early unfortunate interactions. But, as you and I conferred, we are stronger together. As such, I desperately want to bring these two into our fold."

"Why do you assume *I* can help you?" Connor said.

"Because you were spotted being spirited away by one of them upon first entering the tower," Sephora said. "Mitsuko Takenaka, I believe her name is? I assume you've also then met her associate, Min Wang."

"Ah," Connor said, realization lighting his eyes. "I see. And you want me to bring them to you then?"

Sephora's smile returned. "To quote from your holy book, 'Blessed are the peacemakers.'"

"Even if I wanted to help, I don't know where they are," Connor said. "We were separated during the… shift."

"I think I may be able to assist with that," Sephora said. "Would you mind accompanying these two gentlemen, Connor? They will help you track down Min and Mitsuko."

"All right," Connor said. "I'll go with them. As you say, we will be stronger united. Where are my clothes?"

Sephora laughed again. "Bring the man his uniform," she said.

Connor stepped out of the hospital room into a place that looked more like a science laboratory than a clinic. Maybe it served as both.

"Welcome to my humble abode," Sephora said. "It might not be much, but it serves its purpose."

"It looks like you've settled in nicely," Connor said. "Does this place not… shift like the hotel rooms?"

"Not everywhere in the skyscraper does that," Sephora said. "Only the most dangerous areas on the periphery seem susceptible to it. Some places are more or less fixed."

"Good to know," Connor replied.

"Your friends were recently spotted in a semi-stable area,"

Sephora stated. "Trevor and Simon will escort you."

Connor turned to Trevor and Simon with a smile. "Hullo, gents," Connor said, extending his hand. "I'm Connor Durham."

One of them took it. "Trevor Hill," he said with an Australian accent. It was like he was trying to learn how to smile for Connor. "This is Simon." Simon just nodded his head.

"Charmed," Connor said, trying not to feel like bugs were crawling over his skin every time he looked at them. "By all means, lead the way, boyos."

Trevor and Simon set out across the room. Sephora briefly turned Connor back toward her, though, placing a hand on his shoulder. "Thank you for your help, Connor," she said. "I won't forget it."

"You're right, Sephora," Connor said. "We won't survive if we're divided."

Sephora winked again and then ushered Connor out of the room. Outside the laboratory, Connor saw that Trevor and Simon had donned protective vests and picked up weapons. They had also strapped on helmets.

"Any more of those available?" Connor asked.

"Sorry, Connor," Trevor said. "This is all we have on hand."

"Sure, of course," Connor said, trying to push past the unsettled feeling growing in his guts. "Onward then."

Trevor and Simon turned toward the door. Connor's eyes darted quickly around the room and spied a thin metal pipe lying on a chair nearby. It was better than nothing. As he stepped past the chair, Connor snapped down and snatched the conduit, sliding it up the left sleeve of his black jacket. Trevor heard his rustling and looked back, but Connor was already striding after them. The three men stepped through the door.

Connor was surprised to discover that Sephora's clinic/laboratory was in the middle of what seemed to be an indoor mall-turned-settlement. Outside the clinic, they strode onto a broad thoroughfare with a white tile floor and an arched glass ceiling that hung thirty or more feet overhead. Makeshift tents, supplies, and provisions littered the ground – enough to have taken quite some time to amass and organize. *How long had these people been here?*

More and more haunted faces peered out of the storefronts and tents lining each side of the hall, trying to catch a glimpse of the newcomer dressed like a preacher. Connor smiled at them, but only a few children returned the gesture. Connor's heart went out to them. One young boy dared to wave at Connor, and Connor warmly waved back.

"How many of you are there?" Connor asked. Neither man replied, which Connor supposed he could understand. After all, they currently had about as much reason to trust him as he did them.

At last, the three men reached the settlement's border. They passed through a gate punctured into a jury-rigged wall and stepped onto a rounded platform jutting out like an inverted tree conk from the skyscraper's main shaft. Broad walkways branched off from it along either wall, while its far rounded edge was lined by a squat glass and metal railing broken up like an eight-year-old's teeth by escalators stretching upward and downward to destinations unseen. Connor was struck by just how oddly *normal* it was.

"So, we're just going to take the escalator like regular folks now, are we?" Connor said.

"Your friends are on level three," Trevor said. "We head up."

Trevor took the lead on the ascending stairway. Simon motioned for Connor to go next, then stepped on behind him.

Connor experienced a severe sense of cognitive dissonance as he juggled the feelings of extreme imminent danger with the sensation of riding calmly up the escalator like any average consumer.

The escalator terminated one level up in front of a line of hotel rooms. Connor found his pulse quickening dramatically at the sight of them. Instinctively, he took a step backward.

"Don't worry, preacher," Trevor said. "They're not in the shifting places. This way."

Trevor and Simon turned right and started down the walkway toward what looked like another strip of businesses. Connor hurried after them, glancing nervously back at the hotel rooms. The two escorts seemed to become warier as they continued their advance, and Connor felt his muscles tensing even further. His fingers absentmindedly grazed the end of the pipe hidden up his sleeve.

Once they reached the storefronts, the three men pivoted right and trailed down the row. Connor quickly scanned the shops, but they unanimously seemed to be dark and deserted. Looking over the railing, he took in the building's cavernous central shaft. It was somewhat square with rounded accents and architectural flourishes scattered about liberally. Hotel rooms ran down the left and right sides while a towering glass elevator shaft blocked off what he assumed were more rooms directly opposite from him. He wasn't sure if it was a trick of the eye, or if some of those doors actually bulged and twitched. Looking upward, Connor saw that the edifice rose for what seemed forever. Looking down, he saw the lobby where he had first stumbled into the skyscraper two floors below. A twenty-foot-tall waterfall adorned the last level-and-a-half of the elevator shaft, water dashing down its staggering levels into the shallow basin mounted near the floor.

The line of shops ended, but the pathway didn't. It continued past the tower's endless shaft, becoming a corridor that soon mushroomed outward into a new courtyard. At the back of this place, Connor saw a line of floor-to-ceiling glass windows with several revolving doors set between the panes. In the center of this wall of glass was mounted a large sign which read "THE DEPOT."

Trevor, Connor, and Simon pushed through one of the revolving doors to find themselves standing in a dimly lit megastore. A happy mannequin near the entrance greeted them, a word bubble that dangled next to its face declaring, "Hey, friends! Welcome to The Depot! We're so glad you stopped by today!"

"What now?" Connor asked. "Is this place safe?"

"Nowhere here is truly safe," Trevor replied. "But this place should be all right. Hopefully." He and Simon scanned the area briefly, and then Trevor looked back at Connor. "Call them," he said.

"What, right *here?*" Connor said. "Shouldn't we take a more covert approach, just in case something *else* is in here with us?"

"And risk being ambushed?" Trevor shook his head. "I think not. Here we have a clear line of sight. We'll see if something is coming at us and be able to decide what to do about it."

"Okay, boss," Connor said unsurely. "Whatever you say." Then he cleared his throat, and yelled out, "Min! Mitsuko! Are you two in here? It's me, Connor!"

He stopped yelling and waited, listening for any sounds of movement. Nothing. "I made it out, would you believe it? What are the odds? Guys?"

He paused again, but still, there was no response. "I'm here with a couple of gents who'd very much like to talk to you," Connor said. "Their people saved me after the hallway stopped moving. Um, they say you all might have gotten off on the wrong foot before, but they want to make amends!"

Connor halted once more, and all three of them listened. "I don't know that they're here," Connor murmured. "It's pretty quiet."

"Give it time," Trevor said. "Try again."

Sighing, Connor took a deep breath to resume his yelling. Before he could start, though, a familiar voice said, "I think you should learn the invaluable power of silence, Connor."

Connor whipped his head around, looking for the voice, and then beamed when he saw Min appear out of the shadows near the end of one of the farthest aisles. "Couldn't agree with you more, Min. It's good to see you again."

"I am greatly relieved you didn't die in the hallway," he said. "I felt I had failed you, and I am glad to have a chance to beg your forgiveness. Who are your two new compatriots?"

"This is Trevor and Simon," Connor said. "They came with me from a little settlement on the second floor. Sephora Jenkins sent them, as well as me. She's a doctor, but I think she's also the leader of their group. She seemed to think you three had gotten off on the wrong foot, and she wanted to rectify that."

Min nodded. "That is very kind of her to extend an olive branch to us. I have no doubt we would be honored to discuss her offer of peace, though, of course, I will have to confer with my companion first. Tell Sephora we will meet her at a neutral location tomorrow at this time. Say, one of the tables in the lobby?"

"That's awfully exposed," Trevor said.

"Indeed, it is," Min said. "But, forgive me if I do not yet trust Dr. Jenkins's intentions."

"Is the girl here?" Simon said, his voice a bottomless, rumbling bass. Connor was startled to hear the other man speak.

"What difference would her presence make?" Min asked. "I am here. Is that not enough?"

"Is the girl here?" Simon repeated, his voice growing even

deeper.

"Simon?" Trevor said. "You okay, mate?"

"Show me the girl," Simon said, his voice now like truck tires on gravel.

"I think not," Min said. "Connor, RUN!"

"Okay, that's enough of this!" Trevor snapped. Reaching inside his armored vest, he drew out a pistol.

Connor didn't even think: He just reacted. His wrist flexed backward, the pipe dropping into his waiting palm. Wrapping both hands around it, he swung with all his might at Trevor. Trevor's arms jerked as the metal bar connected with his forearm, causing the bullet he then fired to sail off into the depths of The Depot.

"Why you little –" Trevor snarled.

"No one's shooting *anyone* today, Trevor!" Connor snapped. "This was a mission of peace, you thick eejit!"

"That wasn't very godly of you now, was it, Preacher?" Trevor said, swiveling toward Connor with fire in his eyes.

"Oh, I think it's *plenty* godly to stop you from blowing a man's brains out for no effin' reason!" Connor yelled back. Trevor's eyes grew wide. And that's when Connor remembered Simon.

Connor dodged to the right as Simon stabbed at his back. The long, tapered talons which had replaced Simon's fingers shot past Connor's shoulder and embedded themselves instead in Trevor's armored vest, punching right through the hardened material. Trevor let out a wheezing sound as his surprised gaze dropped to his chest. Simon snapped his hand back, blood coating the top two inches of his icepick fingers. Slowly he swiveled toward Connor as Trevor collapsed to the ground. Simon's face was elongating, his eyeballs literally rolling backward in his head to leave two empty chasms peering out through his visor. Most of his teeth were the size of thumbs now; his incisors were as long as a middle finger.

"What in God's name…" Connor breathed.

"Mitsuko, NOW!" Min roared.

Mitsuko lunged over the nearest register, her sword in one hand and her machete in the other. She was blindingly fast. Simon started to turn toward her, but his elastic body couldn't currently muster the speed necessary to stop her. Her blades sliced through the air, meeting Simon's neck with a wet *thunk*. Simon gurgled and thrashed at Mitsuko, who released her blades as Simon stumbled and sprawled on the ground. It was trying to pull itself back up, the pulsing flesh of its head wrapping around and absorbing its helmet. Mitsuko lunged at the thing that had been a man and let out a primal cry. Dislodging the machete, she started hacking at Simon's neck wound, cutting deeper and deeper. Blood sprayed up onto her face and chest and hair, but she didn't stop. At least, not until Simon's still elongating skull rolled away from the spurting stump of its neck, the final sinew severed.

Mitsuko freed both of her weapons and stood. Connor saw that her body was shaking.

"Mitsuko, are you all right?" Connor asked, stepping toward her.

"Don't, Connor," she muttered, turning from him. "Just… don't."

Min was there now, and he put a hand on Connor's shoulder. "She may be a champion fencer, but that doesn't make killing someone any easier," Min said. "Even someone like that. Give her time. She will recover." Then he stepped in front of Connor. "I am greatly relieved to see you alive, Connor. How are you? Are you unharmed?"

"Yeah. Yeah, I'm fine," Connor said. "Physically, at any rate."

"Thank you," Min said. "For stopping him from shooting me. Perhaps he was only going to threaten, but I always prefer not to have a pistol pointed at my head."

Connor almost smiled. "I thought you might." Then he looked down at the twitching, groping body of Simon lying on the ground. "So, this is why you said people weren't our friends," he said.

"Indeed," Min replied. "This isn't the first time we've been… accosted."

Connor stared at Simon for a moment longer. "Do you think Sephora knew…?" he murmured. Then he shook his head. "Screw this. I'm getting out of here. The things outside may be hell incarnated, but at least there's a sliver of hope beyond these walls that we could escape this madness." Connor looked back up at Min. "Are you two coming with me?"

"Yes," Mitsuko whispered. "We will."

Min smiled wearily. "The lady has spoken. Let's gather some provisions for our journey."

FOUR

MUTATIONS

"In all honesty, these newest scans of the anomaly could only be described as… unusual, even by the standards of previous metrics. There is a ghost pinging back on our scans, which perfectly matches the facility's previous specifications. I know it's impossible. But… It's almost like somehow, perhaps in some sort of overlapping space-time configuration, an echo of the facility remains. I hope you can make better sense of these reports than I have."

Phillip Reed – Leng Corp. Specialist

KADATH FACILITY

"As the OCEA representative for this facility," Lucas said, "it is my duty to take regular surveys of this area and ensure that no damage is being done to its habitat. But I can't do that if I don't have access to a submersible!"

"Dr. Kane," Commander Wade said, "I understand your

position. But it does not change the fact that I cannot give out submersibles to anyone who asks – especially one whose file is mysteriously absent from our databases! To be perfectly honest, as far as I can tell, you're not even supposed to *be* in Kadath!"

Lucas sighed, rubbing his eyes with his fingers. "It's a clerical error," he repeated. "A blip in the system. Commander Wade, I ask you: with the level of security and secrecy surrounding this place, how on earth would I have a laboratory, private quarters, and a reputation here if I wasn't an authorized Leng Corporation asset? For that matter, how would I have even *gotten* here?"

"And that benefit of the doubt is the only reason you are not locked in a security cell until this matter is cleared up," Wade said. "Though perhaps I should reconsider that course of action, just to ensure you're not a saboteur."

Lucas shook his head. "My job is to ascertain that this facility is not posing an active threat to the ocean, and to study the interplay between this place and the surrounding ecosystem," Lucas said. "You are directly impeding my contracted purpose for being here, Commander."

"I'm sorry you feel that way," Wade said. "I could always authorize a transfer back to the surface for you. Or my offer of a change in accommodations is still on the table, should you prefer." Wade stood up from his desk. "Now, I'm afraid I'm a busy man, Dr. Kane, and I fear I will have to draw our session to a close. I'll let you know when I have word from the surface. Good day."

Lucas turned and stalked toward the door. "Thank you for your time, Commander."

"My pleasure, Doctor."

"I can't believe Wade's busting your balls about checking out a short-range sub," Rachel said, her fork roving through her salad.

Lucas shrugged. "Ah, well. I suppose this record issue will be taken care of soon enough."

"Yeah, but still," Rachel said. "I mean, what are you going to *do* with it? Hook up with a Russian outpost to spill all of Leng's secrets?"

Lucas laughed. "I think that's *exactly* what he expects me to do."

Rachel looked down at her salad, studying it intently. Then she looked back up. "This is nice," she said. "With you, I mean."

Lucas smiled, leaning forward slightly. "Likewise, Rachel."

"Really?"

"Yeah. When I'm with you, I'm… I don't know. Happy."

"Aw, you're just saying that," Rachel said, her eyes sparkling.

"Nope. Not just saying that."

"So, what? Without me, you're just a miserable head case?"

Lucas laughed again. "You have *no* idea."

Rachel scooted her chair back. "Well, I think I'm about done," she said. "You want to go for a walk?"

"Hey, it's not like I have a sub to take out," Lucas said. "What else do I have going on?"

Rachel snorted. "You sure know how to make a girl feel like the most important thing in the world."

"I try."

Lucas and Rachel had been eating in a little open dining café on the promenade. Now, standing, they left the shop and set off down the wide paved path, the artificial sunlight glowing down from its rendered blue sky. They passed a park on the right and stores on the left, which at last gave way to an immaculately adorned little temple. In front of the temple was gathered a small group of people, their heads lowered. It seemed a man was leading them in some kind of ritual.

"Who's that?" Lucas said. "What're they doing?"

"Oh, that's Summerisle, Kadath's resident chaplain," Rachel said. "Some people still feel the draw for that stuff here, so they brought Priest Summerisle to see to those needs."

"It doesn't look Christian," Lucas said. "Buddhist or Muslim, either. Or *any* kind I'm familiar with."

"No, he's part of a smaller religion," Rachel said. "I think they call themselves the Golden Dawn. Apparently, some of the higher-ups in Leng are members, so they brought their beliefs along with them when they came here."

"Huh."

"Hey, did you hear the new 'megastore' finally opened?" Rachel asked.

"No, I didn't," Lucas said. "I still can't believe they spent all that space and money on it."

Rachel shrugged. "Nothing says home to people like consumerism. Want to check it out?"

"Sure."

They walked along the promenade until, at last, they came to its far edge. There, carved into its surface, was an immense glass wall. Several revolving glass doors were further cut into the bottom of the wall, beckoning to Rachel and Lucas as they turned slowly on their silver shafts.

"'The Depot,'" Lucas read. "They really couldn't think of anything more creative to name this place?"

"Oh, stop being a wet blanket," Rachel said. "Come on!"

Rachel pulled Lucas into the store, where they were greeted by an automated mannequin waving jovially, a word bubble suspended above its shoulder, declaring, "Hey, friends! Welcome to The Depot! We're so glad you stopped by today!"

"Whoa," Rachel said. "Because *that's* not creepy at all."

"They might be taking the old-time feel a bit far," Lucas

replied.

"Oh, well," she said. "Let's look around."

Something flickered in the air beside Lucas. It seemed almost to have the shape of a human, but it was so deformed that it could hardly be considered one. It squealed, its gaping jaw impossibly wide, its eye sockets black pits into oblivion. It drew one hand back, flexing its terrible icepick fingers as it prepared to strike –

"Gah!" Lucas cried, jumping backward.

"Lucas!" Rachel said. "What is it? What's wrong?"

Lucas blinked. The apparition was gone as if it had never been there at all. "I just – You didn't – But it was just there!"

"Don't go crazy on me yet, Kane," Rachel said. "You still owe me a shopping trip."

"I… Yeah," Lucas said, taking a deep breath. "Sorry, I don't know what came over me. Maybe a trick of the light or something. Let's go."

Lucas and Rachel wandered through the aisles, making small talk and looking at the bureaucrat-approved products on offer. One necklace, in particular, caught Rachel's eye. She leaned in to study it closer, and Lucas craned down beside her. Her hair smelled like lavender and cucumbers.

"You know, I think I could help you with your sub problem," she whispered.

"What?" Lucas said. "No! I won't let you put yourself on the line so I can go sight-seeing."

"It's no problem," she said. "I know the system better than anyone. I'll be in and out, and no one will ever know. Besides, when you make your big find, we'll *both* come out looking like heroes. Wade'll never be able to shut you down then. I'll just partner you up with someone who's already going out."

"Who'd be the pilot?" Lucas asked.

Rachel smiled mischievously. "I know a guy."

Lucas chuckled. "You sure about this?"

"Absolutely," Rachel said. "If you buy me that necklace."

Lucas strolled into the submersible bay, trying to act as though he belonged there. Rachel had told him the time and the place, but that was all she'd said. Lucas swept his gaze over the few subs cradled in their tubes, watching as one was readied for launch while another was double-checked for maintenance issues. That left only one other option. Was it his?

"You must be Lucas," a deep, gruff voice said. Lucas jumped, then turned to see a towering, muscular man with wavy black hair and a goatee approaching him. He looked grizzled. Imposing.

"And you are…?" Lucas asked.

The man's stony face cracked in a smile. "Charles Ryan, your pilot for the day," he said, extending a hand. Lucas took it. He felt like his fingers were about to be crushed.

"A pleasure," Lucas said. "I appreciate you doing this."

"Hey, when Rachel asks…" Charles said with a wink. "Besides. The nature of this operation has piqued my interest. Shall we go? She's all ready for us."

"By all means, Charles," Lucas said. "Lead the way."

The sub was a small, light craft designed for speed and distance more than comfort or capacity. It only had two seats arranged in a line and almost no pathway beside them to get around. Behind the seats was a small enclosed receptacle that served as a bathroom. Lucas loathed the thought of actually using the thing.

"Watch your head, Doc," Charles said, settling into the first chair. "It's kind of a squeeze."

Lucas snorted as he climbed into the back. "Probably more so for you than me, Charles," he replied.

Immediately Lucas felt immersed in a sea of screens and control pads as he sank into the chair. Looking around, he stared at the wide viewports lining the sides, the transparent material fashioned from the same thick composite as the observation gallery windows. His smile crept into a grin.

Charles laughed. "Point taken. I'm sealing us in now." The hatch and its secondary safety layer sealed above them, and Lucas could hear the hiss as the sub pressurized.

"Control, this is submersible *Endeavoring Truth*, requesting permission to launch for routine recon," Charles said. "Please acknowledge. Over."

"Acknowledged, *Endeavoring Truth*," a female voice said. "Permission granted. Go in the light. Over."

"Thank you, Control," Charles said. "Beginning launch procedures and engaging chrysalis. Over."

Lucas watched on the myriad screens as the top of the launch tube folded over the submersible, pressurizing to create an airtight seal and form the chrysalis. Charles's fingers danced over the controls, bringing systems online and double-checking safeties before he finally flooded the tube, opened the airlock, and launched them out.

"Control, butterfly is free of the chrysalis," Charles said. "Over."

"Understood, *Endeavoring Truth*. Happy hunting. Over and out."

"So, just in case Rachel didn't mention it, I'll still need to perform my normal recon while I'm out here," Charles said. "But it seems to me our missions are pretty complimentary, so I don't foresee that causing an issue for either of us."

"I'm just glad to be out here, Charles," Lucas said. "Do whatever you need to do." Lucas unfolded a screen and propped it on his lap, but then the sight of Kadath lit up below them drew his attention and caught his breath.

The facility sprawled across the seabed like a sunken metropolis from another world, its illuminated structures pushing defiantly upward into the inky abyss. The station's domes and towers seemed like the last bastions of light and reason still standing in an endless Stygian wasteland. It was hypnotic, dreamlike, and yet somehow inexplicably solid. Lucas could make out the shuttle tubes running between the three main domes, as well as to the smaller, squarer outposts and middle structures. He could even see the primary enclosed drilling site not far off from the main facility, connected to Dome Three by long, spacious tubes.

"It's been a while, huh?" Charles said, glancing back.

"Yeah," Lucas said. "You forget, I guess."

"It is a sight, there's no doubt," Charles nodded.

"Have you seen anything strange out here, Charles?" Lucas asked. "Anything that seems… unusual?"

"I've seen my share," Charles replied.

"Can the systems on-board map the sea life by area as well as the minerals?" Lucas asked.

"In the right hands, you bet they can, Doc," Charles said. "And those hands have already engaged said systems."

Lucas chuckled. "Thanks, Charles. I appreciate it. Now, all we need are some samples from the various sectors and we should be set."

"On it." Then he glanced backward. "So, if you don't mind me asking, what are we really looking for out here, Lucas? Is this really because you want to check up on the local ecosystem?"

"I'm absolutely interested in that," Lucas said. "But I also kind of hope to find *this*. I'm currently lovingly referring to it as the kraken." Lucas drew up an image of his squid and passed it to

Charles. Charles whistled.

"So, we're on a monster hunt," Charles said. "Okay. I can get on board with that. Let's see what we can find, Doc."

The whispers drilled into Lucas's ear canals afresh without the slightest warning. Lucas jerked in his seat, his eyes growing wide. Quickly his gaze darted around, looking for the source – but of course, there wasn't one. The original voice was joined by others this time: he could make out unique tones and cadences layered on top of each other, interwoven with one another. As their chattering continued, Lucas realized he was beginning to understand them. God help him; he knew what they were saying. There was nowhere he could go; nothing he could do. Suddenly the submersible seemed unbearably tight around him.

We give ourselves to this, knowing – Why is everyone so bloody soft that – It churned like a maelstrom of lightning and eyes…

You're not real, Lucas thought. *You're not real, and I'm not actually experiencing this.*

Create a Kadath as a housing for – We're too exposed here – Direct exposure to the catalyzer – like a siren to a sailor.

Lucas squeezed his eyes shut. *Leave me alone!*

"Lucas? You okay back there?" Charles asked.

"Yeah," Lucas said. "Yeah, fine. Just a momentary wave of vertigo or something. It's almost passed."

"Do we need to head back?"

"No," Lucas replied. "No, it's already over. I'm okay. Thanks."

"All right, if you're sure," Charles said. "It would not look good to have a dead scientist on my record. That's all I'm saying."

Lucas laughed. "Understood."

We are waiting, the first whisper said, its voice the deepest and clearest of all. *We have been for so… very… long.*

"How's it going back there, Doc?"

"Doing fine, Charles," Lucas said. "Nothing to report."

"Good to hear. How's the view?"

"Astounding." And Lucas meant it. The whispers had undoubtedly left a dark tint on his mind, but the glorious underwater world engulfing the *Endeavoring Truth* had done its best to wash that stain away. The limitless expanse enraptured and entranced him, almost like a drug. Or, perhaps more accurately, like he had ventured into his true home.

"Glad you're enjoying it," Charles replied. "I've got some bad news, though. I'm about to reach the end of my charted run. They're going to expect me to start heading back soon."

Lucas sighed. "Well, I guess it had to end sooner or later. I certainly appreciate everything you've gathered for me."

Charles glanced back briefly. He cleared his throat. "Okay, so here's the deal. There's another sector that thus far is still uncharted, which I've been meaning to check out. And, honestly, if we're going to find your beast, it's probably going to be there. I can maybe run a bit long and wide if you're interested in checking it out."

"Would that cause problems for you, Charles?"

Charles shrugged. "Nothing I couldn't handle. Especially if we end up finding something interesting. You want to check it out?"

"Do you have to ask?" Lucas replied.

"All right then," Charles said. "Once more unto the breach."

The sub banked slightly, its speed increasing. Lucas watched the seafloor speed by through the windows as they traveled deeper into the unknown. He felt a little rush of adrenaline, knowing this was a place no human eyes had likely seen before.

"Preliminary telemetry says there's a relatively shallow trench up here somewhere," Charles said. "We should be almost on top of it now…" Charles paused, leaning forward in his seat. "Whoa.

Check this out, Doc."

Lucas followed Charles' gaze and frowned. "What are they doing?"

"I was hoping you'd tell *me*," Charles replied.

Outside they saw a fissure cut deep into the seafloor – no doubt Charles's trench. But the fascinating and perplexing thing was the vast array of sea creatures circling endlessly around it, like a vortex of life. It wasn't just one variety or species, either. It looked like dozens. Possibly hundreds. Lucas thought it looked a bit like a dazzling neon light show as so many different bioluminescent animals swirled in their psychedelic loops and patterns.

"Have you ever seen anything like that, Lucas?" Charles asked.

"Not with this many species, or at this depth," Lucas replied. "It's almost like they're… in a trance or something."

"I have to get some scans of that trench," Charles said.

"Please do," Lucas said.

Charles dropped the sub down to the seabed, collecting geological samples and animal specimens as he went.

"These creatures are *bizarre*," Lucas said.

"Are they new varieties?" Charles asked. "Or mutations?"

"I don't know," Lucas said. "Maybe."

"There's so *many* of them," Charles murmured. "It's like a reef with no reef. But we're too *deep* for that!"

"Are you picking up anything strange in your scans?"

"There are some promising readings to be sure, but nothing that I could concretely say would cause *this*."

"Strange magnetic activity?"

"Mmm, maybe… I mean, there's got to be *something*, right?"

A light began flashing on Charles's display. He cursed. "Well, it looks like time's up for today, Lucas," he said. "Power levels are running low. If we don't head back now, we might be out here for longer than even *we* wanted to be."

"Another time then?" Lucas asked.

"Oh, most definitely," Charles replied. "This is one of the most interesting things I've seen in ages. We're coming back out here as soon as I can get clearance."

"That's good enough for me," Lucas said. "Take us in, Charles."

"You got it, boss."

Charles guided the sub back into its chrysalis and then pressurized the airlock. The chrysalis unfolded, and then Lucas and Charles piled out onto the platform.

"Well, that was indeed an enlightening excursion," Charles said. "Let's do it again soon, Doc."

"I couldn't agree more, Charles," Lucas replied. "Thanks for letting me stow away."

"Any time. Now, let's get you your specimens."

The two men unloaded all the biological samples they had collected and then stowed them on an antigrav cargo bed. Charles finished shutting down and sealing up the *Endeavoring Truth*, then grabbed the back of the transporter. Lucas steered it from the front, and together they set out for Lucas's lab.

It was a long jaunt to the science wing. After walking for what felt like an hour, Lucas and Charles finally arrived at Dunwich Station. Requisitioning one of the shuttle's pods, they transported their cargo to Dome Two's Innsmouth Station and made the final trek to Lucas's laboratory.

"It's still pretty quiet around here, isn't it?" Charles said.

"It is," Lucas said. "Many of the scientists haven't arrived yet."

"I think I saw there was a submersible from the surface inbound with a few lab coats onboard," Charles said. "Maybe you'll have company soon."

Lucas shrugged. "I don't mind still being able to think."

Charles laughed. "I hear you, Doc."

They loaded the specimens into the lab's cold storage as well as into various tanks. "Thanks again for your help, Charles," Lucas said. "I couldn't have done this without you."

"Not a problem, Lucas," Charles said. "Hey, do me a favor, though, will you? Let me know what you find. I'm itching to learn what you uncover."

"Absolutely," Lucas said. "You've certainly earned that."

"All right," Charles said, heading for the hatch. "Well, I'll leave you to it, Doc. Happy hunting."

Lucas nearly jumped out of his skin when the knock came at his laboratory's hatch. Whirling around, he saw Rachel stepping through the open portal. He huffed, forcing his heart to settle back down in his chest.

"So, how'd it go?" Rachel asked.

"Extraordinary," Lucas said. "We hit a proverbial platinum mine."

Rachel cocked an eyebrow as she strode into the lab. "There was no *actual* platinum in that proverbial mine, was there? Because I'd be *very* interested in that," she said. "So, do you think Kadath has damaged the local ecosystem?"

"I don't know if anything's outside of acceptable limits, but it's not what we found *near* the station that was interesting," Lucas said. "We found a fissure in an uncharted sector. It's utterly *swarming* with species that may be unlike anything humanity has ever encountered before."

"May I?" Rachel asked.

Lucas wheeled his chair backward and extended his hand. Rachel came over and peered into the aquarium containing the specimen Lucas had been studying. She gasped. "There are so many colors…" she murmured. "I've… never seen anything like it."

"Neither have I," Lucas said. "And this is what I do."

"Bioluminescence?"

"On a whole other level."

"So, how many species do you think you've discovered?" Rachel asked.

"It's too early to say with certainty," Lucas replied. "But maybe dozens."

"Extraordinary."

"I want to thank you, Rachel," Lucas said. "This wouldn't have happened without you."

Turning, Rachel smiled. "You're welcome, Lucas. I'm glad I could help." She turned back to the creature. "So, what comes next?"

"I examine these," Lucas said. "I catalog them and study their genetic code. And then I get back out there. Charles has already agreed on a second trip."

"Well, when you're a world-famous scientist, don't forget us little people down here at the bottom of the ocean," she said with a wink.

Lucas laughed. "Who's to say I'm not bringing you with me?" he retorted.

"Ooh, big talk, flatterer," she shot back. "And who's to say I'd go?"

"Ouch," Lucas said. "That one cut me deep."

"Mm, did it?" Rachel said. "I'm so sorry. Maybe I can ease the pain." Then, stretching upward, she kissed Lucas's cheek.

Lucas arched an eyebrow at Rachel.

"Well?" she asked innocently. "Did that fix it?"

"It's feeling much better," Lucas said. "Thanks."

Something is coming down the next street. You hear it slithering, slushing along, accompanied by the screams of any who see it. Whatever it is bellows, setting the few windows that remain rattling in their frames. You hear someone shriek and then gurgle. Something wet slaps against the concrete.

You try to collect yourself as others scramble in a frantic frenzy around you. It is not appropriate for you to lose your composure as they have, though. You must help others to safety.

Quickly you try to usher anyone who will listen into the temple and away from the encroaching horror. Perhaps, if you get deep enough inside it, the monster will pass by without even a second glance.

Too late. It unfolds from around the corner up ahead, wriggling tendrils and writhing tentacles and bulging putrescence slurping as they slide over the buildings and across the pavement. Despite all your years pursuing enlightenment, even though you should be above such things, you can't help but scream along with everyone else.

Lucas awoke with a shriek ringing in his ears. It took him a minute to realize it was his own. Wasn't it?

Lucas wiped the sweat from his forehead with the back of a shaking hand. The nightmares had been less frequent in recent nights, but this one had certainly made up for the relative calm. It had felt *so real…*

Taking a deep, shuddering breath, Lucas lay back down on his bed. What did these dreams mean? Why were they tormenting him? They didn't seem to reflect his life or experiences at all. And even if they were explainable, what about the whispers and the waking visions?

An icy tingle crept along Lucas's spine. Was there something wrong with him? Was he losing his mind?

Lucas forced himself to close his eyes again. He needed more sleep. There was so much to do tomorrow, and he needed to have a clear head for it.

Lucas lay there tossing and turning beneath the covers, willfully ignoring the way the walls inhaled and exhaled around him. He further disregarded the phantom standing at the foot of his bed, its head vibrating incessantly. It was all just his imagination trying to run away with his mind. Nothing more.

The science wing was crammed with new faces as Lucas made his way toward his lab. It seemed Charles's promised sub had arrived. Lucas sighed. So much for his peace and quiet. Slowly he wormed through the jostle of people and paraphernalia, hearing men and women in lab coats shouting orders or berating the technicians for mishandling their equipment.

Finally, Lucas made it to his lab and shut the hatch with a sigh. Time to get to work, and hope the mob remained outside. Sitting down at his terminal, he pulled up the analyses he had run overnight. First, he looked at one of the samples collected near Kadath. He frowned. Unexpected genes that he didn't recognize were presenting in its DNA. How interesting.

Unable to wait, Lucas flipped to the next sample. And the next. They were all radically altered from the expected sequences. He turned to the following one – and stopped, his jaw dropping. It must be a mistake. There was no way this was possible.

Hurriedly, Lucas pulled up the information for his current sample. It had been collected directly above the fissure. Lucas returned to the results, leafing through them. His heart was racing. There had to be an error, but he didn't see where it was. Leaning back in his chair, Lucas covered his mouth with his hand.

He was looking at a DNA strand on the screen, or at least he should be. But what he saw was not a double helix rotating in front of him. It was a *triple* helix.

His hand trembling, Lucas tapped his node and called Charles.

"Hello?" came Charles's gruff voice.

"Charles, this is Lucas," Lucas said.

"Oh, hey, Doc," Charles said. "What's up?"

"When's the next time you can go out again?"

It was the following day that Lucas's node chirped in his ear with strange tidings. "Incoming call from Station Liaison Judy Blake," the calm female voice said.

Lucas frowned. Judy Blake? What did *she* want with him?

Uh oh. Was this something to do with the sub?

Reaching up, Lucas tapped his node. "Hello, this is Lucas Kane," he said.

"Ah, Dr. Kane," Judy's voice rang like chimes in his ear. "A pleasure to speak to you. I hope I'm not interrupting?"

"Not at all, Ms. Blake," Lucas said. "How may I help you?"

"Well, some fascinating information has come to light, and I would very much like to discuss it with you," Judy said. "When might be your first opportunity to stop by my office?"

Lucas grimaced. "Information?" he said. "What sort of information?"

Judy chuckled. "Let's not be coy, Dr. Kane," she said. "I know all about your sight-seeing, and I would appreciate a few minutes of your time to go over the details. If you don't mind."

Several unpleasant thoughts rushed through Lucas's head. Had he just ended his time at Kadath? Would he get Charles and Rachel shipped out as well? "Okay, I could probably find some time tomorrow —"

"What time today would work well for you?" Judy asked.

Lucas squeezed his eyes closed. "I can be there in two hours."

"Wonderful," Judy said. "I look forward to our discussion, Doctor."

The call disconnected. Lucas cursed under his breath, then hurried to document as many of his findings as he could. Just in case.

Lucas sat outside Judy Blake's office, shifting uncertainly in his chair. Her receptionist had assured him she would be with him as soon as she had finished up one small task, but Lucas had a bad feeling she was trying to make him sweat. If that was her intention, it was working.

"Lucas?" a voice said to his right. Lucas turned and saw Charles walk through the hatch. "Uh oh," Charles said.

Lucas sighed. "I was really hoping you wouldn't be here."

Charles sat down next to him. "No regrets, Doc," he said. "It was worth it, no matter the cost."

"I just hope they didn't find Rachel, too," Lucas said.

Charles nodded but didn't say anything further.

The door to Blake's office opened, and Judy Blake stood in the hatchway, smiling. "Ah, Mr. Ryan!" she said. "So glad you could join us. Please, come in." Stepping aside, she gestured for the two men to enter. Standing, they did.

"Have a seat, Lucas; Charles," Blake said, motioning to two chairs in front of her desk. "May I call you by your first names?"

"I suppose that depends on the purpose for our little rendezvous," Charles said with a lopsided smile.

Judy laughed as she slid behind her desk. "I take your point," she said. "To ease your minds, why don't I start. You may both call me Judy." Once she was in her seat, Judy leaned forward across her desk, her fingertips pressed together. "Now. Gentlemen. Let's cut straight to the chase. There is very little that escapes my notice here in Kadath. And, while Ms. Wilkins thinks no one knows the system better than her, she is mistaken. Everything in this facility is an asset of the Leng Corporation, and I make it my business to keep an eye on those assets' usage – especially when rogue submarine expeditions are illicitly conducting research following direct orders from Commander Wade forbidding this very activity."

Lucas tried to remain calm, but inside he was finding himself winding up tighter and tighter. They knew about Rachel. About *all* of them. It was over. "Ms. Blake, I take full responsibility for this," he said. "Charles and Rachel were just –"

"Please, call me Judy," Blake said. "I insist."

That caught Lucas off-guard. He cocked his head to the side quizzically.

"I am not here to punish you, Dr. Kane," Blake said. "On the contrary. I have been monitoring your research closely, as well as all the readings from your recent outing. And I find them to be singularly compelling. In fact, I feel you two are very, very close to uncovering something that the Leng Corporation is *incredibly* eager to find.

"So, I am here to make a proposition to you. I am aware of your current clerical problems, Dr. Kane. But this research is too important to allow it to be sidelined. As such, I have made those problems disappear. There will be no further inquiries. You have just become a top asset for the Corporation, and you will be treated accordingly.

"Next of all, I am going to ask that you both begin making reports directly to me. We cannot have your work held back by petty squabbles with station leadership, and my superiors would prefer a direct link to your findings in any case. Does that sound agreeable to you?"

Within seconds Lucas had gone from nearly panicked to dumbfounded. He was having a tough time processing what he was hearing. "So… You want us to…" he managed.

"Continue with your research," Judy said. "And posthaste, should you be agreeable to it. I am also prepared to meet whatever needs you may have, whether that's more pay, additional staffing, etcetera. And all I ask in return is that you keep me informed with regular progress updates. As of right now, your research has become one of the top priorities for the Kadath facility."

"I realize what we have found is incredibly important," Charles said, "but why is it suddenly a top priority for the facility? What do you expect us to find out there?"

"Why, the *future*, Mr. Ryan," Judy said. "And Kadath exists to drive mankind into the future."

"I think you can call me Charles, Judy," Charles said, his lip quirking up into a smile. "And I could definitely do with a pay raise. As well as better quarters. And I either need the *Endeavoring Truth* upgraded for longer excursions or swapped out for a new sub."

"Very good, Charles," Judy said. "Consider it done. Have your list of desired upgrades to me by tomorrow." Then she turned toward Lucas. "And what about you, Dr. Kane?"

"You can call me Lucas," Lucas said.

"Wonderful, Lucas!" Judy exclaimed. "I'm so glad you've both come around. Now, though, there is the slight matter of Ms. Wilkins. It is a bit problematic to have someone who both has the means and the tenacity to game the system as she does in Control. Unlike in certain areas, it is a bit harder for me to be lenient in this one. I'm sure you can understand the predicament in which I find myself with this."

"I'll take her as my lab assistant," Lucas said quickly, the idea springing to his lips nearly before it had crossed his mind.

"Excellent," Judy said. "Consider it done. She will retain all but her highest level clearance so that she will be of the maximum use to your work. And, of course, if you require higher privileges, you are more than welcome to contact me for them."

"Great," Lucas said. "Th-thank you, Judy. This is… very unexpected."

"We like to reward forward-thinking at Leng, as well as bet on promising prospects," Judy said. "And, if I'm not mistaken, yours are very promising indeed. Now, I think I've kept you both long enough. Charles, I trust that you will also assist Lucas in any capacity he needs, in addition to continuing your geological research and scouting expeditions."

"Certainly," Charles said. "I planned on doing that anyway."

"Great," Judy said. "And, Lucas, I will wait to inform Ms. Wilkins of her change in position until tomorrow, should you wish to inform her yourself first."

"Okay," Lucas said. "I'll tell her tonight."

"Fantastic," Judy said. "Well, if there's nothing else I can do for you gentlemen currently, then I will let you get back to your research."

"Yes," Lucas said. "Of course. Have a good day, Judy."

"And you as well," Judy replied. "We'll be in touch shortly."

Charles and Lucas both stood and hurried from the room. The hatch swished shut behind them.

"Charles, what just happened in there?" Lucas asked.

"Blake gave us carte blanche, Lucas, that's what!" Charles exclaimed, slapping Lucas on the back. "We are in business, Doc! We've got to celebrate. Find out when Rachel's shift is over, and let's meet on the promenade for dinner. We have a lot to discuss."

The smile took a little while to spread across Lucas's face, but when it finally did, he couldn't make it go away. "Okay. That's a great idea. All right. I'll talk to you soon, Charles."

"You better believe you will," Charles said. Then, with one final slap on Lucas's back, he strode off, leaving Lucas alone. Well, almost alone.

Lucas caught sight of the four beings out of the corner of his eye. They were blurry and light grey but had the rough shape of humans. He thought they were trying to speak, but all he heard was a muffled, humming mumble.

"You're not real," Lucas muttered. "You're not there, and you're not going to steal this from me. Leave me alone. Go away. Go *away!*"

Lucas didn't look back to see if they had.

⁂

"Okay, you've got me here," Rachel said after she and Lucas had ordered their food. "What was so urgently important?"

"You know how you're always saying you get fed up with the bureaucracy in the control center?" Lucas replied.

"Yeah?"

"And how you sometimes get bored with the menial tasks in your job?"

"Well, sure."

"What would you think about coming to work with me?" Lucas asked.

Rachel's expression was shocked. "What are you talking about, Lucas?"

"Judy Blake found out," Lucas said. "About everything. She called Charles and me to her office, and we were pretty sure we would be on the next sub home. But she didn't reprimand us in the slightest. Instead, she gave our work top priority. She said we could have anything we wanted. And I said I wanted you."

"Wait," Rachel said. "Whoa. What? I –"

"I know, it's a lot to process," Lucas said. "I've been trying to wrap my head around it for hours, and I still haven't succeeded. But this could be *it*, Rachel. This actually could be our chance to change the world. We're a great team, and I want you by my side. You're the reason this is happening in the first place, and you deserve to be a part of it."

"But I don't have any training or anything," Rachel said. "I –"

"You're quick on your feet, and you have that sense of wonder," Lucas said. "The rest I can teach you. So, what do you say, Rachel? Will you join me?"

"I… Yes, of course, I will," Rachel said. "How could I pass this up?"

Lucas beamed. "Thank you, Rachel," he said. "That means so much to me. I hope you don't mind, but Charles is going to join us in a few minutes. He wanted to give us a little bit to talk about this before he dropped in. We have a lot to plan, though, and we want to get moving as quickly as possible."

"Sure," Rachel said. "That's great." Then she shook her head. "Is this really happening, Lucas? Are we really doing this?"

Lucas placed his hand on top of Rachel's. "You better believe we are, Rachel," he said with a smile. "This is as real as it gets."

Lucas hoped he wasn't lying to her. On the other hand, perhaps he did. He still felt the four entities behind him, shimmering in and out of existence. They were coming closer again, crowding in around him. Their murmurs were still a muted jumble, but now he almost thought he could make out a handful of their words.

"*… Great things…*" "*… Receptor of God…*" "*… light.*" "*Must unlock…*" "*… awaken…*" "*… sphere.*" "*You.*"

Lucas tried to ignore them and just enjoy his time with Rachel. He never let the smile slip from his face as he chatted with her. It wasn't long before Charles arrived.

Lucas threw a couple more items into his bag and sealed it, then stood and headed for the hatch. Charles met him at the shuttle, his duffel slung over his shoulder.

"You ready for this, Lucas?" Charles said with a grin.

"Absolutely," Lucas said. "As long as you think the upgrades weren't just slapped on there with mid-grade adhesive."

"Ouch!" Charles said. "Insulting me is one thing, but insulting my baby? That's harsh."

"I wasn't insulting your baby," Lucas replied. "I was simply questioning the speed with which said baby was enhanced to meet our needs."

Charles chuckled. "Truth be told, I was a little wary of that, too," he said quietly. "But I checked it over myself this morning. It all looks top of the line."

"Well, all right then," Lucas said. "If you say so."

The shuttle slowed to a halt, and Lucas and Charles filed out of it, accompanied by an outpouring of other passengers. The station seemed busier than usual. They found themselves pressed shoulder to shoulder with other travelers –

A hand shot out of the crowd and grabbed Lucas's arm. Lucas frowned and swiveled left. "Edgar?" he said. "Is that you?"

Edgar Kayce panted raggedly, sweat plastering his hair to his forehead. His sunken eyes were wild, his skin clammy. He looked like he had a fever.

"Are you all right?" Lucas asked. "Do you need to get to the med bay?"

"They can't help me," Edgar rasped. "They don't understand, Lucas. But *you* do. I *know* you do. You have the dreams, just like me."

"Hey, buddy, I'm going to need you to take your hand off my friend," Charles said, coming around the side of Lucas.

"It's okay, Charles," Lucas said. "I know him. He *built* this place." Then he redirected his attention to Edgar. "Still having bad dreams?"

"They came to me last night," Edgar said. "Not just in a dream, but *the flesh*. They were standing right there, in my room. And they told me what you're about to do."

Lucas felt a chill run down his spine. "*Who* came to you, Edgar?" he asked.

"Not *who*, but *what*," Edgar said. "Something's coming. Something… *monstrous*. But there's still time. We can still stop it. You can't go out in that sub today, Lucas. You can't. Just stay here."

Lucas's frown deepened. "How did *you* know we were…?"

"You don't understand," Edgar said. "It's out there. Waiting. It *wants* us to find it. It *wants* to be unlocked. It's hungry! *So hungry…*"

The four entities were clustering around Lucas now, clutching at him. He could feel their fluctuating, gyrating skin pressing against his clothes. "**Don't listen…**" "**… doesn't comprehend.**" "**… activate…**" "**… consciousness.**"

"Edgar, you need medical attention," Lucas said. "You're not well."

"If you go out there today, it will set things in motion that cannot be undone!" Edgar shouted. "Please, you must understand! Is your need for discovery worth endangering the entire human race?"

Lucas felt a knot of dread tightening in his stomach. The intensity of Edgar's gaze seemed to bore through Lucas's eyes into his soul. What if he was right?

"Is everything okay here?" a security guard asked, stepping up beside Edgar.

"My friend is very sick," Lucas said. "He needs to get to the nearest med bay. Would you mind making sure he gets there?"

"Of course," the guard said, grabbing Edgar's shoulder. "Come along, sir. Let's get you to the med bay."

"No. NO!" Edgar cried. "Lucas, listen to me! We should never have built this place! It was a *monumental* mistake! But we couldn't stop. Even after the accidents, and the signs – But *you* still have a chance! You can end this, Lucas! Or at least *delay* it. Please, don't go out there! PLEASE!"

"We need to get going, Lucas," Charles said. "We're falling behind schedule."

"I'll… check on you as soon as I get back, Edgar," Lucas said. "I promise. I hope you feel better soon."

"No, Lucas, don't go out there!" Edgar shouted. Turning, Lucas started walking away. "DON'T GO OUT THERE! YOU'LL KILL US ALL!"

Lucas tried to block Edgar's shrieks out of his mind. It grew easier the farther away they walked.

FIVE

THE EXPEDITION

"The latest round of fusion experiments has surpassed our wildest expectations. Never before have we been able to inject an agent into the other worlds while both maintaining a connection to the agent and keeping a core of the agent's mind intact. This breakthrough allows for a level of communication previously unachievable in all our centuries of effort, giving us an unprecedented level of control over the shaping of events. These may be the most stellar fusion trials since the asset's manifestation. And, if separated from that felicitous event, their success could potentially be orders of magnitude greater than any other experiment we have ever conducted."

Dr. Jayce Norton

TOWER WORLD

Mitsuko checked the backpacks one more time as Connor and Min looked over their makeshift armor and secured the weapons they had acquired. At last, Mitsuko handed a pack to each of her companions before shouldering the third one herself. They double-checked their gear one final time, almost fidgeting as they cast uncertain glances through the double doors that stood so near at hand.

"So, I guess this is it," Connor said finally. "You two ready?"

"We will never be ready for this," Mitsuko said. "Let's go."

With one last glance back at the building's expansive lobby, they pushed through the two sets of double doors and stepped out of the skyscraper.

The day was deceptively calm and nearly warm. A soft breeze chilled the group's exposed skin, while the red paving stones before them smoldered in the sunlight. Connor thought he saw something stir in the distant woods, but that may have just been his nerves.

"Let's move," Mitsuko said. "Quickly!"

Turning, the three travelers hurried around the black skyscraper. They clung to its side, keeping one wary eye on the swaying forest beyond the radial roads. Connor was keeping such a careful watch on their surroundings, in fact, that Min's comment completely caught him off guard.

"Does anyone see the sun?" Min asked.

"What do you mean?" Mitsuko murmured. "There's light all around us!"

"Yes, but do you actually *see* the sun?" he said. "Because I do not."

"Maybe it's blocked by the skyscraper," Connor replied. "Or clouds."

"Of course," Min said. "That must be it."

"We're too exposed here," Mitsuko said as they continued around the tower. "We need to break for the woods."

"We don't know what's in there," Connor replied. "They could be on us in an instant."

"Perhaps we cannot see them now," Mitsuko said. "But they can *certainly* see us."

Connor sighed. Of course, she was correct. "Okay," he said.

Angling slightly to the right, Mitsuko dashed forward toward the woods, Min and Connor following in her wake. Their footfalls made dull slapping sounds against the red blocks beneath their feet. A cool breeze gently swept around their skin.

Far away from them, something bellowed wetly. Connor glanced back, his stomach leaping up to his throat. He was now a little less confident the movement he saw in the distance was his imagination.

Mitsuko led them past the edge of the woods, then she slowed. Her eyes warily scanned every tree and shrub. "We move slower now," she whispered. "Stay close to the forest's border in case we must run."

Neither Min nor Connor said anything. It wasn't necessary. Though Connor secretly suspected that, if it came to running, none of them would make it back to the skyscraper's entrance in time.

Carefully they circled the red-bricked courtyard's circumference, dashing across the perfectly straight roads they found striking off from the rounded center. They passed another set of double doors along the building's left-hand side, perfectly centered in the middle of the structure. They kept going.

At last, the three travelers reached the back of the skyscraper. From here, they could see yet another set of double doors cutting into the black edifice's base. Connor realized there must be an entrance on each side. Funny, he didn't remember seeing any exits on the inside but the one.

"All right," said Mitsuko. "We head up from here." Coming to the next road, she turned and began navigating through the forest alongside it.

"It's interesting," Min whispered. "I rather thought we would run into *something* by this point."

"Don't jinx us, Min," Connor replied.

"My apologies," Min said.

"Shh!" Mitsuko hissed. "I hear something up ahead!"

"Bloody hell, Min!" Connor said.

"My apologies," Min replied.

Mitsuko gave them both a dark look before stalking forward and parting the bushes. Min and Connor waited tensely as she looked around, drawing their weapons into their hands. Connor had taken Trevor's pistol, as he didn't think the man would need it any longer. Still, he hoped not to have to use it. Any number of horrible things would undoubtedly hear the gunshot.

Mitsuko returned to them. "There is one of the mutations in the brush up ahead," she said quietly. Calmly. "We're going to try to get around it."

Mitsuko's words doused Connor like freezing water. He knew the creatures were out here. Of course, he did. But to hear that one was so close… Almost near enough to touch…

Mitsuko veered left, and the three travelers crept out of the woods and across the road. They disappeared into the trees on the opposite side just as something shifted and cracked across the way. They each hid behind whatever was nearest, their breath frozen in their chests. Something thudded on the paving stones. It sounded big and soggy. Then they heard the voice.

"Hello?" a woman called. "Is anyone here? I… I could have sworn I heard someone…"

Connor's eyes grew wide. Had they made a mistake? Was this actually a *person?* He looked over at Mitsuko, who vigorously shook her head.

"Please, I'm hurt," the voice said. "I need help. If you're there, I beg you… come out."

Connor could feel every sinew in his body aching to respond to the voice. What if they were wrong? They couldn't abandon someone who was just as lost as they were!

A steady hand fell on his shoulder. Connor looked back to see that Min had snuck up beside him. His eyes were firm as he repeated Mitsuko's action, shaking his head slowly, emphatically, back and forth.

The woman began to cry. Her sobs lasted for what seemed hours, and then they could hear the thick, sodden footsteps lumbering away from them and back into the woods. They waited for a few minutes, breathing shallowly, waiting to see if the woman would come back. She didn't.

"Let's go," Mitsuko whispered. They stole off again down the road.

"Are you sure we weren't wrong, Mitsuko?" Connor asked. "What if it really *was* a woman who needed help?"

"It wasn't a woman," Mitsuko replied. "At least, not anymore."

They kept walking for what seemed a very long time, taking cover whenever they heard noises in the woods around them. The red cobblestone road continued ever faithfully alongside them, as straight as a measuring stick.

"Have you noticed how few animals there are here?" Min said.

Mitsuko nodded. "It is unusually quiet."

"Could they have been driven off by the creatures?" Connor asked.

"Perhaps," Mitsuko replied. "In any case, we are lucky we packed provisions."

"If the mutations are still mainly congregated near the ocean, perhaps we will see more wildlife as we go," Connor suggested.

"That is a big 'if,' unfortunately," Min replied.

Sometime later, Mitsuko bent down to examine a shrub nestled into the crook of a tree's roots. Her hand trailed over to the tree the plant nestled inside.

"What is it, Mitsuko?" Connor asked.

"There is something odd about the plants here," she said. "I just... can't put my finger on what it is."

"Are they conceivably mutated as well?" Min asked.

Mitsuko shook her head with a frown. "I don't know. Maybe it's nothing." She stood to her feet again. "Never mind."

The trees and foliage around them began to thin. It shortly became clear that the forest was about to come to an end. Connor felt his heart leaping inside of him. Soon they should see some other signs of life. Soon they'd be able to find help.

"Do you hear that?" Min asked.

"Hear what?" Connor replied.

"It sounds like... waves."

Mitsuko frowned. "Yes, I do," she said. Connor frowned, too, and inclined his ear.

"Yeah," he said. "I do, too."

And then he saw the drifts of sand sifting over the road beside them.

"Bloody hell," he said.

Mitsuko followed his gaze. Her shoulders sank. "This must be a peninsula," she said.

"Let's keep going," Min said. "Perhaps we will see some landmarks we can use to get our bearings."

"We'll be awfully exposed," Connor cautioned.

"We will try to stay out of sight," Mitsuko said. "And then we will retreat as soon as we've surveyed the area."

Carefully, quietly, the three descended toward the beach. Soon their eyes were overwhelmed by the blinding white sand, the cerulean sky, and the turquoise waves. It all seemed so peaceful. Almost idyllic. Yet, at the same time, Connor couldn't help but feel that it looked very, very familiar. His pulse was racing, despite the picturesque scene.

"This looks oddly similar to the other shore," Connor said.

Mitsuko snorted. "It is a beach, Connor," she said. "They tend to look alike, especially when they're part of the same piece of land."

"Of course," Connor said. "You're right. It's just my nerves."

"Do you see anything in either direction?" Min asked. "Perhaps something that might hint at where the landmass is?"

Mitsuko and Connor scanned the horizon in both directions. "Nothing concrete," Mitsuko said.

Min sighed. "Neither do I."

"Is the air… shimmering?" Connor asked.

"What do you mean?" Min said.

"Look out over the water," Connor replied. "Away from the land. It almost looks like the sky is a mirage. Or a heat haze."

"You are describing an incredibly common occurrence," Mitsuko said, sounding only a little exasperated. "There is nothing strange about that."

Connor just nodded.

"Oh, over there," Min said. "I see a shed. Perhaps it's a boathouse?"

"Are you very interested in going for a ride right now?" Mitsuko asked.

Min shrugged. "I was just noting a point of interest."

The ground beneath them shook. It was almost like a miniature earthquake, but Connor knew instantly that's not what it was. The earth rumbled again. "It's time to go," Connor murmured. "Right now."

Mitsuko nodded. "I agree," she said. "Completely."

The trees further down the beach rustled. Something snapped. Turning, the three travelers ran.

The sand kicked up beneath their feet in little plumes. Their movements seemed so slow, considering how badly they wanted to move quickly. The forest covering seemed so far away.

The chimeric behemoth pushed through the trees in the distance and bellowed. It was so large. Connor dared a glance back at it and felt a shock of recognition. He would never forget those clusters of glistening black eyes.

Min slipped. The sand erupted around him in a cloud as he landed face-first in it. Connor and Mitsuko frantically scrambled to help Min back up to his feet.

The towering beast was thundering down the beach directly toward them now. Its mandibles churned; its multitude of limbs and tendrils writhed. Connor tried not to look at it. Even a glance made him want to start screaming and not stop. *How many mouths did it have?*

They were almost through the brush and into the grass now. Connor had a dizzying sense of déjà vu as they raced toward the forest. He wondered briefly if either Min or Mitsuko were feeling the same thing.

Mitsuko veered left, directing them to the red road. Their feet thudded over the stones, finally granting them some traction. The tall grass waved and weaved around them before being replaced once again by the looming forest. Connor and the others practically dove between the trees. They zigzagged between the trunks, feeling branches and bushes clutch and rip at them. This time they didn't try to stay by the road but instead raced as fast and deep as they could into the woods. Behind them, they heard the pines give way to the behemoth.

"We are losing our way," Min said between huffing breaths.

"That is currently not our chief concern," Mitsuko replied.

The ground sloped downward up ahead, and Connor noticed that a large section of hillside had sloughed off below some tree roots. Even better, a tree had fallen over the top of it, partially concealing it. Jumping over the tree, Connor appraised the hollow. It would have to do. Connor threw himself into the little alcove and motioned for Mitsuko and Min to follow him. They did, scrambling in beside him. It was a snug fit.

"What if it can smell us?" Min asked.

"Then we're screwed," Connor said.

The woods shook around them. It was getting closer. So much closer –

The world shuddered and then held its breath. The only sounds now came from the monolithic horror standing directly over them. Connor and the others covered their mouths.

The beast paused. Was it listening? Was it looking? Was it smelling?

One of its enormous, gnarled legs came into view, its foot digging into the soft dirt. Connor noticed it wasn't a cohesive whole, but rather a collection of disparate parts fused together. Arms and legs pressed out of the central mass, intertwining with thick, ropy tendrils. And there were faces, too.

One of the faces opened its eyes, and Connor began to tremble. They were looking directly at each other. The face's mouth opened as if it were trying to draw air into lungs that no longer existed. Connor noticed its eyeballs were milky as if it was blind or suffered from thick cataracts. He so hoped that was true…

The creature took another step. Then another. And then it

lumbered off into the woods. Connor, Min, and Mitsuko all took a deep, shuddering breath in unison. Realizing they were clutching at each other, they slowly released their grips.

"I am very ready to be away from this bloody place," Connor growled. He was trying desperately to get the face's gaze out of his mind. Not to mention the fact that, as the beast walked away, one of the arms on its leg had extended like it was reaching for Connor. Begging him for help.

It was nearing dusk by the time they managed to find their way back to the tower. They were all exhausted, their previous adrenaline surge having worn off some time ago.

"Do we go back inside and try again tomorrow?" Min asked.

A look flashed across Mitsuko's face. One of failure, sorrow, and loathing. Connor noticed it, and said, "Why don't we choose one of the other directions and make camp for the night. It's not too cold out here, and I think we can manage."

"And if the mutations find us in the night?"

"One of us will have to keep watch," Connor replied. "And, honestly, are we any safer back inside the tower?"

Mitsuko cleared her throat and nodded. "I agree with Connor. Let's keep going and make camp when we must."

"Very well," Min said. "Which direction shall we try now?"

"Right's as good a way as any," Connor said.

"True enough," Min said. "Right it is."

They wound toward the path parallel to the tower's right-hand doors and turned, walking beside it until the dusk's light had bled to dark.

"Another," Mitsuko said, shaking her head.

"One more… effin'… beach," Connor murmured.

Min sighed. "Any sign of land this time?"

"I doubt we would see anything from here," Mitsuko said. "The only hope of land now lies directly behind us."

"Look," Connor said. "Another boathouse."

"Ah, so it is," said Min.

"Doesn't this beach look strikingly like the others?" Connor asked.

"What are you trying to say, Connor?" Mitsuko said. "That these beaches are duplicates? That we're just going to the same one over and over again, thinking they're different?"

Connor paused, then shook his head. "I don't know," he said. "Maybe I'm just babbling nonsense."

"No, I fear you could be correct," Min said. "I just don't know how. Or what it means."

Picking up a smooth stone, Mitsuko chucked it into the sedately lapping waves. The rock disappeared with a plop. Then, seconds later, another splash answered it a little farther out from the shore.

"Time to go," Min said. "Before we're noticed."

It wasn't long before trees once more enveloped them. Noises to their left forced them to delve deeper into the woodlands again, creeping ever farther into the unknown belly of the forest. Connor let his eyes wander upward, taking in the canopy overhead. Spanish moss dangled like beards from the groping branches above them, adding an otherworldly, ethereal quality to the place. The trees moaned as the wind gusted between their limbs.

"I wonder if we're near a swamp," Mitsuko said, following Connor's gaze. Connor nodded.

"What do you do, Mitsuko?" Connor asked. "When you're not swinging swords about or avoiding mind-shattering abominations, of course."

"I was a scientist," Mitsuko said. "A botanist."

"Is that right!" Connor said. "I wondered, from your comments about the local plant life."

"You never asked me what *I* do, Connor," Min said with a smile.

Connor chuckled. "I kind of figured that was as necessary as someone asking *me*."

Min laughed. "Indeed."

"It is strange, though, isn't it?" Connor said. "Two holy men and a scientist. Why us? What called us to this place?"

"You assume there is some reason beyond blind chance," Mitsuko said. "Often, *it* is as good a cause as any."

"Perhaps," Connor replied. "But even beyond that, why have *we* remained intact when so many others have been… altered?"

"Survival of the fittest," Mitsuko said.

"So, you're seriously suggesting that a preacher and a monk are the two fittest of everyone who emerged from the ocean?" Connor asked. "No offense, Min."

"Some taken," Min replied. Then he gasped, stopping dead in his tracks. "Mitsuko, I think I know what is wrong with the foliage here." Mitsuko doubled back to Min and followed his gaze up a tree. She gasped, too.

Worked into the bark of the tree, about twelve feet off the ground, was a face. Its mouth was twisted in an eternal wail; its eyes were empty tombs.

"Look closer at the limbs, also," Connor said. "Do they seem just a bit like… hands? With branches for fingers?"

Min and Mitsuko nodded.

"Come on," Mitsuko said after a couple of minutes. "We need to keep moving."

Now that they had seen one, the wanderers spotted the people trees all around them. It was a wonder that they hadn't noticed them before. But then, they'd had other concerns previously.

Min was walking forward, his eyes on the canopy above, when Mitsuko placed a hand on his chest. "Min, stop."

Min looked down. Mud was squelching up around his boots. He had been about to step into the swamp Mitsuko had predicted earlier.

"Look," Connor murmured, pointing across the expanse of softly stirring green water. As they watched, they saw the cattails part at the far edge of the swamp, and one of the mutated people shamble forward. It walked on all four of its appendages, which had become long, pointed spears of bone. Its neck had elongated until it looked like a thick snake, while its mouth opened like a petaled flower crammed with teeth.

The monster surveyed the water before it, then stepped in. It shuffled forward on its four bony extremities, a long, low moan ushering from its gullet. It moved out ever deeper into the swamp, more and more of its body disappearing below the surface. Connor couldn't tell if the ripples were distorting its appearance, or if its physical form was actively dissolving.

At last, only the creature's head was still above the water. It let out one final mewl, and then it submerged completely.

"Did it seem to anyone else like the swamp just… ate him?" Connor said.

The water burbled and splashed near the center of the bog. One of the monster's limbs bobbed to the surface, no longer encumbered by a body. The bony thing floated there for a moment, bubbles popping around it. Then it sank slowly back into the miry depths.

The three travelers stood very still, their jaws slack. Connor shivered as if a breeze were encircling him from off the fen. It called to him, urged him to plunge into its unknowable heart. It would be such a little thing to offer himself to it…

"No closer," Mitsuko said. "I think it really did eat that thing."

"Could the trees…?" Min said.

Mitsuko shook her head. "It doesn't make any sense. But they *would* draw water from this. I wonder… how many of these swamps there are…"

The air above the swamp was shimmering. Electric. Fungi growing around the water's edge seemed to glow. The Spanish moss swayed in the trees.

"Perhaps this is why we haven't seen more of the mutated people," Min offered. Mitsuko nodded.

"Mitsuko's right," Connor said, shaking his head. "We need to go. Now. Before we all decide to take a swim."

"I feel its pull as well," Min said. "It calls to me, like a siren to a sailor."

Wrenching their eyes away from the swamp, Min, Connor, and Mitsuko stumbled away into the woods. Mitsuko stopped after only a few minutes, though, in front of one of the human trees. "Wait," she said. "I need to know."

"Know what, Mitsuko?" Min asked.

Mitsuko didn't reply. Instead, she pulled out her machete and found a rock lying nearby. Looking up at the face staring down at them, she whispered, "I'm sorry." Then she pressed the knife's tip against the tree's bark and started hammering the rock into its hilt. The machete pushed deeper into the tree with every hit. After about a quarter of the blade had punctured into the wood, she yanked the knife back. Sap that was as red as blood clung to its tip. Reaching out a finger, she scooped up a small amount of the watery fluid and brought it to her nose.

"Copper," she said, sniffing it. "It's not sap. At least, not entirely." Her mouth was drawn into a grim line as she wiped off her blade and sheathed the knife. The sap came off much too easily.

"Let's keep moving," she said. "I want to be far away from this place."

Min and Connor nodded.

Sometime late in the day, they made it back to the black tower. The thing seemed to stretch into the troposphere, its glinting windows capturing the last glimmers of the day's light. There was something dark, sinister, and almost alien about it. Perhaps it was just their experiences in the woods that led them to feel even more uncomfortable than usual standing in its shadow. Maybe it was the time of day. Or possibly it was something else.

"I assume we still don't want to go back in there?" Min said.

"Not a chance," Connor said. "Though… I'm also less inclined to camp in the forest than I was yesterday."

Mitsuko nodded. "Still, going back in there would feel like an utter defeat. And we are not yet defeated."

"Do you think we can cut straight across?" Connor asked. "Rather than creeping through the woods now?"

"If we're quick and cautious about it," Mitsuko said.

They looked around to make sure the coast was clear, and then they dashed across the red cobblestones toward the skyscraper. Trying to keep a healthy distance from the doors, they hurried around the tower's perimeter. Then, when they had finally reached the opposite side, they ran for the final road lined up with a pair of doors – their last hope of escape.

The creature leaped at them from the gathering gloom between the trees, its shriek inhuman and guttural. Mitsuko dodged to evade it and meet it with her sword, but it was too quick. It knocked her to the ground, its mouth opening wider and wider to make way for another mouth, and another, each one sliding out in succession on thin, waving stalk-throats. Mitsuko was trapped beneath it, unable to get free from its long, twisting fingers.

Connor felt the world slow down around them. He and Min wouldn't be able to stop it before it killed Mitsuko. She had pulled slightly ahead of them, and they were now running to catch up. He felt his hand move toward the gun of its own accord. Then his arm pulled it up, and his eye aimed. His finger pulled the trigger. Then again. And again.

The aberration squealed as it was blown off Mitsuko and flopped on its side, its mouths swiveling and snapping at this new threat. Mitsuko was on her feet in an instant, her sword and machete in her hands. Before it could recover, Mitsuko's blades became silver blurs, slicing its flesh. Its visible eye was a long, milky white gash, and Mitsuko drove her sword through it into the thing's brain. It twitched and spasmed a couple of times, and then it lay still.

Mitsuko's gaze darted up to Connor. "You just made things very difficult for us, Connor," she said.

"Better that than you dead, Mitsuko," he replied.

"We need to move," Min said. "Now."

The jungle all around them was stirring to life. Bellows and yips and squeals echoed off the ground and the tower and the trees. Leaves and branches and pine needles rustled and cracked.

The three humans ran as their surroundings awoke to devour them whole. They didn't bother to hide in the woods now. Their feet pounded over the paving stones as, behind them, they heard something much bigger shake the ground.

"If this isn't a way out, I fear we will be in great trouble," Min said.

"We need to lose them somehow," Mitsuko replied.

Connor looked back. The road behind them was swarming with

undulating, jerking, churning nightmares. And also…

"The big one's back," Connor said, looking forward again.

Talons, fingers, tendrils, and legs like lances were bursting out of the woods on either side of the street, reaching for them, seeking them. Twisted faces peered at them from between the tree trunks – and sometimes looked down on them from the trees themselves. Connor, Min, and Mitsuko pressed closer together, forcing their feet to move faster.

A squeal arose behind them, higher pitched and more desperate than the rest. New sounds were emerging now, as well. Min glanced back, and then he slowed.

"The big one is… *eating* the others," Min announced, cocking his head to the side.

Connor and Mitsuko looked back as well. The towering monstrosity had indeed scooped one of its smaller brethren up in one limb and was holding it out in front of its face, considering. Then its mandibles parted, exposing the much too small orifice behind it. Bringing the smaller being up to its mouth, it experimentally chewed one limb off the mutation and swallowed, causing its prey to scream afresh. At last, the behemoth seemed to make up its mind. A seam formed in the monster, running from its mouth down its neck and over its chest. The seam flexed, rippled, and then burst open, exposing a new gash full of vibrating razor teeth. The new flaps extended outward and wrapped around the lesser beast. The big horror devoured the smaller one in one swallow.

The other aberrations slowed as if considering their options. And then they scattered into the forest. The behemoth jerked one of its other arms down, snaring a second creature.

"Quickly," Mitsuko said. "This is our chance."

The light was seeping slowly from the day, dousing the world around them deeper and deeper in shadow. Connor watched the encroaching darkness with growing anxiety. There could be anything waiting for them in those pools of night. Just because they were quiet now didn't mean –

"No."

Looking forward, Connor searched for the reason Mitsuko had suddenly stopped. It didn't take long to spot it.

"Another beach," Min said.

"We're on a bloody island," Connor murmured.

Mitsuko sank to her knees, defeated.

"What are you doing?" Min cried. "Get up, Mitsuko!"

"We're done," she said. "There's no way we can get back to the skyscraper. And there is no way to escape into the ocean."

"Like hell, there isn't," Connor said. Turning right, he saw another small shed. It *could* be a boat storage. It certainly could be. "Come on!"

Connor raced across the beach to the shed. Skidding in front of it, he threw open the doors which were blessedly unlocked. His heart leaped up to his throat. "A boat!" he almost screamed.

Min was by him in a flash, and together they were hauling the small boat out of the shed. It wasn't huge, but it would do for the three of them. There were oars in the boat, and…

"It has a motor!" Connor exclaimed. "Would you look at that little beauty!"

Mitsuko reached them and got behind the boat, pushing it as Min and Connor pulled. They had gotten to the waves when they heard the giant bellow behind them. It had lost interest in the smaller mutants. Even from this distance, they could make out the giant's footfalls shaking the cobblestones.

Connor had Min and Mitsuko climb aboard, then he got behind it and pushed it out into the calm waves. The water rose, soaking more of Connor's pants the farther he pushed the boat. At last, he was up to his waist, and Min and Mitsuko hauled him up into the ship. The hulking thing roared again, and Connor looked back to see that the horror had reached the edge of the beach.

"Not today, beastie," Connor said. Then he lowered the motor's blades into the water and thumbed the ignition. The engine whirred to life, and its propeller started churning. They lurched forward. All three of them let out a triumphant yell as the shore began to shrink behind them.

After they were confident the behemoth was no longer pursuing them, Connor shut off the motor. There was no way they could tell what direction was best to head in at night, and the engine was running low on solar power in any case. After this, they settled down as best they could to try to get some sleep.

"The sky is strange," Mitsuko said. "It's almost like I see something, but I don't know what it is. I don't think it's stars."

"Perhaps there are clouds playing havoc with our sight," Min suggested.

"Yes, maybe," she said, lost in thought. Then her gaze dropped back to Min and Connor. "Thank you," she said. "For saving my life."

Connor smiled. "My pleasure, Mitsuko."

"I'm… not used to relying on other people," she admitted.

"I think it's safe to say we all must count on each other in this place," Min said. "I am thankful for you as well, Mitsuko. I doubt any of us would still be here if not for you."

Mitsuko smiled and bowed her head slightly.

"We should try to sleep if we can," Connor said. "Do you think we need to keep a watch?"

"I will take the first shift," Min said. "You two sleep. I will let you know if anything happens."

"Which direction should we head?" Connor asked.

"Any direction is as good as another at this point," Mitsuko replied. "We have as much chance of finding the mainland regardless of our choice."

"I motion we move as far away from the island as possible," Min said.

"That works for me," Connor said. Setting the island directly behind them, he gunned the outboard.

The sky was overcast, but no rain was falling. The clouds were moving, too, in a lazy pattern that seemed almost circular. Connor felt strangely unsettled as he remembered his first glimpse of the tower.

"The sky is bizarre even still," Min said.

"Yes," Mitsuko said. "It is indeed."

"So, what's the last thing you remember?" Connor asked. "From when you were home, I mean."

"It's all… fractured," Mitsuko said. "I may have been running. There was someone with me. And maybe something else."

"I seem to remember being in the temple where I serve," Min said. "But the rest is a confusing jumble."

Connor nodded. "That's about as much as I can recall, too. I think I was inside my church. And I think it was burning."

"Connor, STOP!" Min yelled.

Connor slammed the motor into reverse and swerved. The boat rocked as the waves crashed against it, but before long, they had come to an almost complete standstill. "What is it, Min?" Connor asked.

"Look," Min said. "Your shimmer."

Connor blinked his eyes. Min was right. The clouds had parted slightly overhead, and the shimmer he'd seen the other day had returned. It was not, however, in the far distance: it was only a few boat lengths away from them.

"Does the ocean look strange beyond it?" Mitsuko asked.

"Yes," Connor replied. "Almost like… it's a reflection."

A lump was forming in Connor's belly that felt like a ball of steel. He brought the motor to quarter power, and they began slowly moving forward again. The hazy shimmer moved closer and closer until it was directly in front of them. Connor guided the boat up so that they were alongside it. Then, grabbing an oar, he poked at the gleaming mirage. It pushed back.

Dropping the oar into the boat, Connor tentatively extended his hand.

"That may not be wise, Connor," Min said.

"I have to know," Connor replied.

Connor's hand hovered just before the shimmer. Then, with one final push, he touched it. The surface gave slightly below his fingers, but it was undoubtedly solid. Connor moaned.

"Draw us closer, Min," Mitsuko said. Retrieving an oar, Min drove their boat flush against the surface. Standing, Mitsuko placed both of her hands against the barrier, and then slowly drew her face in toward it. It almost looked like her face passed through the haze, submerged in the image of the ocean and sky that it showed them. She gasped.

"No," she said. "No, no, no, no *no NO!*" Stumbling backward with a sob, she looked like she was about to fall out of the boat. Jumping up, Min grabbed her and steadied her, then helped her sit down.

"What is it, Mitsuko?" he asked. "What did you see?"

Both Min and Connor saw tears streaming down Mitsuko's face before her balled-up fists pressed into her eyes, trying to shield her from the world. Connor and Min shared a look of steadily growing alarm. "Nothing," she sobbed. "There was nothing but an endless, throbbing nightmare. It churned like a maelstrom of lightning and eyes. *It saw me.* It looked into my *soul*…" Lowering her fists, she finally opened her eyes, which were so bloodshot they were almost red. "We can't escape. There's *nothing* we can do. We're not even on *earth* anymore…"

SIX

THE SPHERE

"It is becoming more and more difficult to keep knowledge of the anomalies contained. As they continue spreading to more and more densely populated areas in increasingly influential countries, our ability to repress the events in the public discourse persistently declines. It is only a matter of time before these activities become public knowledge (as it always was.) I recommend beginning phase two implementation, prepping the public-focused clean-up crews as we prepare to seize the narrative."

Lawrence James – Leng Corp. Public Relations

KADATH FACILITY

"You going to be okay, Lucas?" Charles asked as the chrysalis closed over the top of their submersible.

"Yeah, I'll be fine," Lucas said. "It rattled me a bit is all."

"Alright," Charles said. "Then let's do this." Flooding the tube,

Charles opened the airlock, and the *Endeavoring Truth* burst out into the ocean's depths.

"Control, butterfly is free of the chrysalis," Charles said. "Over."

"Understood, *Endeavoring Truth*. Happy hunting. Over and out."

"So, who *was* that guy?" Charles asked.

Lucas chuckled. "He's the engineer who spearheaded the construction of Kadath."

"You're kidding me."

"No," Lucas replied. "When the facility was still barely a skeleton crew, he and I bonded over nightmares."

"Wow," Charles said. "He may have been down in the dark for a little too long."

"Yeah," Lucas said. "Seems that way."

"Well, it's time to forget about that nastiness, Lucas," Charles said, glancing back. "Now, we focus on hunting monsters."

"You're right, Charles," Lucas said. "Let's go."

Today they didn't make slow passes over different sectors. Instead, Charles propelled them at full speed toward their target. Before long, they were there again, staring in wonder at the slowly revolving cone of sea life centered above the seabed's long rocky gash.

"There it is," Charles said.

"And just as captivating as ever," Lucas replied.

"I'm engaging the new scanners now," Charles said. "Launching mapping drones."

Twin drones burst like torpedoes from either side of the submersible, streams of bubbles jetting behind them. A few seconds later, two more fired. The first two angled down, spreading out in either direction, while the next two swerved upward.

"I have control of three and four," Lucas said.

"Beautiful," Charles replied. "I've got the other two. Let's see what we can find, Doc."

Lucas guided his two drones up into the living vortex of sea animals, watching enrapt as innumerable species flitted around them. Many of them twinkled, pulsed, or glowed with unique patterns of light, creating a spectacle a bit like an underwater fireworks show. It was a stunning, wondrous sight.

The hours passed in relative silence, both men engrossed in their displays. At last, though, Charles swiveled around. "I'm picking up some interesting readings in the fissure," he said. "Mind if I take us in for a look?"

"Be my guest," Lucas replied.

Nodding, Charles guided them toward the cleft's jagged opening, the sub's lights playing over the rock and warring with the silt. "There's something extraordinary going on in there," Charles said. "I've never seen anything like it before."

"Mind sending me the scans?" Lucas said.

"Sure," Charles said, flicking the readings back to Lucas. Lucas frowned.

"Wow," he said. "What in the world is causing *those?*"

"Exactly," Charles said. "Let's go find out, shall we?"

The sub passed over the lip of the fissure and began a slow descent. Its floods bathed the sides of the trench in circles of light, shadows flitting in the rocks and hollows as the wide beams slid past. Lucas's heart beat faster as the submersible sank deeper. The number of animals was thinning now, almost as if –

The whisper thundered in Lucas's mind: *Welcome, Herald. We see you. We greet you.*

"Huh," Charles said.

"What?" Lucas said with a wince.

"I just lost one of the drones," Charles replied. "There went the second one, too –"

The beast unfurled from the depths, its jagged tentacles lashing out at the *Endeavoring Truth*. Charles yelled out in alarm, jerking back on the sub's controls. It was closing in on them, its churning beak growing larger, larger…

Lucas gasped. "That's it."

"That's *what*, Lucas?" Charles yelled.

"The kraken," Lucas replied. "My sea monster."

"Well, hold on!" Charles cried. "Your sea monster looks like it wants to open us like an anchovy tin!"

Charles engaged the emergency deterrent system as he blasted the sub's turbines. Lucas watched, hardly breathing, as the nightmare squid barely missed a beat. It was truly magnificent this close. And it was also absolutely terrifying.

"Sorry, Doc, the show's over," Charles said. "I'm going to turn off the lights and see if I can lose it."

"I don't think that'll be enough."

"Maybe not. But it's worth a try."

Charles flipped off the exterior and sparse interior lights, and the soft glow of blue instrument panels filled the sub. Almost immediately, they felt their little sanctuary, their tiny oasis of air amidst the limitless crushing liquid, quake as the monster's tentacles slammed into them. They heard the hull squeal as talons inside some of its suckers scored gashes into the metal.

"I'll recall the other drones," Lucas said, hands flying over his controls. "Try to distract it and give us some time."

"Good idea," Charles said. "Get them here quick!"

Lucas set the drones on a return trajectory at top speed, sending them whizzing through the ocean's depths. Quickly they approached the sub, and the kraken temporarily released its quarry to investigate these new playthings.

"I just lost drone four," Lucas said. "And… there goes three, as well."

"That was fast," Charles replied. "I was hoping it wouldn't be quite *that* efficient."

There wasn't time for Lucas to reply. The squid was on them again in a matter of moments. Emergency alerts burst to life all around the two men as the creature squeezed the submersible, its beak trying to pierce the hull.

"Are there any weapons built into this thing?" Lucas asked. "Anything we can defend ourselves with?"

"If we could get it beneath us, I could try to tangle it up in a sample net," Charles said. "But, apart from that, all we could really use are some robot arms. Oh, that might work! Hold on."

Charles killed the main propulsion turbines and used jets to rotate them from horizontal to vertical. Robot arms sprang to life, snapping out at tentacles and grabbing hold of them, keeping the squid in position. Then Charles ejected the specimen net over the beast. The netting closed reflexively around as much of the "sample" as it could, constricting around its contents. Charles severed the connecting cord as the kraken disengaged from the sub to free itself from this nuisance. Quickly Charles leveled the sub back out and engaged the propulsion system, retracting the robot arms back into the *Endeavoring Truth*.

"That won't hold it for long," Charles said. "But maybe it'll be enough. Just enough…"

They rocketed back toward Kadath, Charles pushing the sub to its limit.

"Control, this is submersible *Endeavoring Truth* requesting emergency docking," Charles said. "Hostile organism is in pursuit. Recommend recalling all submersibles immediately and activating station defense measures. Over."

"Acknowledged, *Endeavoring Truth*," an officer replied. "Can you return to the chrysalis? Or will you need to land on a docking pad? Over."

"Better leave the bay open for us just in case, Control," Charles said.

"Acknowledged," the officer said. "Docking pad three is empty. If you can't make it to the chrysalis, I advise you to land there. We'll try to give you some breathing room when you're in range. Over."

"Roger that, Control," Charles said. "See you soon. I hope."

The sub shook again, twisting in the water. A long, sinewy tentacle wrapped around the front of the craft, its muscles flexing as the long black claws scratched against the viewport.

"No!" Charles cried. "Not yet! We're not in range!"

"What more can we do?" Lucas asked. "Jettison the samples?"

"I don't think that'd work any better than our other distractions have," Charles said. "I'm going to try to blind it."

Flipping the sub around again, Charles flashed on every light the sub had. The sea monster recoiled, momentarily caught off-guard by the flood of illumination. Charles rotated the sub back around and sped toward the facility once more.

"Almost there," Charles murmured. "Almost there…"

"It's coming again!" Lucas said, his eyes glued to the displays.

Charles jerked the controls, trying to keep it off them. He swerved randomly and erratically up and over and side-to-side, but the beast somehow matched him move for move. It grabbed hold of them again, and this time it enveloped the sub in a mass of tentacles and started to squeeze.

The submersible began to warp and twist around Lucas and Charles. The two men sat there, helpless, as the craft deformed around them. This was it. They weren't going to make it —

"Endeavoring Truth, we have you on scanners," the operator said. "Engaging defense systems."

Lucas saw several streams of bubbles blast by the sub, and then the small transport quaked violently. The emergency warnings had never turned off, but they had undoubtedly been joined by more notifications now.

"What's it looking like back there, Lucas?" Charles said.

Lucas studied what rear feeds were still active. "The kraken seems hurt," he said. "Maybe even dead. It's barely moving."

"Well, that's a plus," Charles said. "Too bad it didn't let go before it decided to die on us." Slowly he engaged propulsion, trying to ease them free of its grip. "Uh oh. The navigation's damaged. It looks like the jets are, too."

"Are we stuck?" Lucas asked.

"One second," Charles said. "I'm going to try rebooting those systems and see if that helps."

"Um, I think it's starting to move again, Charles," Lucas said. "It may still be alive."

"Not yet," Charles mumbled. "Not yet… I need a little bit longer…"

"It's twitching," Lucas said. "I'm starting to think it was just stunned."

Charles growled. "It's still cycling. It's not coming online as it should."

"Is there any way for us to move?" Lucas asked.

Charles tapped a few more options. "Hold on," he said. "Let me try this."

Lucas was slammed back in his seat as the sub rocketed to life. The squid still clung to the sub, its bulk trailing behind them in the water. It was starting to rouse.

"It's not working," Charles said. "This isn't working!"

"What isn't?" Lucas said.

"The propulsion is misfiring," Charles replied. "And the controls are sluggish at best. Plus, with that thing still clinging to us, landing is going to be… interesting."

"How can I help?"

"Strap in," Charles said. "Control, this is *Endeavoring Truth*. Can you hear me? Over."

"We hear you, *Endeavoring Truth*," a voice said. "What's your situation? Over."

"Your blast hit the creature and damaged it," Charles replied. "It has not yet recovered. We're coming in hot on docking pad three. The creature is still attached to the craft. Internal propulsion and guidance systems are damaged. I think we're going to crash. Over."

"Understood, *Endeavoring Truth*," Control said. "We will evacuate the area and have a repair and rescue team ready to engage as soon as you land. Over."

"Appreciate it, Control," Charles said. "See you soon." Then he glanced briefly back at Lucas. "Okay, Lucas. I'm going to try to land us, but there is an excellent chance that it won't be pretty. I don't know if it was the blast or the squid that did it, but, regardless, we're in rough shape. I'm transferring propulsion controls back to you. My hands are going to be full trying to land us, so I'll need you to kill the turbines at the exact moment I tell you. Got it?"

"Got it, Charles."

"Good. Transferring now. I figure you're not a praying man, but if you are now is a good time to do it."

Lucas took a deep breath as he saw the propulsion system controls pop up on his screens. Charles engaged the manual steering system and maneuvered the craft to the left. It seemed like he was putting a lot more muscle into it than would be necessary under normal circumstances.

"Okay, get ready, Lucas," he said. "You're going to fire downward for two seconds, and then completely cut the rear thrusters and apply the front ones. You're going to leave those on until I tell you to stop." He paused briefly. "Now, Lucas! Fire down!"

Lucas jammed the top thrusters, and the craft dropped downward.

"Stop!" Charles snapped. "Cut rears! Engage in front!"

Lucas killed the rear turbines and flipped on the fronts at full blast.

"Come on," Charles said, gritting his teeth. "Come on!"

Kadath was coming up quicker and quicker. Lucas could see the flashing lights of the recessed docking pad not far away from them. The outer airlock was already open, waiting for them. The bay was empty, but even still, that space seemed so small. The facility drew closer. Closer.

"Okay," Charles said. "Okay, we can do this. Get ready, Lucas. I'm going to activate emergency measures just in case… All right, kill it now!" Lucas turned off the front thrusters.

The squid woke up.

Tightening its arms, it wrenched them to the side. They were too close to the docking pad's bay to do anything about it. Lucas watched in what seemed slow motion as the sub careened into the docking pad's metal wall and crumpled inward like a tin can getting flattened by a baseball bat. Lucas saw water erupting inside the sub, and then he blacked out.

… He was still alive.

Lucas didn't know how much later it was that he opened his eyes, but it couldn't have been *that* long. His mind was woozy, and he tried to clear it by shaking his head and rapidly blinking his eyes. Looking up, Lucas saw that the docking pad airlock doors had closed above them. He could also see the kraken's vicious appendages entwined limply over the *Endeavoring Truth*'s hull. The world still looked so blurry…

Someone moaned. Who…? *Charles.* That's who was in here with him.

"Lucas…" Charles managed. "I think something's wrong…"

Lucas almost laughed at that, but then he peered over the back of his friend's seat. His eyes grew wide. Blood. There was so much blood.

"Hold on, Charles," Lucas said, fumbling at his restraints. "Hold on. I'm going to get you out of here. You're going to be fine." He tapped his node and called Control. "Help! This is Lucas Kane in docking pad three! We need emergency medical attention! Repeat, we need emergency medical attention!"

Lucas entered the med bay, Rachel by his side. Learning the location for Charles's room, he wound his way through the clinic, knocking as he stepped in the door. He winced when he saw his friend.

"Lucas! Rachel!" Charles said. "Good to see you guys! How's it going, Doc?"

"Better than you, Charles," Lucas said, trying for lighthearted and failing miserably.

Charles looked down at his body. He nodded. "Yeah, that's probably true," he said. "They… couldn't save the legs. Or my left arm. They said the damage was too extensive, even for nanobots. I guess my days of piloting subs are over." He almost chuckled, but couldn't quite manage it.

"Well, you're alive, and that's the most important thing," Rachel said, trying to stay upbeat. "The world would be a darker place without you in it, Charles."

Charles smiled. "Ah, you'll make me blush," he said.

Lucas sat down in a chair by Charles's bed. "Charles, I…"

"Don't say it, Doc," Charles said. "Don't apologize. Don't feel sorry for me. I'll get through this, just like I get through everything. In fact, I already have a plan. Blake stopped by with an offer from the company. They have an experimental robotics program in place that they think will be a perfect fit for me. They're going to pay me a small fortune to be a part of it, too. And then, when I'm all decked out in my new gear, I'll be right back down here. It shouldn't even take that long. I'll be harassing the two of you again in no time. Who knows: maybe I'll even eat my words about piloting."

"And you're okay with that, Charles?" Rachel said.

Charles shrugged. "It's not like we all don't already have implants and that sort of thing. I'll just have a few more than other people. Let's just say, of all the offers I've received since the accident, it's definitely my number one option at this point."

Lucas actually laughed at that. "When do you go?"

"They have a shuttle leaving in the morning," Charles said. "They plan to have me on it."

"Oh, that soon?" Rachel said. "Will you be okay traveling right after this?"

"Ah, I'll be fine," Charles said. "I feel better every hour. By tomorrow I'll practically be a new man."

"Sounds like that'll be more like in a few weeks," Lucas said.

"Fair point," Charles replied.

"We'll come to see you off," Rachel said.

"You guys don't have to do that," Charles said.

"But we're going to anyway," Lucas said. "It's the least we can do. We owe you a lot, Charles."

"Speaking of, how much data did we lose in the crash?" Charles asked.

"I don't think we lost much of *anything*," Lucas replied. "In fact, we *gained* an enormous kraken corpse to examine. I've already downloaded and transferred all our readings from the wreck."

"Good," Charles said. "So, at least it wasn't for nothing."

Lucas put a hand on his friend's shoulder. "Definitely not."

Lucas pulled back from his instruments and rubbed his eyes with his hands.

"What's wrong, Lucas?" Rachel asked.

"I… can't focus," Lucas said.

"Is it Charles?" Rachel said, walking over to him.

Lucas hesitated. "It's my fault," he said. "He lost his legs because of *me*."

"That's not true," Rachel said, placing a hand on his shoulder. "And you know it."

"I want to believe you're right," Lucas said. "But… I don't think I can. What does that say about me?"

"It says that you have a conscience," Rachel said.

"Why did I escape unharmed?" Lucas persisted. "How did I get out of there without a single broken bone when Charles was *crushed?*"

"It was blind luck, Lucas," Rachel said. "If you had been in the front, then he'd be having this conversation about *you*."

"Yeah," Lucas said. "Of course. You're right." He was silent for a moment, and then he stood. "I'm going to take a walk. I'll be back."

Rachel watched Lucas go, concern flooding her eyes as he trudged out the opened hatch and down the corridor.

Often when Lucas wandered, his feet would eventually lead him to one of the observation galleries. But not tonight. He needed to *see* it. To confront it again. Perhaps now it would finally offer him the answers he sought.

Lucas stepped inside the cold storage locker, and there it was. The kraken was stretched out before him, the culmination of so many hopes and fears dead on a slab. Even now, the leviathan looked ferocious. It was almost unearthly in its viciousness.

Lucas walked down the monster's length, absorbing its every inch. Slowly the feeling of discovery began to well up inside him again, waging war against the morose guilt and disconnectedness he had been wallowing in. Almost reverently, he reached out and touched the sea terror directly above its right eye.

Lucas gasped and fell to his knees, his hand trailing down the kraken and into one of the bloody cavities carved out by the station's defense projectiles. He didn't even notice. He couldn't see it anymore.

What he saw instead was an ethereal orb wrapped in rock and silt. Its surface was iridescent, shimmering with greens and blues and yellows. It was both gorgeous in its otherworldliness and somehow terrifying at the same moment. Lucas realized he had seen it before in his deepest, darkest dreams. Furthermore, he instinctively knew where to find it: deep within the belly of the fissure he and Charles had explored. This thing was the cause; it was the connection; it was the call.

Had the kraken been protecting it? Or had it merely been as overwhelmed by the sphere's pull as everything else? Was this thing the chief whisper picking at his mind? Was it *all* of them?

Lucas felt the four entities shimmer into existence behind him, their beings fluctuating with their excitement. Their flickering fingertips flitted over Lucas's shirt and hair and neck, their pulsating skin causing Lucas's body to shake violently. Their hurried words poured like oil through Lucas, the ones that rose to the surface becoming islands of madness in a sea of viscous nightmare. *"The sphere…" "The sphere…" "… awaken." "… transcend us all…" "You'll become…" "Truth."*

With great effort, Lucas withdrew his hand from the squid's corpse. He collapsed to the floor, his breath searing and ragged as his lungs heaved it in and out. Sweat had doused his forehead, even in the chilled air of the cold storage. It was too much. He couldn't take it. This was… This was –

Lucas retched on the smooth floor. As he did, he found Edgar's words flooding back to him: *It's out there. Waiting. It* wants *us to find it. It* wants *to be unlocked. It's hungry. So hungry…*

Lucas's hand was still shaking as it covered his mouth. He couldn't tell anyone about this - not even Rachel. He couldn't help them uncover it, no matter how badly he wanted to find it. Or to *touch* it. He had done enough damage already. *What would that thing do if it got near human beings?*

Slowly, Lucas pulled himself to his feet. Looking down, he saw the squid's blue blood coating his hand. A shudder shook his body, and Lucas stumbled from the cold storage room. He needed to get it off him. Before he couldn't anymore.

"How are you doing, Lucas?" Judy Blake asked, leaning forward across her desk.

"I'm doing fine," Lucas said. "Just fine."

"Good, I'm glad to hear it," Judy said. "Though when someone who has been through a trauma like you have, it's all right for them not to be. It doesn't make them any less of an asset to be shaken up or to want to talk to someone else about it all. For instance, I could schedule an appointment with Chaplain Summerisle, and no one would think the lesser of you. Just to talk, of course. Unload a little bit."

Lucas imagined talking to Summerisle, and immediately the thought of him accidentally disclosing his vision of the sphere filled him with a panic that he barely tamped down. "I'm fine," Lucas said, forcing a smile onto his face. "It was certainly a difficult experience, but nothing I can't handle."

"Good," Judy said again, scrutinizing his face. "Excellent. Well, your initial findings have been… remarkable, to say the least. Coupled with the data that Charles collected, we have decided to focus all our current exploratory efforts on this sector. The preliminary results have just been too compelling to ignore."

Lucas felt his stomach plummet. "What kind of exploratory efforts did you have in mind?"

Judy chuckled. "Mining, biology, geology, ecology," she said. *"All* of them."

Lucas nodded slowly. Judy read his hesitancy. "Something wrong, Lucas?"

"Well, it's just that it's a very fragile, complex ecosystem," Lucas said. "I worry that we may permanently damage it if we move too quickly or invasively."

Judy's smile widened. "And that's why I want you to spearhead the team," she said. "I feel you've more than earned that. You won't be operating alone, of course. Our chief mining officer will be working with you, as will a group of your fellow scientists. We will also have a security detail along, should any other large predators take an interest in the party. So. What do you say, Lucas?"

Lucas couldn't speak for a moment. Then, forcing his mouth to move, he heard it say, "Yes, of course. It would be my pleasure."

"Wonderful!" Judy said. "That is fantastic news! Now, I would like to introduce you to another member of the team. I want him to help shepherd the expedition alongside you." Tapping her node, she said, "Tammy, send in Dr. West, please."

Seconds later, the hatch behind them opened, and a tall, confident man with sandy blond hair and a pristine white lab coat entered. Walking up beside Lucas, he extended his hand. "Ah, you must be Dr. Kane!" he exclaimed.

Lucas stood and swiveled to face the man. "Yes," he said, taking the offered hand. "Dr. Lucas Kane. And I presume you're Dr. West?"

"Oh please, let's not be so formal," Dr. West said with a laugh. "It sounds as though we'll be working together, after all! I'm Dr. William West, but I insist that my friends call me William. And, for those who simply *must* attach a Doctor to it somewhere, I ask them just to call me Dr. William."

"Okay, William," Lucas said. "I can do that."

"Good, good!" William said. Then he released Lucas's hand and turned to address Blake. "And Judy! Superlative to see you again."

"The same to you, Dr. William," Judy said. "Now, sit, both of you. We have much to discuss."

"*Golden Light* is away," the *Golden Light*'s captain announced over the coms.

"Roger that, *Golden Light*," the captain of Lucas's submarine, Immanuel Martinez, replied. "*Intrepid Voyager* launching now."

Intrepid Voyager lifted off the docking pad, then angled over Kadath. *Golden Light*'s wake was still visible up ahead of them, paving a clear pathway toward their target. Behind them, *Transcendent Day*'s lights flashed and flickered on, dousing its docking pad in illumination.

"*Intrepid Voyager* is away," Captain Martinez said.

"Roger that, *Intrepid Voyager*," the captain of the *Transcendent*

Day said. "*Transcendent Day* launching now."

"I still don't know that we're ready for this," Lucas murmured.

"It's okay, Lucas," Rachel replied, squeezing his hand. "We're as prepared as we're ever going to be. We'll be fine."

Lucas nodded begrudgingly. "I hope you're right," he said.

The three submarines swept across the ocean floor toward the area the expedition members had taken to calling the Mecca Trench. It didn't take them long to arrive. Landing supports extended out of the three submarines, and they all settled near the fissure's craggy mouth.

"Wow," Captain Martinez said. "Look at that."

"It's as breathtaking as you said, Lucas," Rachel said, staring out in wonder as the submarines' lights illuminated the mammoth column of brilliant, almost electric life endlessly circling the trench. Lucas could still feel that sense of discomfort wriggling inside him, but he had to admit seeing this again was undoubtedly enough to renew his sense of awe.

"All subs, engage precautionary measures," Gordon Richmond, their head of security, said, cueing the coms.

"Acknowledged, sir," a voice replied.

Settling into his console, Gordon's dark-skinned hands began tapping displays and adjusting controls. Moments later, a swarm of drones swam up from the submersibles. The humming cloud of machines hovered over the subs, waiting.

"I'm also engaging the onboard weapons systems, just in case," Gordon announced to those gathered nearby him. Lucas could hear the whir and groan as the canons slid out from their recesses in the sub's hull. "All right," Gordon said, running a hand over his bald scalp. "All done here."

"Very good," Captain Martinez said, his eyes like hard flint above his thin mustache. "All subs, extend corridors." Lucas heard a louder moan now as the collapsible corridors mounted into the sides of the submersible accordioned outward, followed by a dull thud as they met their parallel passages on the other submarines.

"All subs, double-check seals," Martinez said.

"Seals look good," one of the other captains said.

"I second that," said the other.

"Great," Martinez said. "Purge corridors." Lucas now heard the loud hiss of water draining not too far away.

"Corridors purged and pressurized," another captain said. "No sign of leaks."

"Then let's open the airlocks," Martinez said.

The airlock behind Lucas hissed and then opened. A few seconds later, Dr. William emerged with a smile.

"Ah, Lucas!" he exclaimed. "We're finally here! Isn't this spectacular? Now, what do you say we get straight to work? I don't know about you, but I can't wait to dive in, as it were!"

"How was the sightseeing today, Ron?" Lucas asked, sitting down in the makeshift cafeteria across from Ronald Myers, the Chief Mining Operator.

"Fine," Ronald replied as he ate. His short brown hair was matted from being inside the heavy miner suit all day, his muscular frame still dressed in the undersuit that helped regulate his body while out in the water. "We found some more interesting deposits that will certainly warrant a deeper look. But still nothing… overly unusual. At least as far as the rocks go. There were still plenty of visitors to keep us company, though none who were too unfriendly. Gordon's guys kindly kept the more curious ones off us, as usual."

"I've been looking over the samples that Ron and his team have been collecting over the last few weeks," said Dr. Stephanie Ming, their resident geologist, as she pushed her glasses up her nose.

The spectacles were more a symbol of choice than anything, as a simple procedure would have removed any need for them within an hour. "And I must make explicit what he is hinting at implicitly. There is still no evidence of anything overly strange, unusual, or even necessarily *profitable* in this fissure. I, for one, am beginning to wonder exactly why we're *here*. I understand that the biological oddities are fascinating, but from my perspective, I have seen little to warrant Leng's sizable gamble on this place."

"Ah, that's because you didn't see what *I* discovered today!" said William, a triumphant smile on his face.

"What did you find, Dr. William?" Rachel asked.

"A field," William said, unfolding another display with a flourish and presenting it to the group. "An extraordinarily *strange* field, not least of which because it seems so good at hiding its presence from our sensors. It extends outward roughly to the edge of the anomalous sea life's gathering. Of course, Lucas's and Charles's initial scans hinted at something like that, so I always suspected it was there. I'm just ashamed it took me this long to chart it properly. But the most interesting points of my findings are not about the field itself, or its borders: it's where the field appears to be strongest." William's fingers flicked across his display and scrolled across the image of the trench. Then, at last, he pointed to the fissure's eastern edge.

"Mr. Myers, I wonder if you would be so kind as to skip ahead in your search, and instead focus your team's efforts in this area on your next trip out," William said. "I have a hunch that what we're looking for will be found right here."

"Sure, we can do that," Ronald said. "I don't mind skipping. I'll take Team Alpha to the very edge and send Team Beta a little further down, and then we'll meet in the middle."

"Spectacular!" William said. "Perhaps this is our last night of frustration. Eh, Lucas?"

Lucas forced a smile on his face and nodded. "Maybe so, William."

Be absorbed into some endless ocean of oblivion – The abyss was so cold – Join hands.

Almost there.

"All right, what's wrong, Lucas?" Rachel asked when they were finally alone.

"What do you mean?" Lucas asked.

"You've been dragging your feet ever since Blake handed you this team," Rachel said. "And tonight, when West was talking, it was almost like you were trying to hide a toothache. What's going on? Is this still about Charles? Do you *want* this expedition to fail?"

"That's absurd," Lucas said. "Why would I want us to fail?"

"Don't lie to me, Lucas," Rachel said. "I know you too well for that. Something has been upsetting you this whole trip. What is it?"

Closing his eyes, Lucas took a deep breath. He knew he should still hold back his feelings, but he realized that wasn't possible anymore. So, opening his mouth, Lucas let the dam burst. "Please don't think I'm crazy," he blurted. "I don't know if I could take that. Not from you."

"I won't, Lucas," Rachel said, walking over to him and putting her hand on his face. "I promise. Just tell me."

Lucas licked his lips. "Sometimes, I see and hear things I can't place or explain. It even feels like I'm experiencing other people's memories once in a while. But one thing that I have seen several times now is a sphere. It's massive, iridescent, and hidden somewhere, I believe, in this fissure. I think it's the causal agent we've been searching to locate. And what's more, I feel it *wants* us to find it. The problem is, I don't know if we *should*.

"Every time I've seen it, it's seemed… alive somehow. And hungry. It's spoken to me in inaudible whispers, calling us to it. And the more it calls, the more terrified I become."

Rachel exhaled slowly and nodded. "Is there anything else?"

Lucas looked away from her briefly. "Yeah. Edgar Kayce, the lead engineer who spearheaded Kadath's construction, told me that, if I went out with Charles a second time, we would find something that would bring an end to Kadath, and maybe all of humanity. But even more than what he said, there's… the four entities."

"The four entities?"

Lucas cleared his throat. "I see them sometimes, out of the corner of my eye. They try to speak to me, though I only ever catch fragments of their words. For some reason, they seem almost *familiar* to me, but at the same time, they are so *monstrously* alien. They want me to find the sphere, too. And, honestly, the last thing I feel like doing is to give them what they want."

Rachel tried to conceal her shock by clearing her throat, glancing momentarily down at the floor. Then she looked up again into Lucas's eyes. "Thank you for telling me," she said. "You've been under so much stress recently. It's honestly no surprise that the strain is coming out in some… unique ways. But, Lucas, you can't lose sight of the prize, especially now that it may be so close. West is going to steal this from you if you're not careful. And, frankly, he doesn't deserve it. *You* do. You're the reason we're here. Not him."

"But do I really?" Lucas said. "Is it actually in better hands with me? I think… maybe I'm starting to lose it, Rachel. Ever since I came to Kadath, I've felt less and less like me. More fractured, somehow. I'm caught between two possibilities. On the one hand, what if it's *not* there? Then am I truly crazy? But, on the other hand, what if it *is?*"

Rachel kissed Lucas gently. "You're not going crazy," she said. "You're the most brilliant man I know. You're dealing with a kiloton of stress right now, but that doesn't mean you've lost anything. And anytime you start to fall apart, I'll be here to put you back together. Okay?"

A smile flickered across Lucas's face. "Okay."

"And that's what I'm doing right now," Rachel said. "We're pulling you back together so that you can lead this expedition. Because no matter what he thinks, this isn't West's find. It's *ours*. And regardless of what it is, I would want it to be in the hands of someone with a conscience. Which, to be honest, I don't know that West possesses."

Lucas nodded. "I've begun to wonder the same thing."

"So, you're going to be okay now, right?"

"Yes," Lucas said. "For you, I'll be okay."

"That's what I like to hear," Rachel said, giving Lucas another kiss.

Lucas had a difficult time focusing on his work the next day. He kept finding himself drifting into the control center module where Rachel, Gordon Richmond, Captain Martinez, and a few others had gathered. It seemed the feeling was not exclusive to him, as he noticed that William also hovered around the room much of the day.

"Ben and I are moving a bit further down," Ronald said over the coms. "Vic, keep an eye on the rest of the guys."

"Roger that, Ron," Vic replied.

"Ah, you don't trust us, boss?" another of the survey team, Gerald White, said.

"About as far as I could throw you," Ron said. "And you look pretty heavy in that suit."

"Ouch!" Gerald replied. "That stung me deep, Ron."

"Behave," Ronald said. "We'll be back."

The idle chatter continued between the teams as their members drifted across the ocean's floor in their heavy miner suits. It seemed like maybe it was going to be just another day, despite Lucas's deep foreboding and William's jubilation the previous night. Lucas almost felt himself relaxing. Just a bit.

"Ron, come look at this," said Ben.

"What is it, Ben?" Ronald asked.

"It… looks like a tunnel," Ben replied.

There was silence for a moment, and immediately Lucas could feel the tension swell in the room.

"Huh," Ronald said.

"It's like something *drilled* this," Ben mused.

"The rock looks melted," Ronald said. "Attention Team Alpha, home in on my coordinates. Ben and I found something highly unusual."

"What *is* this, Ron?" Ben asked.

"I have no idea," Ronald replied. "Let's go find out, shall we?"

"Ronald?" Rachel said. "What's your status?"

"We've found something, Control," Ronald replied. "A tunnel. Ben and I are going to take a look down it. Initial impressions are that it is deep. Maybe really deep. It also does not appear to be a natural formation. It's surprisingly symmetrical. In fact, just eyeing it, I'd say it may be perfectly cylindrical. It could be twice our height, too – possibly more, and it's angled. We should be able to walk down it."

"I'm dispatching drones to your location," Rachel said. "Hold tight for just a couple minutes, and they'll make sure the path is clear for you."

"Roger that, Control," Ronald said. "We'll wait for the drones."

"This is it," William said. "This is *it!* We found it! Ha HA! We found the source!" He leaped into the air, pumping his fist.

"Now, hold on," Captain Martinez said. "We don't know *what* we've found yet. Let's not break out the champagne this minute."

"And we also don't know what's down there," Gordon said. "It could be a kraken lair for all the information we have."

"Perfectly cylindrical," Lucas murmured. He suddenly felt chilled.

"You all right, Lucas?" Martinez asked. "You look like you just saw a ghost."

"I'm… fine, Captain," he replied. "Just eager to see what we have, like everyone else."

Rachel gave him a considering look but said nothing.

A few minutes later, the drones had passed by Ronald and Ben and were skimming down the tunnel. Rachel had the image pulled up on every display. The group kept growing in the control center, but, regardless, there was a rapt – almost reverent – stillness in the room.

"It really is a perfect circle," Dr. Ming said in hushed tones. "I don't think this could be a natural formation."

"Judging by the angle, I'd almost think that something *had* drilled this," William replied. "Or burrowed, perhaps. Or crashed, though one would expect a bigger impact sight in that case."

"Could another corporation have done this?" Gordon asked.

"No," Lucas said. "Look at the growth inside it. The tunnel is old. Maybe *extremely* old. At the very least, no one dug it in the last few decades. Or maybe even centuries."

"Wish you guys could see this first-hand," Ronald said over the coms. "It's unreal. Almost spooky."

The drones' images blurred. And then they devolved into static.

"What?" Rachel said, frowning. "Ronald, we've lost the drones' eyes. Do you have a visual of them?"

"No," Ronald said. "They were too far ahead of us."

"Ronald, I want you to come back," Gordon said. "Without the drones, we aren't able to ensure your safety. Let's regroup and move everything we've got to this site tomorrow."

"It almost seems like there's a glow up ahead," Ben said. "It's faint, but… Do you see it, Ron?"

"Yeah, I see it," he said. "Roger that, Gordon. This place is starting to give me the creeps. We'll pull back and return with all the equipment tomorrow."

"Wait, we're just going to stop *now?*" William said. "But we've come so *far!* We're so close!"

"The safety of our people is my top priority, Dr. West," Gordon replied. "I won't jeopardize them just because you want to adventure a little further. Tomorrow will come soon enough."

"We need to reconsider our priorities here," William said. "I think, if Leng officials were now present, that they would encourage us to continue onward!"

"Well, they're not, Dr. William," Captain Martinez said. "But, if you want to pursue that line of reasoning, we can put it to a vote. You, me, Mr. Richmond, and Dr. Kane. Who says we pull back and regroup tomorrow?" Martinez, Gordon, and Lucas all raised their hands.

"Lucas?" William said. "For shame! Where is your sense of curiosity?"

"Our people's safety comes first, William," Lucas said firmly. He wished that were the only reason he had voted to postpone the expedition. The truth was, he was terrified of what lay just ahead. And he was petrified that he was right.

"I'll report our findings to Kadath," Rachel said. "I have a feeling they are going to be *extremely* interested in what we've found."

"Lucas? Wake up!"

Lucas's eyes snapped open, sweat beaded on his forehead. The sphere. *The sphere…* "Rachel? What is it?"

"It's time to get going," she said, tossing him a shirt. "The calvary's on its way."

Shaking his head, Lucas scrambled up. "What do you mean?"

"Kadath's sending several more subs, advanced drilling equipment, more crewmembers, and increased firepower," Rachel said. "They're pouring just about *everything* into this. I guess they must have been intrigued by our findings. Ronald and his team are already climbing into their heavy miner suits."

"Wow," Lucas said. "Okay. I'm on my way."

Several minutes later, Lucas arrived in the control center. The screens were displaying a variety of images today. Feeds were running off the miners, drones, and submersibles. Ronald and his team were just offloading from the transport sub with their equipment when Lucas stepped into the room.

"Okay, keep tight, and don't disconnect," Ronald said. "We'll go in on two lines, one for miners and one for security. Miners, if something flares up, hang back and let security do their thing. Stay out of their way. Okay?"

"Got it, boss," Vic said.

"We'll go down at regular intervals," Ronald continued. "Try not to bunch up. If something goes wrong, I don't want us all to get wiped out in one go. Plus, I want those of us in front to be able to get back up if we can." Ronald took a deep breath. "You guys ready?"

"Lead the way, Ron," Ben said.

"All right," Ronald said. "Let's do this."

Ronald engaged his jets and pivoted down the tunnel.

The team descended for what seemed hours. The shaft proved deeper than anyone had thought it could be, and all the time, it had the same smooth roundness as it had at its entrance. There were several times when it seemed the feeds would go out again, but always at least a few remained intact.

"There's that glow again," said Ben.

"Yeah," Ronald said. "It's faint, but I can see it, too."

"There's something up ahead," Jasper, the lead security officer, said. "You see that?"

"What… is it?"

"Holy…"

"It's – it's beautiful."

"Are you guys seeing this?"

"The feeds are cutting in and out," Rachel said. "Can you describe the visual, Ronald?"

"It's… a sphere," Ronald said. "It's enormous, almost exactly the width of the tunnel. And it's… exquisite."

Rachel's eyes grew wide as her gaze swiveled toward Lucas. Lucas was staring back at her, his body starting to tremble. A sphere. *The* sphere. Just like he had seen. Just like Edgar had said. Just like the entities had impressed upon him.

"I think this is the big one, everybody," Ronald said. "This is what we've all been waiting for."

Lucas had never before been so terrified by being right.

The *Intrepid Voyager* docked with Kadath, and Lucas stumbled numbly out of it. Somewhere nearby, they were unloading the sphere. They had actually brought it back here. Right inside the facility. Exactly where it wanted to be.

Lucas dropped his things in his quarters and collapsed on his bed. He didn't know what to do or where to go. On a whim, Lucas looked up Edgar Kayce's quarters. He wandered there in a dream-like fog and buzzed Edgar on his hatch.

"Wh-who is it?" Edgar's voice called through the com.

"Edgar, it's Lucas," Lucas said. "Can I come in?"

The hatch opened to reveal Edgar standing there. His eyes shivered back and forth as he searched the corridor, then motioned Lucas in. "They keep sending their emissaries for their false gods," he muttered. "Trying to glean what I know. But I see through them now. I understand. I'm trying to get out of here, but they won't let me. They say I'm not fit for travel. I need to escape before it's too late." Then he looked up at Lucas. "You did it, didn't you?"

Lucas took a deep breath. "I think I did," he replied. "And I don't know how I can fix it."

Edgar shook his head. "If it's here now, then I think we've already lost. All we can do is hope for a quick end."

"There has to be *something* we can do, Edgar!" Lucas said. "Haven't you seen any way out of this?"

"Have you?" Edgar replied. "You dream just like I do. You see them. Or perhaps you see *more* than me. I don't know. I can't tell. Maybe it hasn't unlocked inside you yet. Why are you *here*, Lucas?"

"I… I needed someone to talk to," Lucas said. "Someone who understood. And… I needed to say I was sorry. For not listening to you. For letting this happen."

Something growled in the back room, the sound wet and bubbling. Edgar glared as he looked over his shoulder. "Not now, Mother! I'm talking to my friend!" He turned back to Lucas. "Sorry about that. For what good it does, I forgive you. But it's not worth much. It changes nothing."

"What do we do, Edgar?" Lucas said. "How can we stop it?"

Edgar's mind seemed to clear, and his gaze locked directly onto

Lucas's. "You run, Lucas," he said. "You steal a sub or find some way out of Kadath. It was a beautiful dream, but it's about to become a nightmare. So, save yourself. Escape from it. Right now, though, it's time for you to go. The Golden Dawn puppet is coming."

"Who?" Lucas said. "You mean that Summerisle guy? The station chaplain? What's *he* got to do with this?"

"Everything," Edgar said. "Who do you think is pulling Leng's strings? Who do you think is so keenly interested in the thing you found? Who do you think won't let me leave? It's all that Golden Dawn cult. They're the power behind Kadath. And they're about to unleash hell on us all. Don't let them catch you, Lucas. Don't let them learn what you are."

Something shifted in the room behind Edgar. It sounded like squelching meat.

"Go now," Edgar said. "I doubt we'll speak again. I won't allow them to steal what's left of my soul. If they don't let me leave, then I'll find my own way out. Goodbye, Lucas."

Lucas thought about objecting, about trying to stop Edgar. But that thing was creeping through the shadows toward them, and he frankly didn't want to see it in the light. Nodding, Lucas turned. "Goodbye, Edgar," he said. "I'm sorry. For everything." Then he left.

Lucas and Rachel jostled through the crowd of people gathered in the loading bay, making their way to the front with the rest of the expedition team. The atmosphere was jubilant, the occupants almost humming with excitement. And why shouldn't they be? Right there, cozily nestled into its recessed platform, was the sphere, the very object they had all worked for so long to unearth and transport to the facility. It sat there like an orb from Olympus, the light glinting off its pristine metallic green surface.

"Isn't it gorgeous?" William whispered, leaning over to Lucas.

"We did that, Lucas. You and I. It's here because of *us*. I cannot *wait* to see what secrets it will unveil."

Lucas managed to smile politely at William. Rachel squeezed his arm in reassurance.

Commander Wade ascended to a small dais to address the crowd. "Thank you all for being here on this historic day," he said. "This is the very reason Kadath exists: to strike out into the depths boldly and to unveil its forgotten secrets. I could not be more excited to be here with you at this moment. Firstly, I wanted to extend my congratulations to the intrepid team who made this discovery, starting with the three who initially uncovered this sector: our very own Dr. Lucas Kane and Mr. Charles Ryan, aided by Ms. Rachel Wilkins! Let's give them a round of applause!"

"Wait," Lucas said, his eyes widening. "Is Charles back? Is he here?"

"I didn't see him," Rachel replied, scanning over the crowd. "If he is, why isn't he up here with us?"

"Maybe he felt out of place?" Lucas ventured.

"Now, I don't have to tell you all how momentous an occasion this is," Wade continued. "And there are far more questions at this point than there are answers. But we…"

"Pardon me, but I was wondering if I could introduce myself to you two gentlemen," a man said, coming up behind Lucas and William with a grin on his face. His thinning hair and hooked nose made him look uncomfortably like a vulture. "I'm Dr. Norman Cohen. I arrived at Kadath the very day your crew discovered the sphere."

"Ah, you don't say!" William said, turning to shake Cohen's hand. "A pleasure, Norman! I'm Dr. William West. This is Dr. Lucas Kane."

"The pleasure is entirely mine," Cohen said. "It sounds as

though I will be assisting you, gentlemen, as we move forward with tests on the sphere."

"Oh! Spectacular!" William said. "I look forward to collaborating with you, good sir!"

"… Now, without further ado," Wade continued, "I'm told one of the dive team members who unearthed the sphere will send out a delegate to be the first to touch this marvel. Would the lucky person please step forward?"

Nearby, Ronald cursed, and Vic crowed. "Aha!" Vic said. "I got it! It looks like yours truly will be making the first contact!"

Ben growled. "I knew drawing straws was a bad idea."

Vic didn't appear to be listening anymore to his colleagues. Inhaling deeply, he gathered his courage and advanced toward the sphere. A hush fell over the assembled crowd. Slowly, Vic pulled his glove off his hand. Then, with one final glance back at the onlookers and a last grin, he extended his palm and touched the flawless round surface.

Vic gasped. "It feels so smooth. Metallic, but also vaguely like a crystal or glass. There's something else, too, like an energy that's radiating off it. It's funny; it doesn't seem to reflect anything in the bay except for me. It's… It's warming to my touch!"

The surface of the sphere awoke, drawing gasps from the crowd. At first, a soft glow arose from its depths, growing brighter as it seemed that the illumination spread to the surface. Then it appeared as if its surface started to move, drifting like clouds traversing the sky. Impressions like vague shapes began to blossom across its surface, bringing with them more colors, more vibrance. Vic stood there slack-jawed, transfixed by the wondrous tableau coming to life inches from his face.

Finally, Lucas couldn't take it anymore. "Vic, get back!" he cried.

Vic frowned, prying his gaze away from the sphere to glance back at Lucas. "Why?" he asked. "This thing is incredible!"

Vic's arm slipped into the sphere, the surface tension completely dissolving below his palm. Vic screamed, his eyes bulging. The sphere's surface had solidified again, though, and no matter how hard he yanked or pulled, he could neither get his arm out nor put more into the object. The sphere rotated upward, and Vic was lifted off the ground. Then the rift in the sphere closed completely, and Vic dropped to the floor, blood spraying from the stump of his severed arm.

Vic's screams were deafening in the bay. People panicked. Some raced toward the young man, some darted for the door, and others just ran. Lucas, for his part, was running toward Vic, his heart hammering in his chest. Vic stared at him, wild-eyed, as his remaining hand, shaking with shock, clamped around his pulsing wound in a vain attempt to stanch the blood flow.

"D-Dr. Kane?" he said.

Tendrils lashed out of the sphere, curling around Vic's neck and waist and legs. Vic squealed like a trapped animal as it yanked him backward, and then he was completely absorbed into the shimmering globe. Lucas screeched to a halt. The only sign that Vic had ever been there was a pool of his blood on the ground. The sphere was as perfect and pristine as ever.

"Wondrous," William gasped beside Lucas, his hands drifting toward his face.

Lucas swiveled toward William, a look of pure horror contorting his expression. He tried to make his throat work, to force his tongue to form words, but they had both constricted uselessly within him. So, instead, he staggered backward, staring in revulsion as the one monster appraised the other, reverent in his steadfast gaze.

UPWARD

"Our teams have been able to reach several of the most active hot zones, and in almost every one we have found at least a single hyperactive conduit. We have been able to cull many of these exemplary units and transport them to Leng facilities for further studies. Initial results have shown these to be some of the most receptive specimens for fusion experiments that we have encountered, even surpassing the grand fusion trials of the 20th century."
Dr. Jayce Norton

TOWER WORLD

"What do we do now?"

It was the question they were all wondering, and, as such, no one had an answer when Connor finally asked it. Mitsuko sat curled up in the belly of the boat, rocking back and forth, while Min and Connor perched on either side of her. Their combined

119

silence spoke volumes.

"Connor, I have been giving it some thought, and do you want to know why Mitsuko and I never tried to escape before?" Min said.

"Why, Min?" Connor said.

"I think it's because the thought had honestly never occurred to us," Min replied. "I think that, somehow, we had accepted the tower as our new lot in life. I wonder, too, if that's what the people in the settlement feel. That this is all there is now, and that we must make the best of it. I wonder if that's why more people don't try to leave."

"I *refuse* to accept that this is all there is," Connor said. "Even after everything we've been through. I've spent too long believing in things that are unseen to stop now."

"What if it is nirvana which lies beyond this bubble of being?" Min said quietly. "And our strivings are stopping us from achieving the ultimate enlightenment of cessation?"

"Min, do you honestly want to cease to exist?" Connor asked. "For all you are to wink away, or to be absorbed into some endless ocean of oblivion?"

"We *can't* go out there, Min," Mitsuko whispered. "The abyss was so cold… And vicious… And *hungry*."

Min paused, then sighed and shook his head. "Then what do we do?"

"We go back," Mitsuko said quietly. "We go up the tower. Maybe… If there's no way out below, we can find an escape above."

Connor nodded. "As the lady commands."

"Do you truly think we will find salvation up that hideous thing?" Min asked.

"It's our only chance at this point, Min," Connor said. "It's either that or we all just give up and die right now."

"Very well," Min said. "To the tower then."

Connor turned the motor back on.

They were nearing the shore again, so Connor killed the engine. There was no use drawing more attention to themselves than was strictly necessary. Slowly they coasted toward the beach, their little boat rocking softly on the waves.

"No sign of the big one," Connor said.

"Perhaps we should count ourselves lucky," Mitsuko said. "Wait – what's that?"

The two men frowned. They could see that there was a strange creature lying prone on the sand. "I have no idea," Min said. "It looks dead."

"Should we make for the other beach instead of this one?" Connor asked.

"Perhaps so," Mitsuko replied. "No reason to risk it, just on the off-chance it's *not* a corpse."

Connor nodded and started to turn toward the motor. That's when the sea began to boil.

"Oh, dear!" Min said.

"What's going on?" Connor cried as the water went from boiling to seething.

"Isn't that obvious?" Mitsuko replied. "More are coming!"

Hands breached the surface of the water. They writhed and flailed, grasping at the air as they sought for any purchase they could find. Some looked ruddy and perfectly normal, while others were pallid and rotting. And some were not human in the slightest.

The hands grabbed the sides of the boat, their desperate grips wildly rocking the small craft and threatening to either capsize it or tear it completely apart. Mitsuko grabbed an oar and started beating the hands, while Min began trying to pry them off.

"Connor, get us to the shore!" Mitsuko cried. "Now!"

Connor didn't reply with words. Instead, he flipped the engine back on and ratcheted it up to full power, sending them careening toward the beach. The boat lurched forward, ripping most of the hands free. A few still clung firmly, though, their grips almost inhuman in their tenacity. The vessel cleaved the waves in two, gaining speed every instant. Then it hit something.

The hull bounced into the air as some unseen obstacle slid by beneath it, the motor whining and then stopping as whatever it was got caught in its blades. Connor looked back, his eyes wide in alarm, as he saw a cloud of blood burst out behind the boat. They had just eviscerated a person.

The boat crashed down into the waves with a jarring thud. Connor heard something crack in the ship's underbelly as it hit the sea. Water started spraying into the bottom of the vessel.

"Connor, the motor!" Min cried.

"I think it's done for!" Connor replied. "The blade's mangled!"

The boat was still coasting forward, but it was slowing down every moment. The hands were groping at it again, trying to get enough purchase to pull their adjoining bodies upward. Connor almost fancied he could see elastic faces rising toward the surface.

"Bail out!" Mitsuko yelled. "Jump as far away as you can and swim for shore!"

Grabbing her bag, she tossed it toward the beach and then followed it out, coming down in the water with a splash. She swam to her duffel and slung it over one shoulder. Breaking into a freestyle stroke, she paddled as quickly as she could toward the shore. Min looked at Connor and nodded. He jumped first, and then Connor followed him a second later. Behind them, they heard the boat capsize.

The two men started kicking frantically after Mitsuko, their arms slicing through the waves. Connor could feel cold fingers pawing at his skin, grabbing at his clothes, bag, and body. They were trying to pull him under -

Connor took a small spluttering breath right before his head was submerged. He felt himself being dragged down, down into the depths. Connor kicked and thrashed, but the new arrivals' fingers held tight. Some were even beginning to elongate, constricting around his limbs like little snakes with fingernails. Connor was starting to panic. The surface was moving farther away. The ocean wasn't *that* deep here, but it was certainly more than enough to drown in.

Something grabbed Connor from up above, followed by another. Connor fought with all he had to move toward these new forces jerking him upward. Bubbles burst from his mouth as his breath fled him.

At last, he got free of a few of the hands. It was enough. Min and Mitsuko hauled him above the surface, and Connor took a deep, searing breath.

The three of them fought their way through the surf until, at last, they felt the damp sand below them. They scrambled up the beach, away from the groping, half-formed people in the water. In their blind scramble, they hardly realized they were moving toward the prone object until they were almost stepping on it.

"What… is it?" Min asked, gulping down air.

"No time," Mitsuko said. "Just get to the tower!"

Connor swept his eyes quickly over the thing. It was almost assuredly a carcass, and it was also incredibly long. The corpse looked like an enormous, monstrous squid, but it was scarier and more vicious than the average cephalopod. Even in death, it sent shivers up his spine.

It didn't matter. Min, Mitsuko, and Connor stumbled over the body's tentacles, then hurried for the safety of the trees once more. Something stopped them halfway there, though. It was a sound: A vile, impossible sound. Against their best impulses, they stopped and looked back.

Many of the people had crawled out of the sea, their bodies fluctuating and stringy. Several of them had even made it far enough up the beach to reach the beast's corpse. Except… that's not what it was anymore. Not really.

As Min, Mitsuko, and Connor watched in dumb, frozen horror, the new arrivals started crawling over the creature. Rather than making it over the body, though, they began to be absorbed into its bulk. The men and women wailed as their chests and abdomens fused into the squid's flesh, their skin becoming like sticky, stringy, melted cheese. The squid's eye was no longer milky and lifeless, its ragged gash of a pupil flicking around in search of prey. Its tentacles were coming alive, too, thrashing against the sand. Its beak clacked before letting out a keening screech.

"Do you see what it's doing?" Min asked.

"It's growing limbs," Mitsuko gasped.

Most of the people had disappeared now except for their arms and legs. Those were migrating to the creature's belly, sliding across its mass until they were evenly distributed on both its left and right sides. With a faltering movement, the kraken-centipede stood, its multitude of fingers and toes digging into the sand below it.

"Run!" Connor screamed. Turning, they did.

It seemed a small eternity before the three travelers made it to the plaza of red cobblestones encircling the base of the tower. The black skyscraper loomed over them anew, eclipsing everything with its Stygian immensity. Their pace slowing, they looked up its immense heights – from its wide, angular base to the crowning needle that pierced the sky.

"I never wanted to see it again…" Mitsuko murmured.

"True," Min breathed. "But I am so blasted tired of running."

Mitsuko nodded. "Let's go."

Exhausted, the three survivors moved as quickly as they could manage toward the entrance. The forest swayed ominously around them as their feet thudded over the blocks. At last, they reached the indented alcove at the skyscraper's base where the doors were nestled.

"Is this the same way we entered before?" Connor asked.

"Who knows?" Mitsuko said. "No, I don't think so, but I frankly don't care right now."

Throwing open the double doors, Mitsuko stepped inside. Min and Connor followed her. Pulling open the second set of doors, they all froze in their tracks, their jaws dropping.

"Apparently, it matters," Min murmured.

They had stepped into the aftermath of a smoldering inferno. Crossbeams cracked and fell, blackened and charred. Flames still licked in charcoal hollows, and smoke choked the warm air.

"This place," Connor said. "It looks so familiar…" He drifted forward as if he were in a dream, his eyes trying to dissect the secrets of this place. He could feel the heat warming his body, drying his clothes. The smoky smell stung his nostrils as the world beyond faded away.

Something inside Connor told him that this place was bigger than it should have been. Grander somehow. But how could he know that? Had he been here before? Or – Then Connor saw it. And he gasped.

The cross was charred, its lower half broken off completely. But that didn't stop him from recognizing it, or from realizing where he now was. This was *his church*. Or at least a fire-gutted, somewhat overblown approximation of it. But why was it in *this* place? And why had it appeared here in flames?

"Connor," Min said, placing one hand on Connor's shoulder while the other one covered his mouth and nose with a damp cloth. "We need to try another entrance. We can't stay here."

Connor's mouth gaped, his eyes widening. "Sophie!" he cried. "Sophie was in here when the fire started! I was trying to save her and…" Swiveling left then right, Connor called out, "Sophie! Sophie, where are you?" Then he darted deeper into the smoldering church.

"Connor!" Min cried, stumbling after him. "We must go! This place will kill us if we linger!"

"I remember hearing the steel buckling around us," Connor rambled, not listening to Min. "She was trapped. I couldn't reach her. And then… something happened. I think… I think I may have caused it, whatever *it* was." Abruptly Connor stopped dead in his tracks. "Oh no," he said. "We weren't alone."

It rose slowly from beneath a pile of burning detritus. Its eyes were flashing coals, and, when it opened its mouth to scream, molten light glowed from between its twig teeth. It was as tall as a tree and as thin as a charred log. Antlers like branches sprouted from its temples and growths like gnarled knots twisted upward from its shoulders.

"We are leaving, Connor!" Min snapped. "Now!" Grabbing Connor, he jerked him back. Connor finally seemed to break from his reverie, stumbling backward with Min. Turning, they ran for the doors where Mitsuko awaited them, her body tensed and her eyes wide. They heard the fire beast careening through the church's ruins behind them, its hungry cries crackling like kindling in a blaze.

Mitsuko already had the doors open for them. Min and Connor ran through the opening, then flung open the second set of doors. Finally, they were outside again.

"Is it coming through?" Min asked, whirling around.

"Hopefully, the barrier works both ways," Mitsuko replied.

The fire beast didn't push through the doors. It just stood there stupidly, staring at them with its burning eyes. The thing shrieked, its knotted hand trailing down the glass.

"What the *hell* was that?" Connor cried. "Do each of the tower's entrances lead to a slice from one of our lives?"

"What if they *do?*" Min said, his eyes wide. "Could it be true? Should we investigate? It may be the only hope we have of recovering some of our pasts, but, at the same time, we just saw how dangerous those could be. Is it worth the risk?"

"I don't think it's one *I'm* willing to take," Mitsuko replied. "I'll learn all about my life again once I get back to it. And if our only potential hope is to ascend this blasted tower, then that's what I want to do as soon as possible."

"What if the elevator is present in all of them – or at least some variant of it?" Min asked. "It would make sense for there to be something like it in each of the tower's versions."

"Better the devil I know," Mitsuko said. "And, right now, that's the hotel and shopping center."

A shriek ripped the relative silence apart. Looking back, all three of the travelers felt their breath freeze in their lungs. They had been so preoccupied with Connor's world and the burning thing that they had forgotten all about the kraken-centipede they had escaped on the beach. It, however, had not disregarded them.

The squid monstrosity was bearing down upon them, its myriad tentacles thrashing in the air, its open beak teaming with row upon row of human teeth, its body supported on and driven forward by dozens of pairs of arms and legs.

"That thing is unbelievably horrifying," Connor murmured. Then, turning, he fled once more, Min and Mitsuko at his side.

They were coming upon the doors that led into the hotel. They were getting so close now. It was going to be tight, but maybe, just maybe, they'd make it.

The trees to their left snapped, each one seeming to let out little moans as they did. Then a whole medley of mouths bellowed. Looking left, Connor saw the giant nightmare behemoth lumbering onto the red cobblestones. When it saw them, though, it no longer plodded but instead broke into a run that made the ground shudder with each footfall.

Connor reached the door first and yanked it open. Min and Mitsuko ran through, then Connor jerked it closed. They all took a deep, ragged breath as they collected themselves, staring through the doors at the oncoming monstrosities. They were safe.

"That was a close one," Connor said.

"Yes," Mitsuko agreed. "It was."

The kraken-centipede reached the door and stopped. Behind it, Min, Mitsuko, and Connor could see the behemoth slowing as well. The two beasts appraised each other, then returned their gazes to the doors.

"Strange," Min said. "I rather thought they would be ripping each other to pieces by this point."

"Maybe they figure it's not worth the effort?" Connor said.

"Perhaps," Mitsuko said thoughtfully. "But why?"

The kraken's tentacles were drifting over the door as if they were searching for something. The suckers on each tentacle tasted the textures of the glass, the metal, and the cobblestones. The creature's serrated beak clacked consideringly, as did all the jaws lining its gullet. Connor felt an unpleasant knot forming in his stomach.

"Maybe we should get going," Connor said.

"None of the mutations have come through the doors before,"

Mitsuko said.

"Just the same," Connor replied. "That thing looks awfully interested in them."

The kraken retreated slightly, and then it folded backward on itself until its first few pairs of arms and legs were dangling in the air. It advanced again until the top feet pressed against the glass, the soles sliding down the slick surface with little squeals. The feet were not the troubling part, though: what was unsettling was that its hands appeared to be groping for the door handles.

"Okay," Min said. "I'm with Connor on this one. Let's go."

Mitsuko nodded. Opening the next set of double doors, they once more entered the lobby of the hotel and shopping center. Behind them, the kraken's hands wrapped around the metal handles.

Connor kept one eye on the doors behind them while Min and Mitsuko scanned the lobby. They scrambled toward the waterfall feature that concealed the base of the elevator shaft, then hurried behind it. Whirling around, they came face-to-face with the elevator doors. Mitsuko jammed the button and was rewarded with a friendly "ding" sound, as well as a softly glowing down-arrow.

While Mitsuko was doing this, Connor craned his head around the corner and hazarded another look at the entrance. A lump rose in his throat as he watched the kraken's hands successfully pull open the first set of doors. Pawning off the gaping entries to two tentacles, the wriggling terror shuffled forward. It maneuvered its bulk into the relatively small space between the doorways, then extended its hands once more.

"It did it," he murmured. "The effin' bugger is actually coming in."

"How long do we have?" Min asked.

"Not very," Connor said. "It's already working on the second set of doors."

"They've never entered here before," Mitsuko said. "I don't understand what's changed now."

"Maybe it's not *like* the other monsters," Min said. "Or… perhaps, by going outside and coming back in, we broke the seal."

Mitsuko jabbed the elevator button again, and then again. She roared in anxious frustration. "Why is this taking so *long?*"

Connor felt his chest tighten. The second set of doors were slowly inching further and further open. At last, the two longest tentacles could squeeze through the gap, and from there, they thrust aside the final barrier to the thing's entry.

"It's in," he whispered.

"Perhaps we should head for the stairs," Min said. "Or the corridors. Or *somewhere*. But we cannot stay here any longer. Mitsuko, we need to *leave –*"

The elevator doors swished open with another welcome chime. Mitsuko, Min, and Connor all leaped through the opening, then Mitsuko slammed her hand on the button for the top floor and the other to close the entryway. Outside, they could hear the terror unfolding itself in the lobby.

The doors slid closed, and all three people gasped with relief. Then the elevator began to rise. It whisked upward, soon passing the waterfall's basin. Now they could see through the glass enclosure. The kraken-centipede was entirely inside the building now, but there was something more – something arguably worse. It was still holding the doors open.

"Oh, no," Connor said.

"Th-they're working together?" Mitsuko stammered. "But no. No, that's impossible. They're just dumb beasts. They're not… No, no, no…"

But it was true, no matter how much they willed it not to

be. The behemoth was already shifting and reshaping itself as it injected its bulk inside the tower. At last, the kraken-centipede withdrew its tendrils from the doorways when the giant was far enough inside, and then it turned its attention to the rising elevator. It bellowed, its unearthly screech piercing even through the glass encasing the three humans.

"It sees us," Min said. "Oh, that can't be good. You don't think it can get *up* here, do you?"

"How could it?" Mitsuko said, sounding entirely uncertain herself. "We're already out of reach of its tentacles."

The kraken skittered forward on its myriad arms and legs, heading directly for the waterfall. It reared backward, scuttling up into the basin, then its tentacles wrapped around the elevators' enclosure, and it began to haul itself upward. Its hands clasped on wherever they could find purchase, and the terror started ascending the shaft.

"Bloody hell…" Connor breathed in stunned disbelief.

"Well, there's nothing for it then," Min said. Sitting down on the floor of the elevator, he crossed his legs and closed his eyes.

"You're going to meditate right *now?*" Mitsuko cried.

"There is nothing better we can do," Min said. "Either it will get us, or it won't. We are presently trapped on this elevator, so we might as well do the only things we can."

Connor nodded. "You're right, Min." Turning, Connor stepped to face a corner and closed his eyes. He quietly began to pray.

"So, I'm just going to stand here alone and watch that thing overtake us while you two mutter to yourselves?" Mitsuko yelled, her voice cracking. Then she laughed, sounding like either they had lost their minds or she had.

"No, Mitsuko," Min said. "Sit with me. Join me."

"I… can't…" Mitsuko said, tears welling in her eyes. "It's

coming. I can't stop watching it."

"Mitsuko, I personally am praying for that thing to slip and impale itself on something particularly nasty down below," Connor said. "Why don't you do that, too, and tell me if we succeed."

The tears finally rolled down Mitsuko's cheeks as she raised her hands to cover her eyes. "Please, God…" she whispered. Lowering her hands, she peeked down at the thing. She lowered her hands completely. "It… stopped," she said wonderingly. "It's climbing off the elevator shaft onto another floor. *What…?*"

Connor turned toward her, frowning. "It's getting off? Why?" Then his eyes grew wide. "What floor?"

"The second one."

Connor leaped over to the glass and stared in horror as the kraken-centipede darted down the walkway, heading directly for the makeshift wall at its end. A strangled moan wrenched free of his lips. *"The settlement!"* he cried. "It's going to eviscerate them!" He whirled to face Mitsuko. "We have to stop the elevator!"

"What?" Mitsuko said. "No! Connor, we can't!"

"There are *children* in that settlement, Mitsuko!" Connor yelled. "They won't stand a chance!"

"Neither will *we* if we go to help them!" Mitsuko cried. "How are we going to *stop* it, Connor? With a sword and a pistol that only has a few bullets left? With harsh language?"

"I can't stand by and do nothing while innocents are *slaughtered!*" Connor roared.

"It doesn't matter anymore," Min said. "It's already over." Min had stood to his feet again and was looking out through the glass. Connor and Mitsuko looked back out to see that the wall had already fallen. What's more, the behemoth had leveraged itself up onto the second story and altered its shape again so that it could fit down the walkway. As the three of them watched, they saw the two mammoth horrors disappear down the hall.

"Maybe there's a back way out of there," Mitsuko offered. "Perhaps some of them will escape."

Connor was reasonably confident he heard the screams of dying people over the hungry roars of the beasts. Shaking his head, he covered his face and sank to the floor. The elevator continued its rise up the tower.

It seemed like a long time passed. Perhaps it was only minutes. Maybe it was a half-hour or more.

The three travelers had been silent ever since the settlement. They sat huddled in different corners on the elevator's floor, consumed by their own thoughts. At last, Min broke the ponderous quiet.

"Was the hotel from your life, Mitsuko?" Min asked. "Because it certainly wasn't from mine."

"No," Mitsuko said. "At least, I don't think so. It never triggered any memories for me as the church did for Connor."

"Then whose is it?" Min asked.

"I don't know," Mitsuko said. "There were four entrances. Perhaps that means there were four like us? Maybe the last one was… in the settlement."

"Which brings up another question that has been weighing on me," Min said. "If there were only four people like us, then who – or *what* – were the others in the settlement? Were they like the unfortunate souls on the beach? Could they have been manifestations of this place, or may they actually have been human? And, if they truly *were* human, then what makes *us* special?"

"We may never know, Min," Mitsuko said. "Besides. We don't really know if we *are*. We never went in the other two entrances, did we? How do you know for sure that the places in them belonged to you and me? Perhaps the only one we would have recognized was Connor's. And, if *that* were the case, it would change the question altogether.

"You and I already suspected the people in the settlement were different from us. We thought that to be truly human, one had to remember coming out of the sea, yes? But who's to say that we were right? What if it was just a way for us to further distance ourselves from them when they were as real as we are? Or, even worse, what if *they* were the true humans, and we're… something else?"

"These questions are pointless," Connor interjected. "It doesn't matter what the fecking difference was between 'us' and 'them.' The only solid distinction that still means anything is that we're still alive, and they're all dead."

"Yes," Mitsuko said. "Of course, you're right, Connor."

"Perhaps we should all eat something," Min said. "Before the elevator finally stops. We don't know when our next opportunity will be, or what will come after this."

The others nodded and pulled a bit of food out of their bags, which were still damp from the ocean. Luckily, the food had been sealed in containers of their own, so it was still edible. They ate quickly and joylessly. At last, though, the elevator slowed. And then it stopped. The doors opened with another chime. Standing, they turned to face the open doorway.

"What… is this?" Connor asked.

"Are we still in the tower?" Min said.

"It doesn't matter," Mitsuko said. "We can't stay here. Let's go."

They stepped out into a corridor that looked industrial and robust like one would expect to find in a space station or a deep-sea facility. Water dripped from the ceiling, then slid between the holes in the grating on the floor and disappeared. But the hallway's most striking highlight was the stuff clinging to its crannies and spreading across its ceiling like a fungal contagion. Looking up, Connor saw one of the gangrenous growths burst. Inside was an eyeball, which stared down at him from the center of a wreath of flexing serrated teeth.

Slowly, cautiously, Min, Mitsuko, and Connor advanced. At the corridor's end, they tapped what they took to be the control for the hatch, which slid into the wall. They stepped through the open portal, and it swished closed behind them.

They found themselves standing in a round room with numerous hatches lining its circumference. A grated pathway ran around the perimeter as well, but the centerpiece of the room was what was *truly* noteworthy.

"Welcome, travelers," the strange being before them said, its deep, flat voice sounding like empty oil barrels and rusty barbed wire. "What brings you to the Nexus?"

"You speak?" Min said. "You're a conscious being?"

"What... is this place?" Mitsuko asked.

The creature shifted in its cradle of tubes, pistons, and harnesses. Its multitude of increasingly mechanical arms flitted around it, each performing their own task in the larger apparatus as the being seemed to focus its attention on the three new arrivals. The top two-thirds of its head almost looked like a pyramid made of either stone or dusty metal, while the lower third appeared at least moderately human. Its lips were shriveled and pulled back from its gums, giving it a ghastly appearance not at all helped by the black oil spilling over and between its teeth. Its jaw made a dry cracking sound as it opened afresh. "As I said before, this is the Nexus," it said. "And I am its Wayfinder. All the memories flow through here. All of the lives coalesce in this place to become one."

"What do you mean?" Connor said. "What... *are* you? What are we doing here? Why –"

Min put a hand on Connor's shoulder. "Apologies for all of our questions, Wayfinder," Min said. "We are just a little confused and overwhelmed, which is why we have rudely not yet answered your question. We are here in an attempt to flee from this world. We traveled to the edge of this realm, and we know escape that way is impossible. So, we came as high up this tower as we could, hoping to find a way out through here. Do you know of such a way?"

The Wayfinder cocked its head to the side, its teeth clacking together. It almost looked like its desiccated lips smiled. "There is a way out of this existence," it said. "But you may not like it. You must continue your voyage skyward, into the tower's greatest heights. There you will discover your path to freedom, festering in a relic from when this world began. But take care: you cannot make it alone, and you will cease to trust everything, including your own being, long before you reach it. The journey upward leads to utter liberation; the journey upward ends in incomparable madness."

The Wayfinder's head snapped the other direction. It was definitely grinning now. "So," it said. "Do you still wish to escape?"

"Yes," Mitsuko said. "We'll take our chances."

"Very well," the Wayfinder said. "Then I have told you all I will. Take… that door." With that, it raised one skeletal rusted hand and pointed toward a hatch to the trio's right, about a third of the way around the circle. "But be quick about it. She is coming and is, in fact, nearly here."

"She?" Connor said. "She who?"

"The one you left," the Wayfinder said. "And she is *not* well pleased. She brings… company."

Connor glanced grimly over at Min and Mitsuko.

"Then we take our leave of you, Wayfinder," Min said, bowing low. "Thank you for your guidance. And for showing us the way."

"It is… my specialty," the wayfinder said. "But do not thank *me*.

I doubt you will feel so grateful in the end."

Without another word, the three travelers headed for the door that the Wayfinder had indicated. As they reached it, though, the Wayfinder spoke again. "You three are a curiosity to me," it said. "I think you will serve him well. He will need the guidance when he is awoken."

"*Who* shall we serve well, Wayfinder?" Min asked. But the Wayfinder didn't reply. Shaking their heads, they left the room.

"Well," Connor said once the hatch had shut behind them. "That was a supremely alarming experience."

"Indeed," Min said. "I thought I had questions before, but now…"

"He spoke as if this world were a living thing," Mitsuko murmured. "Almost as if he were an avatar of the hippocampus or limbic system in this place's brain. Its memory, or maybe its dreams. He said something else that was very disturbing, as well: 'all of the lives coalesce in this place to become one.' Does that strike either of you as terribly disconcerting?"

"Just about every word he said I found to be highly unnerving, to be blunt," Connor said. "Not the least of which was that we were about to have company."

The others nodded, their mouths set in dour lines.

At the end of the corridor, they came to another hatch. Opening it, they stepped through into a cavernous space. The place was dimly lit, with most of the illumination focused in the very center of the domed room. There, all alone, stood a Spartan metal ladder that stretched up into the empty darkness high above before disappearing from sight.

"I guess… we take the ladder?" Connor said.

"I don't like this," Mitsuko mused. "It's too open. Too exposed."

"If it were any brighter, I'd say at least we would be able to see if anything was coming for us," Min said. "But as it stands currently…"

"You couldn't just leave well enough alone, could you?" a new voice echoed across the empty expanse. "You couldn't just be content in the little world we were trying to build. You *had* to try to get out. You had to go against the grain. You needed to go *outside*."

A red mist was rising off the ground now, glowing brighter and brighter as it grew in volume. Streaks of violet lightning arced through it. Beyond the haze, Connor could see someone coming. A trim woman with dark skin wearing a white lab coat. She was cradling a young child in her arms. "Sephora?" Connor said. "Is that you?"

"I wanted peace," Sephora said as she approached. "I sought order. But that wasn't good enough for you, was it? You just couldn't conform. And now, it's all gone. You destroyed everything. There's no one left to save."

"Sephora, we're so sorry about the settlement," Connor said, moving towards the woman. "I wanted to help. Please believe that. But it all happened so fast. I couldn't get there in time."

"Will your words save my people?" Sephora spat. "Will your apologies bring them back to life? It doesn't change *anything*. *You* let them in! They followed *you* through the doors, and then they eviscerated every… last… *one* of my friends. They pulled them *apart*, Connor, like a kid plucking wings off a fly."

"Let's go, Connor," Mitsuko said quietly. "Head for the ladder. There's something… *wrong* with her."

"I had built something here that could have been so beautiful," Sephora said. "Like carbon squeezed into a diamond. I had come here to guide this world and its development while documenting its progress. But it was only when I *got* here that I truly saw its potential and understood what it could become. You don't understand the beauty or the magnificence of what we are trying to do. Of what the Golden Dawn is so close to accomplishing. But how *could* you? It's not *your* fault that you're no more than glorified guinea pigs. I *shaped* this wonderful, malleable place. I shaped *him*. But now your interference has undone so much of what I was striving to achieve. And all my old friends are gone."

As Sephora had been speaking, the others had been slowly inching towards the ladder. The closer she came, the faster they hurried, trying to maintain a healthy distance between themselves and her. Only Connor hesitated.

"You don't have to be alone, Sephora," Connor said. "Come with us. We're going to get out of here and find a way back to our old lives. You can, too. You're like us, I *know* it. Remember when you said we're stronger together, and that we can accomplish great things when we're united? Let's prove it. Join us. There's no reason why we can't work together now to accomplish something magnificent."

Tilting her head back, Sephora let out a deep, lilting laugh. "There are so many fallacies in what you just said, Preacher," she replied. "I don't even know where to begin. First, and perhaps most importantly, I'm *not* alone. I have *new* friends now, and they are closer to me than any I've known before. They brought me to this place through the secret ways of the tower and told me how to find you. They have wanted to meet you properly for some time. In fact, they have positively *hungered* after you.

"But words so often fail to express the fullness of something, don't they? Here. Let me show you instead."

Sephora set the child on the ground and knelt behind him. The boy was sobbing quietly, tears and snot running down his face. Connor realized he recognized him from the settlement: He was the one who had waved at Connor.

"At least let the boy come with us, Sephora," Connor said. "Give him the best chance he can have. Please."

Sephora looked down in surprise at the young boy, and then she guffawed. "This thing? It's just a collection of cells! Isn't that right, Jeremy?" Leaning down, she affectionately pinched Jeremy's cheek. "It's mine to do with as I see fit, and I'm feeling a mite peckish."

"Wh-what do you mean?" Connor said. "Sephora, let him go! He's just a kid!"

"Oh, Connor," Sephora said, chuckling. "You're so charmingly naïve." Then her jaw dropped lower and lower, her teeth elongating into brilliant white needles. Leaning over, she engulfed Jeremy's head in her mouth and bit down. The boy's body spasmed and flopped over as blood pumped from its neck. Sephora tipped her head back as she chewed, crunching bone and mashing brain, and then, at last, she swallowed Jeremy's head down her throat.

Connor found himself frozen by shock, unable to move. Sephora was experiencing no such hindrance, however. Opening her lab coat, she unbuttoned her blouse. The mist pulled back from her on every side before spiraling upward, swirling into a helix around her. Sephora leaned back further and further until her hands were pressed flat against the ground. Her stomach bulged as it expanded, and then it opened.

"Run!" Connor cried. "Get to the ladder, quick!"

The hole in Sephora's stomach continued to widen, and soon Connor could see the writhing mass of tentacles and claws and mouths contained within her. The beings let out mewls and squeals as they pressed outward, pushing against the limits of the opening. They would be free soon.

Connor finally made his limbs work and raced after Min and Mitsuko. Reaching the ladder, they started to climb. The mist entwined up the poles and rungs, licking at their feet as they ascended. When he was a reasonable distance off the ground, Connor dared a look back. The red and violet light illuminated a tableau straight out of a surrealist's nightmarish fever dream. The squirming sights and metallic smells twisted his stomach and made him clench his teeth. He knew they weren't free of what was being unleashed down there. No matter where they next arrived, the terrors below would haunt them.

Turning his gaze upward once more, Connor continued his climb toward the pendulous darkness above. The iron bars were cold against his clenching grip, warmed only slightly by Min and Mitsuko's previous passage. The obsidian gloom grew closer every moment. He would be there soon.

EIGHT

THE CATALYZER

"Progress report. Lord Zeiss's eyes only. Sir, we have collated information gathered since the incident, and recent developments have brought us to several tentative conclusions. It appears that multiple planes are colliding at ground zero. One could almost describe it as a war, with each dimension clashing for supremacy. But there is more, Sir. Our eyes in the Otherworld's realms are reporting a dramatic uptick in activity, with the Otherworld as a whole appearing agitated at a level previously undocumented. Even some of our most recent experiments seem to be advancing in most promising ways, rising toward dominance in their respective realities. We are very close to something, Sir. It will either be an unprecedented cataclysmic event or the miracle of transcendence we have been working toward for so long. Perhaps both."
Victor Northwood – Leng Corp. Executive of Sciences

KADATH FACILITY

It throbs inside your head, burns before your eyes. It spins, endlessly spins, its surface beautiful and terrible and maddening. Something lies within it – beyond it – another world, or perhaps much more than that. It calls to you; speaks to you. It wants you to touch it.

The woods whip past around you, branches snapping against your face. You clench her hand tightly in your own, trying to will you both to move faster. It's still behind you. You can hear it stalking you through the trees. You stumble over a tree root, and moments later, your face grinds into pine needles and dirt. She is pulling at you, trying to get you to stand again. Looking up, you see the lab through the treeline up ahead. But your pursuer is almost on top of you now.

The lab is set up. You have your memory in mind: the one that you will focus on and actualize upon your arrival. It will serve you well in the next world. Quietly you organize and double-check everything one more time. It's only fitting that you ensure everything is in order, after all. This place is your temple. This is your gateway into awe.

The temple quakes around you. The terrors are coming in through the front entrance now, the people clustered in a shivering clump behind you. You don't think there's any way you can stop the creatures. There is nowhere left to run. You are trapped.

She is trapped. You can't get her free. You hear it coming through the flames: anger and sap given shape and form. Closing your eyes, you unleash a bellow from the very core of your being. This is not how it ends.

It calls to you. It speaks to you. It says it's time you wake up and let the true nightmare begin.

"Lucas! Wake up!"

Lucas jerked, his eyes snapping open. Sweat drenched his body once again, matting his black hair. It was as if he had been fighting a fever all night. But slowly he realized it wasn't night, and he wasn't in bed. He was in his lab, lying on the metal floor. A red light was strobing overhead.

"Rachel…?" Lucas managed, trying to force his eyes to focus.

"Lucas, are you all right?" Rachel asked, kneeling beside him. "Are you hurt? Or sick?"

"Hull breach detected near science wing," a voice calmly droned. "All personnel, please evacuate sector immediately. Decompression and flooding detected. All personnel, please evacuate sector immediately."

"I… What happened? I was studying a sample and…" Lucas shook his head, trying to clear it. Rachel grabbed his arm and helped him up, guiding him into a chair.

"Was it the sphere again?" Rachel said, her voice low. Lucas nodded, and Rachel ran her hand over her face.

"We've got to get out of here, Lucas," Rachel said. "They're saying there's been a breach. The science wing's flooding. Everyone's being evacuated."

Lucas shook his head. "I can't leave my work," he said groggily. "I…"

"Lucas, your *life* is more important than this stuff!" Rachel said. "Now come on! We have to go!"

"I don't know that I can walk yet," Lucas said.

"Well, you're going to have to!" Rachel said, trying to hoist him up. "The alarm's been going off for a while now. I don't know where the problem is, but everyone else has already left. The only reason *I'm* still here is because *someone* I know didn't answer his node and worried me! If we don't go now, we may not be able to get help if we need it."

"If it's been going on for a while, we may be safer just to stay here," Lucas said, his head starting to clear. "It hasn't gotten in here yet, and if we don't know where it happened, then we don't know what the safest route out would be. And it's safer in a room with a locked hatch than in a corridor with the whole ocean pouring in to meet you."

Rachel paused, then sighed. "Yeah, that makes sense. Okay."

Rachel pulled up a chair and sat down next to Lucas. At last, the sirens and voice mercifully stopped. They waited in silence for a few moments, the red warning lights still flashing overhead.

"Control must figure everyone got out," Rachel said.

"Yeah," Lucas replied.

"Lucas, what's going on?" Rachel asked. "What is that thing doing to us?"

"I don't know," Lucas said. "And I'm frankly a little scared to find out."

"Is that why you didn't fight back when they put West and Cohen in charge of studying it?"

"West can have it," Lucas said. "The farther I am away from the sphere, the better."

"I've started hearing stories," Rachel said. "People are seeing things all around the station. It's not just you, Lucas. And there have been rumors of people disappearing, too. You were right. We should have left that thing in the hole where we found it."

"Well, it's a little late for that now, unfortunately," Lucas said. "I'm not entirely sure what…" Lucas frowned. He sat up straight in his chair, swiveling his head toward the door.

"Do you hear something?" Rachel asked.

"No, it's not that," Lucas said. "I *feel* something. What in the world?"

Lucas stood shakily and moved toward the door.

"Wait!" Rachel cried. "What if the corridor's flooded?"

"It's not," Lucas said. "There are people in it."

"What do you mean? How do you know that?"

Lucas didn't reply. Instead, he pressed the control, and the hatch swished open. There was an entire procession of people directly outside his door, led by Judy Blake. What's more, while he had never met Leng's CEO, Meredith Waite, in person, there was no denying who the stern, statuesque woman was standing next to Blake.

"Who the hell are *you?*" Meredith Waite snapped. Lucas noticed she was wearing an elegant grey robe with gold accents, the hood pooled around her neck below her short, wavy brown hair. "What are you doing here?"

"Oh!" Judy said. "Lucas! I thought the whole area had been evacuated! Didn't you hear there's been a major breach?"

"I was… indisposed," Lucas said. Then his eyes turned toward the dejected, dark-haired teenage girl walking with her head down directly behind Waite. The girl looked up at Lucas. And then she gasped.

"You," she said, a hushed sort of awe in her voice. "You're like *me*. Aren't you?"

"I… I don't know," Lucas said, moving dreamily, curiously, toward the teenager. Her eyes were the same sea-blue hue as his own, her hair, likewise, was a matching raven-black. "Maybe. I felt you coming."

Reaching out her hand, the girl gently touched Lucas's face. They stared into each other's eyes, and Lucas recognized an insurmountable force stirring to life between them. It was undeniable: Somehow, the two of them were linked. They were alike. They were *different* –

"Regan!" Waite snapped. "Get away from him!" Grabbing the girl's – Regan's – hand, she snatched it away from Lucas. Lucas jerked as though electricity had zapped him. Shaking his head, he looked around and realized a dozen or more people were staring at him with a mix of shock and something bordering on outrage. They all wore robes identical to Waite's.

Judy cleared her throat. "Ms. Waite, allow me to introduce Dr. Lucas Kane," she said. "It was his research that led us to the sphere's sector, and he was furthermore part of the team that discovered and retrieved it. Lucas, may I introduce Meredith Waite, the CEO of Leng Corporation. And this is her daughter, Regan."

Lucas knew he needed to say something. Forcing a thin smile, he tore his eyes off Regan to focus on her mother. "A pleasure, Ms. Waite," Lucas said, offering her a slight bow.

"It seems we owe you a debt of gratitude, Dr. Kane," Waite said, her voice only slightly less icy.

"I was just following where the research led," Lucas replied.

"Mm, indeed," Waite said. There was a new look on her face now. One of the first glimmers of curiosity. Was it because of his interaction with Regan?

"Well, as I mentioned, it's not safe out here right now, Lucas," Judy said. "I'm going to have to ask you to return to your lab until the situation is resolved."

"Of course," Lucas said, stepping backward.

"That specimen is ready, Dr. Kane," Rachel said, wrapping her hand around his arm. "You had said you wanted to look at it as soon as possible?"

"Well," Lucas said. "I will leave you all. It was a pleasure to meet you, Ms. Waite. Regan. Perhaps we will see each other again in the future."

"Perhaps," Waite said.

"Maybe in the next life," Regan said, her voice barely above a whisper.

"Come along now, Regan," Waite said, grabbing the girl's wrist. Without another look at Lucas, she marched on down the hall, her entourage in tow. Lucas stepped back inside his lab and closed the hatch.

"Well, *that* was… unexpected," Rachel said. "What was going on with that girl?"

Lucas was quiet for a moment, his eyes trained on the floor between his feet. Then he spoke. "They're going to do something terrible to her," Lucas said. He looked back up at Rachel. "They're taking her to the sphere. I know it."

"Whoa now," Rachel said. "Lucas, you *cannot* go after them. It's either career suicide or *actual* suicide. You could barely walk a minute ago, and now you want to go *save* someone?"

"I'm not going to let them hurt her," Lucas said. "There's something… special about her. I have to go. Now. Before it's too late."

"Lucas, no!" Rachel cried. "You can't!"

Lucas looked Rachel straight in the eyes. "I'll be back soon. Stay here." Casting his gaze around, Lucas found a nearby tray with an auto-scalpel lying on it. Picking it up, he strapped the instrument to his belt. Then, turning, Lucas opened the hatch again and stepped into the corridor once more.

Every sense in his body sharpening to points, Lucas stalked through the corridors toward the sphere. The abandoned halls were eerily quiet. It almost reminded Lucas of the early days of the facility when it was just him walking with his nightmares. The red warning lights continued flashing in the ceiling, creating a disorienting, almost kaleidoscopic effect. Lucas could feel the sphere pulling on him. Calling him. Coaxing him.

With growing unease, Lucas began to wonder if he was honestly trying to save the girl, or if he was using that as an excuse to give the sphere what it wanted.

At last, Lucas arrived at the intersection closest to the sphere bay's entrance. He could feel the four entities clustering around him, mumbling their garbled wisdom, but he ignored them. Peering around the corridor's corner, he saw the procession that had been following Meredith Waite, as well as the CEO herself. Regan was nowhere in sight, and neither was Judy Blake. The people in the group were lined up in two rows with Waite in the center by the bay doors. They were chanting something while moving in strange synchronized patterns, their hoods up and strange glyphs smeared on their faces. It was almost like some sort of bizarre ritual.

At last, it seemed that a cycle of the ritual completed, and Waite turned. Tapping the hatch control, she entered the bay and closed the entrance behind her. The others in the corridor began the ritual again.

Lucas needed to find a way past the mob immediately. Every second that passed was one step closer to Regan's end. The four beings were gesticulating wildly behind him, their dark mutterings buzzing like static in Lucas's mind. Lucas squeezed his eyes shut, trying both to silence their chatter and to force his brain to think. There had to be a way –

Kadath shook as if an earthquake were trying to rip open the ground beneath it. The entourage stopped their ritual, trying to keep their feet, and then they began to vibrate. The men and women screamed as their bodies pulsated faster and faster, their movements almost seeming to blur. Their voices were changing, growing deeper and wetter. Their bodies were changing, too.

Lucas realized this was his chance. Breaking into a run, he raced for the doors. The once-people didn't even notice him, consumed as they were by their pain and terror. Lucas opened the hatches and stepped inside. He screeched to a halt, his heart stopping in his chest.

The sphere was alive, its surface spinning wildly in a mind-melting psychedelic phantasmagoria. Regan stood before it, her arm extended, black, green, and purple lightning arcing between her fingertips and the orb before her. Actually, Regan wasn't standing. She was *levitating*. Waite was shrinking away from the girl, her eyes wide with terror at what she had unleashed.

Lucas saw that the world around them was beginning to fluctuate and reshape itself. An entity seemed to be arising out of the chaos, its being illusory and somehow primordial. Lucas knew this was his last chance.

"Regan!" he cried. "Don't give in! Look at me!"

Regan's head swiveled slowly toward him. Her eyes were ebony pockets of sparking hellfire. "L-Lucas?" she said. "You came for me?"

"Yes!" Lucas said. "I won't let them do this to you! You can beat this!"

"Too late for me," Regan said, a faltering smile flickering across her lips as lightning sparked inside her mouth. "But not for you. Not yet. I cast you out, Lucas!" Reaching her hand toward Lucas, Regan shot bolts of virulent energy from her fingertips, striking Lucas squarely in the chest. Lucas was flung off his feet and sent sailing backward. He saw repulsive, horrific beings shuffling past him toward Regan and Waite. But then his vision was consumed.

The sphere erupted into his mind, its energy cracking through his paltry defenses. He saw universes within universes, possible worlds bubbling in a quantum sea of madness. He saw a black tower stretching to the swirling heavens above, surrounded by a circular island and a frothing band of ocean. And beyond it, he saw the chaos of unbeing, the miasmic Otherworld of vicious, viscous insanity. The veil between the two was so thin. Such a flimsy membrane was all that kept the oblivion at bay. It would be so easy to pierce it –

His back struck the unyielding metal of the corridor's far side, stars and blackness bursting before his eyes. His vision cleared briefly, though, focusing just in time to see everyone in the room beyond vanish in a swirling vortex of darkness and damp. They were gone. Just… gone.

Lucas passed out.

Someone was carrying Lucas. The ceiling moved bumpily, haltingly by overhead, the smells of saltwater and lubricant assaulting his nose. Whoever – or whatever – held him so effortlessly had to be huge.

It was all too much. Lucas couldn't focus on this right now, or anything else, for that matter. He found himself slipping into unconsciousness again.

"I think he's starting to wake up."

"Lucas? Can you hear me, buddy?"

Lucas groaned, wincing as he felt the bruises screaming from his back and chest. With a concentrated effort, he forced his bloodshot, burning eyes open. Rachel was standing above him. And so was…

"Ch-Charles?" Lucas stammered.

"It's me, Doc," Charles said. "Or at least, what's left of me."

"What… happened to you?" Lucas said.

Charles smiled grimly. "Let's not worry about me right now. How're *you* doing?"

"I feel like vindictive lightning just stabbed me and flung me across a stadium."

"I mean… it doesn't seem like you're wrong," Charles said.

"How did you find me?" Lucas asked.

"Rachel called," Charles replied. "She told me you were doing something supremely stupid, so I got there as soon as I could. Luckily, it was before any other crews arrived, but unfortunately, it wasn't before whatever happened to you and the others was over."

"I tried to contact you, Charles," Lucas said. "I worked to track you down. Were you avoiding me?"

"I'm sort of specialized now," Charles said. "They send me outside a lot, sometimes for extended periods. But, yes. I suppose I was. I've been trying to come to grips with what I am now, and I haven't been doing a very good job of it. I'm sorry for not being in touch. Now. What happened in there?"

"Something bad," Lucas said, trying to sit up. "The sphere – or maybe someplace it had created, or contained – sucked all of them in, including Regan. I didn't get to her in time. But *she* was changed, too. She blasted me with a strange energy she was siphoning off the sphere and knocked me out of the bay. I think she may have saved my life."

"Lucas, what on *earth* possessed you to do that?" Rachel asked. "You nearly died, and for what?"

"I don't know that I can explain it, Rachel," Lucas said. "I just know that I had to *try*. Maybe it *was* a mistake, but there was something about that girl I couldn't shake."

"So, what? I'm not young enough for you now?" Rachel retorted.

"That's *not* what I meant," Lucas replied. "It wasn't like that –"

The station shook violently beneath them. Lucas and Rachel cried out, Rachel trying to brace herself. Sirens blared again along with the red strobing lights, but the sirens seemed unstable. They warbled strangely as if the system was forgetting what it was doing.

"This has been happening since whatever they did with the sphere," Charles said. "Systems have been on the blink across the station, and there has been a metric ton of seismic activity. There's nothing quite like being in a metal bubble at the bottom of the ocean and wondering if it's about to pop."

"Okay, Charles, we covered me," Lucas said, his voice quiet. "Now, what happened to *you?*"

Charles sighed, light glinting off the viewport before his face. "They lied to me," he said. "Or maybe they just didn't tell me the full truth. I don't know. In any case, they cut more of me off and then turned me into… this." Charles spread his mechanical arms. One ended in what almost resembled someone's idea of industrial-strength fingers, but the other one now terminated in two rotating blades that looked ideal for cutting through rock. He still had two arms and two legs, but otherwise, the only sign he was human was his haunted face through the viewport. Rather, he looked like a roughly anthropomorphic machine. Or a particularly svelte heavy miner suit come alive.

"Charles, I'm… I'm so sorry," Lucas said.

Charles shrugged, the pistons and motors whirring in his shoulders. "It's not all bad," he replied. "There's a second 'skin' I can wear when I'm not out on a mission. It's just kind of a pain to get in and out of them. Plus, I can swap out this saw hand when it's called for, and there's something to be said for being able just to take a stroll in the ocean when you need to think for a while." His face darkened. "But what *is* a kick in the nuts is that they sent the bastard who butchered me down here, too. Dr. Cohen."

"Dr. Cohen?" Rachel said. "You mean West's new accomplice?"

"That would be him," Charles said. "I don't know what it says about him, or West, for that matter, that he's under West. But it does give me pause. He's been awfully cozy with Blake, too, since he got here. I'm starting to fear there's a lot more going on here than we signed up for. And it makes me wonder if the people in charge aren't just as dangerous as that thing they pulled out of our sector, Lucas."

Wincing again, Lucas sat up and turned toward his friends. They had placed him on one of his examination tables. The touch of the cold metal beneath his fingers felt uncomfortably like waking up in a morgue. "We need answers," he said. "I just don't know who to talk to about getting them." Raising his gaze, he looked out into the corridor. "It seems people are starting to filter back in," he noted.

"What do you mean?" Rachel said. "How do you know that?"

"People are walking down the corridor," Lucas replied matter-of-factly.

"Uh, Doc, do you hear something we don't?" Charles asked.

"No, don't be ridiculous," Lucas said. "They're just walking right there."

"Lucas, you *can't* be seeing anyone in the corridor," Rachel said. "There's still a wall in the way."

Lucas's eyes grew wide. "Oh," he said. "Uh…"

Rachel walked to the hatch. "Tell me who's coming," she said.

"There are two techs, walking quickly," Lucas said. "Both men with dark hair. They look disturbed."

Rachel opened the door and peered out into the corridor.

"Please stay in your lab until we've ascertained this area's damage, Ma'am," one of the techs said as they walked past her.

"Sure," Rachel said. "Sorry." She closed the hatch again and turned back to Lucas. "What the hell, Lucas."

"I… don't know how I did that," Lucas said. "What is going *on* with me?"

"Is this the one?"

"Yes. This is him."

Lucas opened his eyes. The light in the room was dim, but he was still able to make out two figures. One was a woman, and one was a man. The woman was tall and austere. It didn't take him long to recognize her as Meredith Waite, even in the gloom. The man, though, was someone he had never seen before. He was wearing a suit that looked like it was straight out of the early 1900s, his dark hair and overall appearance fastidiously manicured. In his hand, he cradled a hardcover book.

"Mm, I hazard you may be correct, Ms. Waite," the man said. "I can certainly understand the mistress's interest in him. I sense definite airs of peculiarity swirling around his being."

"I *know* I'm right, Phillips," Waite said. "He's a collective. He just doesn't realize it yet."

"What the hell are you doing in here, Waite?" Lucas said, sitting up straight in bed.

The two invaders ignored him as though he weren't worth their attention. Like they were studying a lab animal. "Where is he from, do you think?" the man, Phillips, said.

"It doesn't matter if he's from anywhere at all," Waite replied.

"Of course, you're right," Phillips said. "Just a writer's curiosity, I suppose. And the mistress does not desire to absorb him?"

"You two stay away from me," Lucas said, climbing to his feet. "I won't go quietly, no matter what you're here to do."

"No," Waite said. "She feels a connection with him. She thinks they're kindred beings. As if it were even *possible* for something to be her kin."

"I'm warning you," Lucas said. "Get out of my quarters. I want you out, *now!*"

"And you don't think he is a threat?" Phillips said.

"That's what we're here to find out," Waite replied.

"Ah, quite," Phillips said. He flipped open his book. The words began to rise off the pages, globbing together and squirming with life as they grew longer and took on shape. Soon they looked like tentacles writhing and rising out of the pages. Lucas stared in disbelief as he watched the tendrils lengthen, fatten, gain definition. And then he screamed as they shot out toward his face.

Lucas jerked back to reality and looked around. He wasn't in his quarters. Nor was he in his lab. This location was someplace else altogether. Why was it every time he opened his eyes recently some new strangeness had just befallen him?

To both his left and right, he could see mammoth conveyor belts loaded with ore. The conveyors were methodically dumping their cargo into the mouths of burning smelters, while machines at their far end poured more onto them every time an empty patch of belt presented itself. *Dome Three.* He was in the processing plant of Dome Three. How the *hell* had he gotten here?

"Hey!" someone called. "Hey, you can't be in here without safety equipment!"

Lucas climbed to his feet. There were two men dressed in safety gear hurrying toward him. Their faces were harder than the people Lucas was used to rubbing shoulders with, their bodies lean and muscular. "Sorry," he said. "My apologies. I'll get out right now."

"How did you even get *in* here?" the second man said. "This area is locked down except for authorized personnel."

"Sorry, I didn't realize," Lucas said lamely. "I'll be going."

"I don't think we can let you do that," the first man said. "We've got to report this."

"Fine," Lucas said. "Get Ronald Myers. We've worked together. I'm sure we can get this straightened out."

The two men froze. "Hey," Lucas said. "Are you okay?" But the men were like statues. One was midway through blinking, his eyelids permanently half-closed. They weren't breathing.

"Hello, Lucas," a voice said behind him. "As I said, we meet again in my next life."

Lucas swiveled around to find Regan standing mere feet away from him. "Regan?" Lucas said. "But how? I saw you get sucked into that other place! I thought you were dead!"

"The old me *did* die in there," Regan said. "But now I am reborn. Or perhaps it's better to say that I am awake."

"Why did you bring me here?" Lucas asked.

"Because I wanted to talk to you someplace free of potential listening ears," she replied. "Somewhere they couldn't find us."

"Who?"

"Whoever," Regan said. "Your handler, the station leaders, the sphere."

Lucas felt a chill. "The sphere can hear?"

"It doesn't need to," Regan said. "It knows your thoughts. But the farther away from it you are, the less its pull on you. At least for now. That won't last much longer."

"What do you mean, my handler?" Lucas asked. "You think someone is in control of me?"

"I suspect someone is watching you, as they watched me," Regan said. "You are too important for them to lose track of you."

"Why do you think that?" Lucas said. "What do you think I am? Why would anyone care?"

"I didn't think there were any others like me in the world," Regan said. "But then, I met *you*. You're special. Different. Just like me. I don't think they know about you here. At least, Meredith didn't, and if she doesn't, then I don't think any other officials would, either. Otherwise, they would have just used *you* rather than bringing *me* down to Kadath."

"How am *I* different?" Lucas asked. "And, if they don't know that I am, why do you think someone's tracking me?"

"They may not know in *this* world," Regan replied. "But I have no doubt they do in another."

"Why?"

"Because we are *more* than human now," Regan replied. "You may not completely feel it yet, Lucas, but it's true. The Golden Dawn and Leng would seek to make us their puppets, or the catalysts for their great transcendence. The sphere and its contents would make us their conduits. But I say we make our *own* fate. Together."

"How do we do that, Regan?" Lucas asked.

"To start with, you must awaken," Regan said. "I will not do it all at once. I don't want to overwhelm you, or to expose you too severely to the sphere's energies. But gradually, you will open your eyes, and you will see. In fact, it seems the process has already begun." She extended her hand. "May I?"

Lucas swallowed the lump in his throat. He wanted to say no, or turn and run. But the little voice inside him, the one that drove him after the kraken, told him he had to see what happened next. Slowly, Lucas nodded his head.

"You are the only person who I ever remember being kind to me just to be kind, Lucas," Regan said. "I will be glad to rule the future with you." Then she touched his forehead with one finger. "Awaken."

Lucas yelled. Then he screamed. Then he shrieked. The facility was closing in around him, and then it cracked open like a Fabergé egg made of metal and meat and water. He felt a strange fire, an eldritch power, coursing through his bones. It was ripping him apart, remaking him into something new. His mind split into pieces, so many pieces, and it took everything within him to pull it back together. There were things inside him moving and raging.

What he didn't know, though, was if what he sensed was an infection or something more. He felt himself expanding, stretching over multiple realities and universes. So many worlds… So many possibilities…

"It knows," Regan said, drawing back from Lucas. "It senses what I've done. We need to leave here, Lucas. Now!"

Lucas was trying to collect himself. He shook his head, forcing his limbs to move. They felt like quivering jelly, and he tripped, falling flat on his face.

"How many?" Lucas mumbled, rolling onto his side.

"How many what?"

"How many realities?" Lucas said. "Or is that even what they are? Is that what *this* is?"

"I don't know," Regan replied. "A great many, and in differing degrees. There are those created by the shockwaves of actions, and those that are like bubbles in an endless ocean. There are some so vast that they effectively become many."

"How many are *we* in?"

"I don't know that precisely, either," Regan said. "I know that I exist in several, at least. You may only exist in this one. You're an anomaly, Lucas. Even more so than I am."

"What am I?" Lucas asked. "Where did I come from?"

"There isn't time," Regan said. "It's sending its emissaries to collect us. We must get you up, Lucas. Now."

Lucas looked at the two miners. They were beginning to move again, but not in a way that made him think they were thawing. They were vibrating like the people who had been at the sphere with Regan and Meredith, or like the four entities sometimes did when they manifested. As Lucas watched, the men's jaws cracked down the middle, splitting open. Their tongues divided into thirds. They seemed to be growing thinner every second, their fingers elongating.

Lucas forced himself up onto his feet with Regan's help. Regan slung his arm over her shoulder, and together they started moving as quickly as they could toward the processing plant's entrance. Something shifted behind them. Lucas glanced back and saw the two workers swivel in their direction. Their split jaws unfurled like wet, red flowers, their tongues probing the air like softly swaying stamens.

They were coming up on the wide double hatches leading out of the room. Lucas tried to push himself to move faster. He could hear the things that had been men starting to shuffle forward.

The doors opened before them. Ronald Myers was entering, his head down, his eyes focused on a display in his hands. "We need to get this new load processed, guys. What's taking so long?" At last, he looked up. "What in the —"

Ronald's eyes jumped from Lucas and Regan to the things pursuing them. Immediately he leaped backward through the open hatchway. "Come on, Lucas!" he yelled. "Hurry!"

Lucas and Regan were moving as fast as Lucas could go now, but the creatures behind them were picking up speed. They were moving faster and faster, gaining ground on them every second. One of them screeched. The sound wasn't even vaguely human.

They were nearing the open doorway, but the things were getting close. Much too close. With a sinking feeling, Lucas realized they weren't going to make it before being overtaken.

"Go, Lucas," Regan said. "I'll find you again."

With that, Regan propelled Lucas forward. Lucas tumbled through the air as if something had slammed into his back. He hit the ground hard and skidded across the grating. Lucas looked up in time to see Regan turn back to the two monsters while the hatches slid shut again.

"Wait!" Lucas managed. "Ron, she's not through!"

"I didn't do this!" Ronald replied. "They just shut on their own! The controls aren't responding!"

Something screamed on the other side of the door. It did not sound triumphant. On the contrary, it seemed panicked. Or maybe in pain.

Ron let out a frustrated yell and pounded his fist into the control pad. At last, he turned back to Lucas. "What in the world were you *doing* in there, Lucas?" he asked. "Who was that girl? Were those things my men?"

"I'm still trying to piece together what happened," Lucas said, trying to pick himself up once again. "I *do* know one thing, though: those two started out as your men, but they certainly didn't end that way. I'm sorry."

"What *did* that to them?" Ron said, propping Lucas up. "And what about that girl? We can't just abandon her!"

"I agree, but how can we get in if the controls won't work?" Lucas asked. "Is there another way? Or a control override?"

Ronald huffed before punching in a code on the keypad beside the standard control pad. Then another. And one more. Nothing worked. "This may be beyond me," Ronald said, looking back at Lucas. "Probably the only people who can get in there right now are security. I don't know what your friend did, but it was effective."

"You don't have override codes?" Lucas asked.

"I do," Ronald said with an exasperated sigh. "Several, actually. But none of them are working." Then he tapped his node. "Security, this is Chief Mining Operator Ronald Myers. Something has invaded the processing plant. I don't know what they are exactly, but they're fast, and they're vicious. Bring weapons. Yeah. They seem stuck in there right now, but I'd get here as fast as you can, just in case. There's also a teenage girl trapped in there with them.

No, this is *not* a prank! I just saw them with my own eyes, and so did Dr. Lucas Kane! How am *I* to know how a teenage girl got down here? She did! Now hurry! And bring override equipment. The room's in lockdown, and even *my* codes aren't working. We'll be nearby awaiting your report."

"How long will it take security to get here?" Lucas said.

"In all honesty, that could be up to an hour judging by how things have been going," Ron said. "That's a worst-case scenario, but the worst-case seems to be the default right now. We're not that close to the security station, and they've had a huge increase in calls in the last day or two."

"She can't wait that long!" Lucas said. "They could have –"

"Lucas, in all honesty, I think that whatever is going to happen in there already has," Ron said. "Either she beat them into pulp, or they ripped her apart. You heard those sounds just as well as I did."

Inspiration flashed in Lucas's mind. "I have an idea, Ron," he said. "One second." Tapping his node, he called Rachel.

"Lucas?" Rachel said, answering. "Where are you? I thought you were coming to the lab first thing."

"Sorry, Rachel," Lucas replied. "I had an unexpected change of plans. Can you still access Kadath's camera feeds?"

"Well, not technically," she said. "But… what do you need?"

"Can you get access to the feeds for the processing plant in Dome Three?" Lucas asked. "That girl might be trapped in there with something pretty awful."

"Are you serious?" Rachel said. "Lucas, what – You know what, never mind. One second."

Rachel was silent for a moment as she worked. Then she gasped. "Lucas, what *were* those things?" she said. "They're…"

"So, they're dead?" Lucas replied. "What about the girl?"

"I see two mutilated corpses," Rachel said. "They look a little like people, but they're certainly not. I don't see any sign of Regan Waite at all, whether alive *or* dead."

"Well, that's… strange," Lucas said. "But, also, kind of a relief. I'll be there as soon as I can. Thanks, Rachel."

"Lucas, what's going on? Why are you in Dome Three? *Are* you in Dome Three?"

"I'll tell you everything as soon as I get there," Lucas said. "See you soon."

"Okay," Rachel replied. "There's someone at the door, anyway. Bye."

"She's… not in there anymore," Lucas said. "At least, according to Rachel."

"What do you mean, she's not in there?" Ron said. "There's no other way out!"

"Well, at the very least, she's not showing up on the feeds," Lucas said. "But the other two are. It looks like they're dead."

Ronald nodded. "Okay. That's good. All right. In that case, I suppose it's okay if we wander off, maybe? Let's get you patched up, Lucas, and wait to hear from security." Slinging his arm around Lucas, Ron helped him down the corridor. "What's going on here, Lucas?" Ron asked. "Is it the sphere?"

"I think it's waking up," Lucas said, nodding. "And I'm pretty sure it's hungry."

"So, the rumors are true?" Ron said. "It wasn't just Vic?"

Lucas shook his head. "No. Definitely not. We need to do something, Ron. We need to stop this."

"Well, first things first," Ron asked. "Pain killers or food?"

"Food sounds great," Lucas said. "Maybe they'll have the room open by the time we're finished."

Ron helped Lucas through Dome Three's labyrinthine depths until he felt strong enough to stand on his own. The farther they went, the more miners they saw hurrying through their workday. Lucas had rarely been to this section of Kadath, and he looked around with an exhausted, detached interest. People dressed in heavy miner suits were loading into transport subs or lumbering toward airlocks, while others checked and loaded up their crew's gear as they departed toward the current mining shaft. A maintenance crew was repairing a console nearby, the thing's guts strewn across the floor, while groups of off-duty workers clustered together, murmuring amongst themselves.

Lucas began to feel a strange cognitive dissonance between seeing this relatively typical buzz of activity and the horrific, life-threatening beasts he had just escaped. As he looked deeper, though, he noticed the workers' haunted gazes and the erratic jittering movements of people on edge. Panic was simmering just beneath the surface here. It was ready to burst. All it would take was the slightest prodding.

They reached the cafeteria. Ronald escorted Lucas to an empty table in the center of the room, then wandered off to fetch them something to eat. Lucas surveyed the people clustered together, dining under an uneasy quiet that was breached only by furtive mutters. They felt it, too: The sense that everything was wrong, and the crackling anxiety that they were nearing a precipice they had slid too far to escape. The tension was almost thick enough to cut.

"Okay," Ronald said, setting a tray down in front of Lucas. "What do you know about what's going on?"

"We started something when we brought that thing back with us, Ron," Lucas said. "There's some sort of conspiracy going on with the station leaders and the Leng Corporation executives. I'm not sure exactly what's happening yet, but I *do* know they smuggled in Meredith Waite and that girl I was with so that the girl could touch the sphere."

"Wait," Ronald said. "What? As in *Leng CEO* Meredith Waite?"

"Yeah," Lucas said. "I tried to stop them, but I was too late."

"Why did they want to do that?" Ron asked. "Didn't they hear about Vic?"

"Regan's different," Lucas said, more of his strength returning as he ate. "She's not a normal girl. I think they were trying to wake the sphere up or change her somehow. And they succeeded on both counts."

"When did this happen?"

"It was at the same time the earthquake hit us."

"No way," Ron said. "Did they *cause* it?"

"I think so."

"Slow down, Kevin," a woman murmured a table or two away from them. "You're going to make yourself sick. It's going to be okay."

"Lucas, if you're right about this, then we need to tell someone," Ronald said. "We need to take action against that thing before it's too late."

"I just don't know who," Lucas said. "Definitely not Judy Blake. She was with them. But I don't know if we can trust Wade, either."

"We've got to try *someone*," Ronald said. "If you say Blake's out, then I think we need to take a chance on Wade. They're the only ones with enough power to make something happen quickly on a station-wide level."

"Hey, have you lost weight?" the girl behind them asked.

The lights went out.

Lucas and Ronald shot to their feet as alarmed chatter erupted around them. The lights snapped back on, and Lucas noticed that many other people had stood as well. The lights flickered out again. When they came back on this time, Lucas saw that many of those standing had turned toward their nearest neighbors. Lucas gasped as he watched their mouths snap, their jaws drawing off to the sides as their multitude of tongues slithered out. The beasts who had been people bleated curiously. And then they lunged.

Lucas watched in shocked horror as the first of the Kadath residents' throats were ripped open. Screams ricocheted throughout the cafeteria.

"What the hell!" Ronald said. "No! No, they were *just normal!*" The lights doused again as pandemonium struck.

Lucas stumbled through the dark as the sounds of clattering carnage and hyperventilating terror soaked his ears and rattled in his brain. He still smelled food and the faint odor of sanitizers, but now there was something else, too: it was a bit like copper. He ran into a table, then skidded over a puddle of something wet and slippery on the ground. Someone clutched at his coat, then was ripped away.

"Ron!" he called. "Can you hear me? Are you still here?"

Ronald didn't answer, but something else did. Its voice was mewling and all too close. Lucas felt long serrated tongues brush over his face. Reaching blindly behind him, he searched for the auto-scalpel that he had previously strapped to his belt. It was still there. Unclasping it, he gripped the familiar tool's handle and pressed its trigger. Its blade hummed to life, and he swung it wildly in front of him. He felt the blade slice cleanly through something, and the thing that was before him screamed before starting to gurgle.

The lights flickered back on. Lucas squinted, trying to get his eyes to adjust to the harsh brightness. "Oh, no," he managed. The cafeteria had become a charnel house. Entrails draped across the tabletops; blood drizzled across surfaces and pooled on the floor. The room seemed only to have two colors: chrome and crimson.

They were everywhere. A dead horror lay at Lucas's feet, but all the rest stalked between the tables, crouching down to feast as their bouquets of tongues waggled in their mouths. Once they registered movement in the new light, though, they paused. Slowly, they swiveled toward Lucas, cocking their heads as their jaws flexed and expanded outward. Lucas clenched the scalpel in his hand. He couldn't escape them this time.

Lucas heard a groan. Looking down, he saw Ronald stirring a few feet away. He must have hit his head on one of the tables. Lucas ducked low and shook him. "Ron!" he said. "Ron, wake up! Come on!"

Ronald seemed to be wrestling with consciousness. Lucas looked up. Several of the things were drifting toward him.

Someone else screamed, and then Lucas heard a man cry out, *"Get the hell away from me!"* Lucas's gaze followed the sound of the voice and saw Gerald White, one of the expedition miners, scrambling to his feet, a rivet gun clutched in his brown hands. Gerald opened fire, cutting into the flesh of the creatures with dozens of hot rivets. His bared teeth gleamed in his dark face, his eyes sparking with rage and panic. A woman near him, meanwhile, was inching toward an emergency unit mounted on the wall. Reaching it, she yanked it open and ripped out the axe it contained. The creatures swiveled toward these two, clearly assessing them as a greater threat.

A hand grabbed Lucas. Looking down, he saw Ron staring up at him with wide eyes.

"Can you get up?" Lucas asked him. Ronald nodded. Wincing, he slowly stood with Lucas's help.

Another woman, closer to Lucas than Gerald and the other lady, had stood up with a crowbar in her hand. Closing the distance with one of the monsters, she swung the metal rod wildly at its head. She connected with it, spinning it around, and then bludgeoned it over and over. In so doing, though, she was too focused to notice the other creature racing up behind her. It leaped on her, its mouth latching onto the top of her head. The woman shrieked as its tongues wrapped around her face, but her cries ceased as its three jaws crunched her skull between its teeth.

The woman was nearer than anyone else, so Lucas hurried toward her with Ronald at his side. It was too late for the woman, but he could still catch her attackers off-guard. Engaging his scalpel, he swung it at the back of the thing's neck as it bent to feast on the woman's brains. The blade cut cleanly through its spinal column, and the ravenous terror pitched forward. The one she had attacked was struggling to regain its feet after being beaten with the crowbar. Lucas didn't give it a chance. Lunging over the corpse of its fellow beast, he plunged the scalpel into its eye.

Looking back, Lucas saw Ron grimly pick up the woman's crowbar. They nodded to each other and moved onward.

Gerald was still riddling the creatures with a steady stream of rivets, making their bodies jitter and flail as they lurched backward. Lucas almost thought he might finish off all the rest of the creatures single-handedly, but then his weapon clicked. It was empty.

"No," Gerald said, checking his depleted reservoir. "No, no, *no!*" He threw the rivet gun aside in disgust. The insatiable humanoids immediately realized what had happened and started racing toward him, jumping over tables and scrambling down aisleways to get to him and the woman with a single-minded intensity.

Lucas ran toward the things, but it was quickly apparent that he was no match for their speed. He saw Gerald take the axe from the woman and tell her to stand behind him. He raised the axe, preparing himself for the onslaught. They were upon him within seconds. Gerald swung his axe, letting out a primal howl as he hacked at the attackers. There were only four of them left now, but their movements were so quick. Their long, skeletal fingers snatched at him, their claw-like fingernails digging into him as their tongues lashed out at his limbs and face.

Lucas reached the beasts and drove his scalpel into the side of one creature's skull. Yanking it out, he pivoted toward another one, which was concurrently turning to face him. Its arms and tongues lashed out at him, its jaws wide and slavering. Ronald cracked its skull with the crowbar, then bludgeoned it over and over until it collapsed to the ground. Gerald swung his axe at the third, the blade cleaving its forehead in two.

"Gerald, look out!" Ronald yelled.

Gerald swiveled toward the fourth monster, but his axe was still embedded in the third one's skull. He wrenched at the handle, but before he could get the blade free, the fourth one dove at him. It knocked him to the ground, its tongues wrapping around his neck and temples. Its nails dug into his flesh as blood welled beneath them –

The girl pulled out a utility knife and jabbed it into the thing's neck. It bucked beneath her blade but, before it could retaliate, she repeated the action, stabbing the vicious beast again and again and again. At last, the creature shuddered and collapsed on top of Gerald.

"Ugh!" Gerald cried. "Get it off me!"

Lucas and Ronald helped pull the corpse off him, and Gerald, at last, was able to stand to his feet shakily.

"You all okay?" Gerald asked, his eyes wild as sweat mixed with blood on his face.

"Yeah, Gerald," Ronald replied. "Largely thanks to you."

"Hey, I wouldn't be here without you three, either," Gerald said.

"Thank you. Good to see you, Dr. Kane."

"Same to you, Gerald," Lucas said.

"You okay, Lizzie?" Gerald asked the woman.

"Did – did no one else make it?" Lizzie said, bringing her hand to her mouth. "It's just us? I can't – No. How?"

"Let's get out of here," Gerald said. "As quick as we can." Slowly, carefully, they worked their way out of the eerily quiet mess hall, picking their way over the corpses. "What the hell just happened here?" Gerald asked. "What *were* those things?"

"They… were our friends," Ronald said.

Lizzie wiped tears from her eyes before tapping her node. "Hello, security? There's been an… outbreak. In the Dome Three mess hall, level two. Four survivors. Everyone else was… *slaughtered* like pigs." She paused for a moment. "Yes. We'll wait for you nearby. How long do you think? You're kidding. Really? What's the situation there?"

They reached the entrance and gratefully stumbled through it. Ronald slammed his fist into the hatch control with understandable malice. The hatch, unphased, slid smoothly shut beside him.

"They're saying that there's a cascade of incidents just like this occurring all over the station," Lizzie said. "And it's getting worse every few minutes. What's going on, Chief? Why is this happening?"

"Did they mention where most of the attacks are taking place?" Lucas asked.

"It sounds like the worst ones are in Dome Two near the sphere, but they're reaching just about everywhere at this point," Lizzie replied.

Lucas felt the blood drain from his face. Tapping his node, he called Rachel again. This time there was no response. He tried once more. No answer.

"Rachel's not answering now," Lucas said, turning to Ronald. "I can't stay. I'm sorry."

Ronald nodded. "Okay," he said. "I understand, Lucas. We'll cover for you. You going to be okay?"

"I hope so," Lucas said. "I hope we all will. Thanks, Ron." Then, turning, he hurried toward the nearest shuttle station.

Even though it had barely been an hour since the last time Lucas had traversed Kadath's corridors, the situation had already deteriorated into a near-panic. People ran through the passages, jostling into one another, their eyes wide and frightened as they glanced over their shoulders or stole paranoid glimpses at those clustered around them. Lucas could only suspect that whatever else had happened was equally as bad as what he had just experienced and that the word – and the fear – had spread like a wildfire pandemic. Lucas realized that he was barely any better. He just kept hearing those words in his head: the worst attacks were happening near the sphere – in the science wing.

Lucas tried calling Rachel again. She still didn't answer. He gave it a minute, then called again: No response.

Lucas pressed into the crowd clustered inside Arkham Station. Winding his way through the crowd, Lucas looked up the information for Dome Two. Shuttles were still running there, and the next one would arrive within five minutes. Forcing himself to stay calm, Lucas joined the queue for the Dome Two shuttle. He noticed absentmindedly that the crowd for Dome Two was significantly less than those heading elsewhere in the facility.

At last, the shuttle pulled in. As it did, Lucas heard the first scream at the far end of the station. Turning toward it to look, he saw… *something*… beginning to spread over the station's far corner. It was like a red fungus of some kind, except that it had numerous traits that seemed disturbingly animal. Lucas shook his head. Usually, he would feel driven to investigate it, but right now, he needed to find Rachel before it was too late.

Climbing on the shuttle, Lucas stared back at the strange substance as it continued crawling up the wall of the shuttle terminal. Then the station moved out of sight and was gone.

Lucas tried his node again. Rachel still didn't answer. On a whim, Lucas called Charles as well: He didn't respond, either.

The shuttle arrived, and Lucas stepped out onto the Innsmouth Station platform. If possible, the uproar here was even worse. Lucas pressed through the throng and worked his way into the corridor beyond.

"Attention all residents," said Wade's voice over the speakers. "This is Station Commander Terrence Wade. We have been made aware of the current disturbances occurring throughout Kadath, and are taking every appropriate measure to both contain and prevent these reported incidents. At this time, we would ask that all residents remain calm and orderly, and that non-essential personnel confine themselves to their quarters until further notice. Toward this end, security has been dispatched to curb any rioting and will be working to clear the corridors – forcibly, if necessary. Rest assured that your safety and security are our top priorities. Together we will curtail these isolated occurrences and advance into tomorrow's golden dawn undeterred. Thank you for your cooperation in this matter."

Lucas shook his head as he continued pressing through the riotous mob. It was getting easier, though, the closer he got to the science wing – and the cargo bay where the sphere awaited. At last, Lucas came to the bay doors concealing the mammoth orb. Two armed guards were standing in front of the hatches, their faces stony, their weapons at attention. Lucas attempted a slight smile and nod, but they didn't return the gestures.

Someone screamed behind the doors. Lucas froze. "What was that?" he said. "Someone's in there! We have to help them!"

"Authorized personnel only, Sir," the closest guard said.

"And who's authorized?" Lucas asked. "You can't just let someone die in there!"

"No one in or out without the strict authorization of Dr. West, Dr. Cohen, Judy Blake, or Terrence Wade," the guard said.

"Do you know who I am?" Lucas asked.

"Yes, Dr. Kane," the guard said. "And you are not authorized."

Another scream came – followed by a significantly less human shriek. Lucas moved toward the door, and the guard raised his weapon. "I ask you not to escalate this situation any further, sir," the guard said. "If you come any closer, I will open fire."

"I'm coming back here with Dr. West," Lucas snapped. "But if anyone dies in there before I get back, their blood will be on *your* hands."

"Have a nice day, Dr. Kane," the guard said. "Please take shelter in your quarters until the current lockdown is lifted."

Shaking his head in disgust, Lucas continued onward.

Lucas paused at the hatch to William West's laboratory. Squeezing his eyes shut, he took a deep breath. So much of him wanted to forget the screams and just find Rachel. But another part of him knew he couldn't leave whoever was in the bay to whatever fate awaited them. Though, did he honestly think whoever was in there was still alive?

Lucas's node chirped. "Incoming call from William West," it said.

"Hello?" Lucas said. "William?"

"Ah, Lucas!" West said. "Wonderful! I had heard from the guards that you were looking for me. And, as it ends up, I'm looking for *you*, as well! In fact, Dr. Cohen and I are in your laboratory as we speak."

Lucas felt an uncomfortable knot forming in his gut. Turning, he once again started walking faster and faster toward his lab, the people in the bay at least momentarily forgotten. "Why are you in my lab, William?" he asked.

"Well, you see, some revelations have come to light from a very reliable source that have greatly intrigued me," William said. "So, I acquired the necessary permissions to pursue the data, and now I have some findings that I simply *must* discuss with you."

"Screams are coming from the sphere's bay, William, and they won't let me go in there without your approval," Lucas said. "Why don't you meet me down here, and we can discuss your data while we get whoever is in there out?"

"Oh, I wouldn't worry about *that*, Lucas," William said. "It's just a little experiment Dr. Cohen and I are running. Nothing to fear there. No, just come here. Someone is *dying* to see you."

William hung up.

Lucas was almost hyperventilating now. He tapped his node again. "Call Rachel Wilkins," he said.

The node chimed a few times, and then the calm voice returned: "Rachel Wilkins is not currently available. Would you like to leave a message?" Lucas cursed and tapped out. Then he broke into a run toward his lab.

At last, Lucas reached the door of his laboratory. Taking a deep breath, he pulled the scalpel off his belt again. Lucas had never thought it would *ever* be used for this. Tilting his head upward, he squeezed his eyes shut. Upon reopening them, though, Lucas was surprised to see that he could see inside the room as if the door didn't exist. West and Cohen stood at the lab's far side along with a short, smarmy, pompous-looking man who Lucas recognized as the station chaplain, Summerisle, while two guards loitered near the hatch. They had strapped Rachel down to an examination table.

Lucas tried calling Charles another time, then Ronald. Neither answered. Sighing, he closed his eyes again. This time when he opened them, he once more saw the hatch. He hit the control pad. The door slid into the wall, and Lucas jumped through it. Pivoting to the left, he punched the guard standing there in the face, sending him stumbling backward. Turning right, Lucas ducked low and thrust his elbow into the other guard's gut, doubling him over.

"Welcome, Lucas!" William exclaimed. "I'm so glad you could join us!"

Lucas swiveled back to the first guard – and that's when Cohen brought the pistol up, leveling it at Lucas's head.

"That's quite enough, Dr. Kane," Cohen said.

"We three are men of *science*, are we not?" West said. "Surely we can have a civilized discourse without resorting to violence!" Then he looked over the two guards. "Though bravo on so quickly incapacitating the help. It's almost like you knew *exactly* where to find them. Perhaps you hacked the security system? Or maybe you had some *other* method of ascertaining their locations? But I suppose we can get to that in due time."

Lucas turned toward the examination table. "Rachel?" he said. "Are you okay? Did they hurt you?"

"Lucas," Rachel moaned, her eyes fluttering open. She looked drugged. "You came. I'm so sorry. I tried to protect you." She tried to crane her head to look for him, but the straps over her body wouldn't allow it.

"Of course, I did," Lucas said. "I wasn't going to leave you to them."

"Lucas?" Rachel said. It almost sounded like the fog was starting to clear from her mind. "No! Lucas, you have to go! Run,

Lucas! *Run!*"

"It's okay, Rachel," Lucas said. One of the guards came up behind him and knocked him to his knees. The other one snatched the scalpel from his hand. "We're going to work this out."

"No!" she screamed. "You're too important! Lucas, you don't understand! *RUN!*"

"Now, now," William chuckled. "Lucas isn't going to do anything of the sort. Are you, my friend? Fetch the man a chair, good sirs! We have so much to discuss!"

"You've chosen the wrong time for us to be enemies, West," Lucas said. "The sphere is wreaking havoc across Kadath. It's manifesting horrors all around us. And you want to attack *me?*"

"Oh, no, no, no, you are gravely mistaken on several counts, Lucas," West said as Lucas was forced to sit, his hands tied to the frame. One of the guards brought West a chair, and he sat, too. "I'm not here to attack you. I'm here to *study* you. And, as for the sphere, it only assaults those who fear it. I do not. We've come to somewhat of a rapport, it and I. I think it is a gift to be treasured, and a resource to exploit. I intend to best it, and I mean to harness it. Just like I plan to do to you."

"What do you think I am, West?" Lucas asked. "How exactly do you propose to harness me?"

"I *honestly* think you don't grasp your true nature," West said. "That is both frustrating and fascinating. But perhaps I can help shed some light on the situation.

"I initially began to think there may be something odd about you during our time in the mobile command center. But it was some recent reports I received – and surveillance feed I absconded with – that *profoundly* fueled my curiosity. Then, when no less than Ms. Judy Blake herself said that corporate executives wanted me to delve a little deeper, *well*, that's when my curiosity evolved into an imperative. So, I began to dig further. Do you know what I discovered? You didn't *exist* before you appeared in Kadath, Lucas. There is no record of you. There is no birth certificate or charming childhood photograph, or even a transfer document to Kadath.

"That was a little passing strange, don't you think? Ah, but it grew even *stranger!* Because I then ran a search on your closest accomplice, the woman who seems to be attached to you at the hip. Or should I say somewhere a bit more… centralized in the pelvic region? But I digress. Imagine my surprise when I discovered that *she* didn't exist, either! Or, at least, she wasn't supposed to be *here* at the Kadath facility. And what's more, it seemed that *she* was the one who had carefully inserted all the needed documentation and paved the way for *both* of you!

"Through a series of exquisitely careful, highly invasive system hacks, suddenly you had a crew quarters, a laboratory, and a pedigree. And, when I traced those dalliances back, I discovered the virtual fingerprints of none other than our own ravishing Ms. Wilkins. What a twist!"

"You're spouting absolute *madness*, West," Lucas said.

"Am I?" West said. "Then tell me, Lucas: What's the first thing you remember? Was it a beloved childhood event? Your first kiss? Your first job, or maybe college? Or was it waking up in Kadath? When was the last time you spent time thinking about your past?"

"I…" Lucas blinked. "You're saying the two of us didn't even *exist* before Kadath? That is a physical *impossibility*. You realize that, right? You realize how *insane* this sounds?"

"Ah, unless you *did* exist before this, but just not in this reality," West said. "Perhaps you weren't *born* into this world but were instead *injected* into it."

"*What?*" Lucas started laughing now. "West, what you're describing is sheer lunacy!"

"Not if one is a student of the works of the Golden Dawn Church, to which Leng is intrinsically intertwined," West said. "Then it becomes staggeringly plausible. Which is why I've invited High Priest Summerisle to join us today, as no one currently present knows their history better than him."

Summerisle cleared his throat. "I must say, it is an absolute pleasure to meet you, Dr. Kane," he said, walking over to stand beside West. "I am High Priest James Summerisle, of the Golden Dawn Church. The order to which, I believe, you owe your very existence." Summerisle chuckled and shook his head. "My, my. We have tried for so long, and now to *see* one in front of me, in the very flesh… A holy moment, indeed."

"I wish I could say I felt the same, Summerisle," Lucas said. "You're the chaplain harassing Edgar, right?"

"Ah, Mr. Kayce and I did have many particularly enlightening conversations," Summerisle replied. "Such a shame to hear about his apparent suicide. I still had so much knowledge to glean from him." Lucas's eyes grew wide, which Summerisle noticed. "Oh, you didn't know? My condolences. I received reports you had visited him, so I assume you were friends."

Lucas swallowed the lump down his throat as the four entities hummed into existence behind him again, their dark babblings strangely subdued. "So, you've got me, West," Lucas said. "Now what are you going to do with me?"

"Oh, I thought that was obvious," West said. "I'm going to take you back to my lab and dissect that beautiful mind you have. I want to find out how it works and why. With your help, I intend to uncover the secrets of consciousness fusion."

"Don't you touch him!" Rachel yelled. "I'm warning you!"

"Okay, fine," Lucas said. "But let Rachel go. Leave her out of this."

West laughed. "Why on *earth* would I let Rachel go?" he asked. "She is *almost* as interesting as you! Plus, if I let her out, the first thing she would do is scheme against me to free you – and it's not exactly like I would be able to avoid her in a place like this. What's more, I have both of you already, so it's not like you're in any sort of a position to bargain. And there is still the burning question of *why* would they inject you into Kadath? That is a question *you* obviously can't answer, but I suspect *she* can. I frankly see *many* reasons to keep her, and *none* to release her."

"Please," Rachel begged. "Please! Release him! Do what you want to me. Ask me whatever questions you want. Rip me open. But let him go! He is the future of humanity!"

"Ah, see, it's statements like that which make me most assuredly *not* want to release *either* of you," West said, laughing. "Oh, goodness, this is a great deal of fun!"

Lucas closed his eyes. He needed to focus. Everyone kept saying he was special somehow. It was time to put that to use.

Regan, please, I need your help.

I hear you, Lucas.

What do I do?

Embrace what you are. Find your core, and unleash it.

"Lucas?" West said. "Where'd you go, Lucas?"

My core? What is that?

You've seen it before. Find it. Grab hold of it. Use it. Start with the four behind you.

"He appears to have just placed himself in some kind of trance," Summerisle said.

"Well, kindly get him *out* of it!" West asked. "I don't want him trying anything before we can get him properly contained."

Lucas mentally seized hold of the four entities behind him and sucked them into himself. He felt their beings solidify, merge, become a concrete part of him. Silencing their incessant mutterings, he fed off their strength to spin out into the place between the worlds.

Lucas spun through the realities he had seen until, at last, he found the one that seemed to call to him – the one that fed his soul. From a distance, the skyscraper almost appeared like a lighthouse on its little island: a beacon in the chaotic abyss. Lucas reached out to it. Pushing through the barrier between them, he broke through.

A flood of images assaulted him: foreign memories and bizarre terrors and – people?

"What the bloody hell!" yelled a preacher, stumbling backward and falling on his butt. "What on God's green earth are *you?*"

Curious. Lucas moved past him and found something to grip. He planted a part of himself in that place, and immediately he felt its power coursing into him. This was it. This was enough. Withdrawing from that place, Lucas returned to his reality and opened his eyes. They were blazing white.

"You wanted me to wake up," Lucas said. "So, I thought I'd oblige you, William."

Lucas pushed against the restraints, focusing intently on their physicality. His bonds vaporized, melting away to nothing. Lucas rose to his feet.

"Incredible," West said.

Summerisle dropped to his knees as if he had just witnessed the return of Christ. "An Enlightened," he breathed. "An Enlightened!"

"Dr. Cohen, would you be a dear and shoot Dr. Kane?" West said.

Dr. Cohen, though, just stood there, his jaw slack, the gun dangling in his limp fingers. "I – I – William, he…" Cohen stammered.

"Oh, very well, I'll do it myself," William said. He snatched the pistol from Cohen's fingers and aimed it at Lucas.

"NO!" Summerisle screamed, slamming into William. West stumbled, his finger jerking against the gun's trigger. The gun fired, and Rachel shrieked.

Lucas focused intently on the pistol for a brief instant and it melted into air from between Williams' fingers. Then he turned toward Rachel. "No," he said. "What did you *do*, West? *What did you do?*"

Rachel was bleeding where the projectile had hit her. A pool of red was spreading beneath her. Lucas was at her side in an instant. Looking at the straps binding her, he willed them away and then started inspecting Rachel's wound.

"Lucas," Rachel murmured. "Lucas –"

"It's okay, Rachel," Lucas said. "I'm going to fix you. It's going to be all right. You'll see."

"Your eyes," Rachel said. "They're beautiful…" Then hers fluttered closed.

Lucas roared in heartrending agony. He heard something shuffle behind him and whirled around to see the guards slowly advancing toward him. He gave them a look of such utter fury that everyone caught in his gaze froze.

"Go," he said quietly, his breath heaving in and out of his lungs. "This is your only chance."

The guards scrambled out of the room, followed only seconds later by Cohen. Summerisle stumbled out of the room, unable to pry his eyes off Lucas. West was close behind him.

"Utterly fascinating," West murmured. And then he was gone.

"Don't leave me, Rachel," Lucas said, whirling back to her. His gaze snapped left and right. He needed tools. He hadn't gotten his scalpel back, but there had to be something else he could use. He saw a pair of scissors stowed in a nearby compartment. Dashing over to it, he thrust the drawer open and grabbed the shears, then returned to Rachel and started cutting away the fabric of her shirt. After carefully pulling the cloth away from the wound, he ripped it into strips to fashion a makeshift tourniquet. He needed medical supplies. He needed nanobots and regen foam. He required so many things right now, and he didn't have any of them. He wasn't set up for emergency treatment…

He wrapped the tourniquet as tightly around her body as he could, then used his newfound gift to peer inside her body. The bullet had passed all the way through, but it had also punctured vital organs. She had severe internal bleeding.

"No," he said. "No, no, no… Stay with me, Rachel…"

Maybe he could restore objects as well as look through them. He *was* a doctor, after all. Wouldn't it make sense that he would have the ability to restore others? Placing his hands on Rachel's wounds, he focused with all his might, willing her flesh to regenerate. Nothing happened.

Rachel was starting to shiver. She was going into shock as she bled through her haphazard bandages. He needed to find a medkit. Surely, he had one here somewhere. He was losing her –

Rachel stopped breathing. Lucas's heart froze. "No," he whispered. *"No, Rachel!"* Raising his blood-soaked hands to her chest, he started performing CPR. There was no response. He kept working, trying to will her to breathe again. Nothing happened.

Lucas let out a wail. Picking up Rachel's still form in his arms, he held her tightly against himself. "I'm not going to lose you, Rachel," Lucas said. "I *refuse* to let you leave me, do you hear? *Do you hear me?*"

Lucas squeezed his eyes shut. "You won't leave me," he growled. "Not now or ever! I won't let you!"

Something burst inside Lucas. He felt an uncontainable surge of power well up within him, and it spilled out of his fingertips and chest and stomach. Lucas's eyes shot open as he let out a primal bellow. He looked down, hoping against hope –

No. No! *What had he done?*

Lucas's body was absorbing Rachel into it. Every second, more and more of her disappeared into him, her physical essence slipping steadily away. Lucas knew, deep down, that there was nothing he could do now. There was no stopping the process he had begun. So, he clutched her to himself as his body consumed her, cradling her in his arms, knowing this was the last time he would touch her in the real world. Lucas ran his trembling hand over her beautiful, still face, pressing his cheek against her forehead. He hadn't appreciated her as he should have. He hadn't given her what she deserved.

Rachel was gone.

NINE

FRACTURES

"Perhaps it was inevitable given the amount of activity taking place at our current location. I certainly should have seen it coming. Even still, the manifestations caught us off-guard. It began in the fusion labs. One of the new candidates we brought in went through a radical transformation, becoming what seemed like a gate of sorts made of meat and bone. I looked through it myself. On the other side was… madness. Crawling, writhing, breathing chaos. They poured through the gate, swarming us within minutes. The lead team barely escaped. Many good men and women were sacrificed to ensure our survival. I almost blame myself for the disaster. The facility is certainly lost, at least until we can assemble a team to retake it."

Dr. Jayce Norton

TOWER WORLD

Connor reached the top of the ladder and clambered off

the rungs onto the tower's next level. He frowned. What sort of material formed this floor?

Shaking his head, Connor looked back down the hole. He had to push past an almost overwhelming wave of vertigo as he stared into that seemingly bottomless abyss. At last, though, he was able to make out the same strange lights he had seen before, which were now swirling upward as the mist curled up the ladder. That wasn't the only thing working its way toward him, though: There was something *else* climbing the rungs, too. Or was it several somethings?

Whatever was coming, they were making steady progress. With the mist clinging to them, Connor couldn't be sure of their size. But he suspected they were big. Possibly enormous.

"It won't take them long to get up here," Connor said, turning to look at Min and Mitsuko. "Any sign of where to go next?" Then he genuinely noticed his new surroundings. "Wow. What *is* this place?"

"It is simultaneously wondrous and terrible," Min said, his jaw slack.

It was like they had just stepped into a magnificent, mammoth cathedral forged from some eldritch, unearthly biomechanical material. Light filtered in through giant vertically oriented stained-glass windows, fashioned into images ranging from beautiful and strange to unsettling and abstract to magnificently brilliant and utterly horrific. The upper part of the structure was completely open, while the lower part was divided up by walls about as tall as two people stacked atop each other. The walls seemed to have grown out of the very structure itself. There was an opening in the two nearest walls set in front and behind them, and Connor expected there would be more openings as they continued through.

"Does anyone see a way to the next level of the tower?"

Mitsuko asked.

All three of them scanned the sides of the cathedral.

"Not off-hand," Connor said. "Maybe we just pick a direction?"

"We must keep in mind that, if we choose the wrong way, it will likely be our last mistake," Min said. "Our enemy approaches swiftly."

Connor looked left towards what he took as the front of the cathedral. "I say we go that way," he said, pointing.

"Why?" Mitsuko asked.

"Because, when you come to a chapel, you go to the altar to meet God, not to the back," Connor replied.

Min nodded. "That's good enough for me."

"Very well," Mitsuko said. "I hope you're right, Connor."

"Me, too," Connor said.

With one more anxious glance down the ladder, they set out through the opening in the first wall. There was another wall only a few paces away, with several gaping portals punctuating its length.

"Do you hear that?" Min asked, his voice low.

"Hear what?" Mitsuko said.

"Yes," Connor murmured. "I do."

Mitsuko frowned, then listened. Her eyes widened. "Whispers," she said. "Hundreds of whispers."

Min nodded. "They're all around us."

"Which path should we take now?" Connor asked.

"I have no idea," Min said. "Though I have a terrible feeling we've just stepped into a maze."

Mitsuko quickly set out to the left. She paused as she reached that door, looking through it. Then she retreated to the center. "The whispers are quieter down there," she said.

Connor jogged down the opposite direction, the others following behind him. The whispers grew louder and louder with every step he took. He leaned through this door and saw a corridor of sorts stretching before him. His hand grazed the doorpost.

"Welcome, Connor," a whisper wriggled into his ear. "You enter the cathedral of the mind." Connor jerked backward with a yelp, and that's when he realized his hand had been resting on a human arm fused into the wall.

"Connor?" Min asked.

"It's this way," he said, shaking his head. They set out down the corridor.

At the end of the pathway, they swerved left, then almost immediately had to turn left again. There were three doors along the right-hand side up ahead, but the corridor didn't end with them: instead, it turned abruptly right not far past the last entry.

"Has anyone else noticed the walls?" Min asked.

"Yes," Mitsuko said.

"There are so many faces…" Min murmured. "Or, at least, the impressions of faces."

Above the sound of the whispers, the three of them heard a screech. Then, moments later, a bellow, which was followed closely by another roar. And, last of all, they heard a voice.

"Connor!" Sephora shouted. "Where are you, Connor? It's time we had that chat!"

The three travelers looked at each other but didn't say a word. Gingerly, Connor moved to the first door and peered through. Unlike the other passageways, a ceiling enclosed this particular corridor. The cathedral's ambient light sifted down the passage, but he could see no other source of illumination down it.

"Step through, Connor," the whispers said. "Take a leap of faith. Come with us. Yes, come, Connor. Come inside."

"This way," Connor said.

"Are you certain, Connor?" Min murmured. "I hear them much

louder down here."

"No, they want us to go this way," Connor said. "I'm positive." He stepped inside the corridor to take a closer look. And that's when the portal sealed behind him.

"No!" Connor cried, spinning around. He pounded on the surface that was growing more solid by the moment. He heard Min and Mitsuko hammering on the other side. There was no way any of them were getting through. At least not without making a terrible amount of noise.

Connor swiveled back around. It was so dark, like being trapped at the bottom of a mine shaft. There could be anything in all that darkness.

Connor found his pulse racing. He remembered now how much he had always hated the dark. It wasn't necessarily the *night* he disliked, but rather the darkness itself. It closed in around him, smothered him, pressed against his chest. Tight spaces. That was it: he was trapped in a confined, dark place again. Just like when…

Groaning, Connor sank to the ground with his eyes squeezed shut. He needed to breathe; to calm down. But how *could* he when there was *no way out* –

"Look, Connor," the whispers said. "Yes, *look*. Open your eyes and see."

Connor did. There was a pinprick of light in the distance ahead. It was barely there, but it was also unmistakable in the otherwise absolute darkness.

"A light," the whispers said. "A light at the end of the tunnel. Do you see it? Do you believe it?"

Connor saw it. He forced himself to climb to his feet and stumble toward that pinprick of hope. The corridor breathed around him. Reaching out his hands, he could feel the walls expand to brush his fingertips before retracting again. As Connor continued onward, though, he began to think the whole area may be contracting around him. Now he felt the biomechanical material any time he extended his arms.

"Our Father in heaven, hallowed be your name," Connor muttered. He smelled the salty sweat running down his face and soaking his clothes. He tasted it on his lips.

"Your kingdom come, your will be done," the whispers replied.

Echoes of the life he may have had arose like electric etchings from a drug-fueled lucid dream, scratched into both the dark tunnel and Connor's retinas. They swirled around him in a feverish funhouse maelstrom, wreaking torment and confusion across his brain. The memories began to speak in voices of their own, joining the whispers in a jumble of words and thoughts and fears.

"Get back in the closet, ya little blighter! Did I say you could come out yet?"

"It's coming, Connor! I heard it in the forest! It's burning like the devil himself!"

"Why can't you seem to make any money at this thing, boyo? There's good money in religion, isn't there? You need to get *you* some of that!"

"They pull at you, Connor. Keep going. Keep traveling through your darkness. Don't lose sight of the light, or you will be lost. Just like us."

"He's dead, Connor. There's nothing we can do now."

Hands were reaching out of the maelstrom. They pawed at Connor, pulling at him. Fingers entwined in his clothing, stroked his hair.

"The monsters are at your doorstep now, Connor. You don't stand a chance."

"Does it matter if the demons are spirits or people? Either way, their evil is undeniable."

Was he still on the ground? Or was he on the wall? Or maybe it was the ceiling? His equilibrium was spinning like a top.

"Where were you, Connor? Was I not important enough to warrant your attention?"

"A Protestant? I thought you said you were a Christian! Sweet Mary and Joseph! What a right shame, a Holy Joe like you throwin' it all away on a false religion. Have you no fear of hellfire, you moran?"

"I told you to shut up, boy! No, 'sorry' sure as hell is not gonna cut it now. Get my belt and be quick about it!"

Connor tripped on a hand and fell forward. Or upward. Or sideways. He started crawling forward. Or was he swimming?

"What did you do, Connor? How did you do that? Are you some kind of a freak or something?"

More voices were pressing in upon him now. Memories that he knew had never been a part of his life. They pressed into his darkness, melded with it, fused with it.

"You're a frigid bitch, Mitsuko. You know that, don't you? I frankly don't know how *anyone* can stand you once they get to know you."

"Where do we go, Wang? What do we do? They're right outside now!"

"Your attempts are lacking at best, Mitsuko. I find you to be a disappointment. Try harder."

"The family is dead, Min. There is nothing more we can do for them."

"Connor? Connor, I can't move! Please, you have to help me!"

"You're throwing your life away for enlightenment, Wang. Why pursue this useless, empty path? You're abandoning your one chance to truly *live!*"

"Who would *want* to work with her, though? She's as frigid as an iceberg! What? Oh, she heard that?"

"You have brought dishonor to this family, Min. I never want to see you again. Be gone from this place. You're no longer welcome here."

The darkness was changing. Becoming… somewhere else.

There were cafeteria tables all around him. Creatures whose jaws split down the middle were devouring people, ripping the meat from their bones. Looking up, they saw him. The darkness returned.

Pandemonium ruled. The crowd was in a panic. Things were coming for them, and they knew it.

The girl stared into his eyes. Her gaze contained volumes and worlds and fire. As he looked into her, though, he was not afraid because of what he saw in *her*. He was frightened because he knew she saw the same thing inside *him*.

The sphere whirled and sizzled and spun. It was alive, so alive. The gate was opening, and behind it was an endless ocean of swirling, maddening thought.

The light blossomed before Connor, and the darkness birthed him into it.

Connor collapsed on the biomechanical floor as the iris closed behind him. His whole body was shaking, his vision blurry. He retched on the ground. Finally, he felt he had the strength to look around, so he swiveled his head slowly from side to side. He was still alone, in a wide-open space. At the far end of the area, he could see the towering wall of the cathedral, which towered upward and ended at a peak. Had he – had he made it to the altar?

Slowly, tremulously, he climbed to his feet and looked back. He saw there were several exits behind him, but they were all sealed. He could only hope that Min and Mitsuko would make it through their portals soon –

Something pressed through the cathedral's ceiling above him. Connor looked up and cried out in surprise and terror.

"What the bloody hell!" yelled Connor, stumbling backward and falling on his butt. "What on God's green earth are *you?*"

The being above him burned like flames, its massive body ethereal and translucent. It was roughly human in shape, except that it had multiple heads and sets of arms – and it was almost as tall as the cathedral. While much of its body shimmered and fluctuated, one thing Connor could make out for sure: its eyes were like miniature suns in its faces.

The being seemed to notice Connor, but it expressed at most a mild curiosity. Gliding past him, it finally landed on the ground beyond Connor at the front of the cathedral. Then it dropped down onto its knees, resting its two lowest hands on the ground.

The whispers metamorphosed into what seemed to be a choir singing on a single note. The sound was not unpleasant at first. In fact, it was almost beautiful. The voices divided until they were singing a full chord. Then they were singing several harmonies. The whole time their volume and intensity steadily increased until at last Connor had to cover his ears. It was like the very air around him was crackling with wild, violent energy – and all that energy was channeling into the being before him.

Reaching up with its top pair of arms, the creature grabbed hold of one of its heads and wrenched upward. The head pulled free of its neck. The hands holding it then maneuvered downward, placing it in the very center of the raised dais at the front of the cathedral. The enormous head seemed to settle there as if the space had been made just for it. The walls and floor reached up to meet it, fusing with it so that it truly became a part of the structure.

The massive being looked upward, and then it jumped. It did not return to the ground, however, but instead continued upwards, gaining speed as it added altitude. It rocketed through the ceiling, passing through it without leaving a mark, and was gone as abruptly as it had arrived.

Connor looked down from the spot the being had vanished, focusing on what it had left behind. The head was a uniform dark gray color now – almost a steel shade – to match the rest of the cathedral's material. Slowly Connor stood back up and warily began approaching the thing.

Connor reached the base of the dais and looked up at the head. It was at least two or three times his height, possibly more. Its eyes were closed, its face so still. Perhaps it was dead – or maybe it had turned to stone. Connor glanced back at the doors out of the labyrinth. They were all still sealed. Sighing, he turned back to the platform and maneuvered over to a curved staircase that wound up to the altar. Connor ascended the stairs, then came closer to the head.

"H-hello?" he said. "Anyone home?" The head didn't reply. Hesitating briefly, Connor extended his hand and touched its cheek.

The head's eyes opened. They still blazed like fire.

"Who are you?" the head asked in a rumbling voice.

"My name is Connor Durham," Connor said. "I'm a preacher from Ireland. Who are you?"

"I am a piece of Lucas Kane," the head replied. "We are a scientist at the Kadath deep-sea mining facility."

"So, you're part of a – human?" Connor asked.

"At least we look like a human, and have always thought of ourselves as such," the head replied. "Whether or not we can truly be called one is a matter of debate, I suppose."

"We were told to seek out a relic, which would be able to get us out of this world," Connor said. "Are you that relic? Can you transport us from this place?"

"I do not think I could be that relic," the head said. "I am not old enough."

Connor sighed again. "Fair enough."

"Is this not your home?" the head asked.

Connor nearly laughed at that. "No. No, definitely not. My friends and I were somehow brought here against our will. We've been trying to find a way out ever since. How are you connected to this world?"

"We don't yet know precisely," the head said. "We felt its pull, like a beacon tethered to our soul. We realized it was somewhere we could gain the energy we needed, so we came and drew from it. We left me here as an anchor to this place." Then the face frowned. "Something is happening," it said. "I sense a disturbance."

"What kind of a disturbance?" Connor asked.

"Someone is coming here," the head said. "Ah, ah, *ah –*"

The head's mouth opened wider and wider. Connor looked in and was startled to see a woman materializing through the soft flesh at the back of the head's throat. She hung there, suspended in the mucous and membrane. Connor glanced up with wide eyes at the head's gaze. It looked even more surprised than Connor, but there was something else, too. It almost seemed to be imploring him.

"I… have to go in there, don't I?" Connor asked. The face just kept staring at him with that same expression.

"Bollocks," Connor cursed. Taking off the backpack he was still wearing, he set it aside. Then he crouched down low and climbed over the head's teeth. Its tongue was wet and slippery as Connor clambered onto it. He quickly realized the only way to truly get through this was to crawl, so he did. He traversed the tongue and made it back to the larynx.

"Hello?" Connor called to the woman. "Miss, can you hear me?"

The woman seemed to stir. At least, Connor thought she did. It also could have been the throat flexing around her. Reaching out, Connor pressed his hands through the membrane encasing her and clasped hold of the woman. Gritting his teeth, he wrenched backward, yanking the woman free with a moist pop. The two tumbled back onto the tongue. She still wasn't moving. Grabbing her under her armpits, Connor clumsily pulled the girl out of the mouth, depositing her on the platform. The head closed its jaws.

"Well," it said. "That was certainly an unpleasant experience."

"For you and me both, boyo," Connor said with a barking laugh. He tried to shake the spit and mucous off himself.

"Who is it?" the head said. "Is the person alive?"

"Bugger if I know," Connor said. "On both counts."

"Miss?" Connor said, leaning over the woman's face. He felt for a pulse, then knelt to listen for breath. "I don't think she's breathing," he told the head.

The woman took a deep, gasping breath, and then she screamed — a sound that arose from the very core of her being. Connor jerked backward, slipping across the ground. The woman jerked up into a sitting position, her eyes wide as she looked left and right. The head gasped as she finally came into view.

"Rachel!" it said.

Looking up at the face, the woman moaned and started scrambling away on her hands and feet.

"Watch out, watch out!" Connor cried, rushing to her to stop her from plummeting off the edge.

"L-Lucas?" she finally managed. "But how? Where?" Her head snapped left and right as she tried to take in the whole area around her. Her jaw dropped, her eyes, if possible, growing even wider. "Oh, hell," she said.

"I take it you two know each other then?" Connor said.

"Why, Connor!" a voice called from the labyrinth. "There you are!"

Connor looked up, and his breath caught in his lungs. A creature that he realized had once been Sephora Jenkins was crawling over the top of the labyrinth. And behind her came a swarm of thrashing, undulating madness.

"You gave us quite a merry chase, good shepherd," Sephora said. "But now there is nowhere left to go. The time of the feast is at hand."

KADATH FACILITY

Lucas didn't know where to go or what to do. He felt cut loose and adrift. Where was he now safe in Kadath? Was safety an illusion? Who could he talk to? Charles still wasn't answering his calls. Chances are he was outside the facility. Should he speak to Commander Wade? But could Wade be trusted if Judy Blake was obviously out to get him? Edgar was dead, so Lucas couldn't ask *him* for advice. Should he go back to Ron? Where was Regan?

And Rachel. Rachel…

Lucas shook his head, keeping the tears at bay. That particular grief would bury him if he let it. He wouldn't allow her death to be meaningless. Lucas would make their attackers pay.

But how?

Lucas sat with his knees pressed to his chest in his lab. He knew he needed to get out of there. Others would come. It was only a matter of time. But he just… couldn't make himself stand.

"Incoming call from Ronald Meyers," Lucas's node said in his ear. Lucas tapped it.

"Ron?" he said.

"Sorry I missed your calls, Lucas," Ron said. "It took them a while to debrief us, and then I went to Wade to try to get him to take action against the sphere. He's refusing to do anything apart from his useless lockdown and security protocols. I swear, the idiot is *blinded* to the threat this thing poses! I even tried Blake while I was in Control, just for a laugh. No big surprises there. I have one other card up my sleeve that I'm going to try but, if that doesn't work, I don't know *what* our next move is. Did you find Rachel?"

"She's… gone," Lucas replied.

"Gone?" Ron asked. "You couldn't find her?"

"No," Lucas said. "They killed her, Ron. West and Cohen and Summerisle. They killed her to get to me."

"Wait. *What?*" Ron said. "Lucas, what are you saying?"

"I don't know," Lucas said. "They came for me, under Blake's orders. They captured Rachel, and then, when I showed up, they shot her. She's dead, Ron."

"Lucas, I – I don't know what to say," Ron said. "I'm… I'm so sorry."

"Thank you," Lucas said, his voice hollow.

"Look, if they're after you, you need to get out of there. Let's meet where we did this morning. Maybe at nine? And you're also going to want to lose your node. Your wrist unit, too, or any other tech you have on. They can track it, and you don't want to make it any easier for them to find you. Just leave it in your lab."

"Yeah," Lucas said, climbing to his feet. "You're right. Okay."

"Get what you need to last a few days," Ron said. "I'll find someplace to stash you. Okay?"

"All right," Lucas said. "I'll see you soon, Ron."

"Okay. Stay safe, Lucas." Ronald hung up.

Lucas collected the few things he thought he might need from his lab, took out his node, removed his wrist unit, and then walked out the door. He glanced back once as he stepped through the open hatch, briefly wondering if he would ever come back. Not that it mattered. He would need to be careful about getting things from his quarters. They could be watching already. Turning, he headed off down the hall –

Lucas blinked. The walls of the corridor were changing around him. This alteration wasn't like the red fungus he had seen earlier, either. This was something else. The only way he could describe this was… biomechanical, perhaps? It almost seemed that pieces of people had been used to help craft the walls. He saw faces staring sightlessly at him, arms and legs and torsos fused into the substance around them.

The path turned. The corridor grew darker. Rounding the bend, Lucas stepped into a Stygian nightmare.

Lucas saw a man up ahead curled into a ball on the ground, his hands covering his head. He was quaking as he was attacked by thin, phantasmal things which Lucas somehow intuited to be the man's memories. They were pulling him off the main path, submerging him in the inky dark. As they did, Lucas saw parts of the man stretching, elongating, as if the apparitions were siphoning him away.

This was not Lucas's day.

"Hey!" Lucas cried. "Hey, get off him! Leave him alone!"

The memories didn't listen to Lucas. He ran at them, wrapping his hands around the man's shoulders and pulling him up as he tried to separate him from the electric apparitions. The manifestations redoubled their efforts and now began attacking Lucas as well. Lucas felt them passing through him and the man, each one bringing a deluge of images and voices. It was overwhelming. There were so many of them that Lucas couldn't make any of them out. They were drowning the two men. Lucas could feel his mind and senses sinking in a sea of lifetime.

Lucas's eyes blazed with light. "I said, GET AWAY!"

The neon nightmares blew away like colored smoke in a gust of wind.

"Can you move?" Lucas asked.

The man nodded. "Yes," he said. "I think so." Lucas helped him up, and together the two men limped deeper into the darkness.

"What is this place?" Lucas asked. "Are we still in Kadath?"

"Kadath?" the man said, frowning. "I've never heard of it. As near as I can tell, this is my crucible. One I was doing rather poorly at until you serendipitously appeared." He looked back up at Lucas. "Thank you. For interceding. I think they were about to consume what remains of me."

"You're welcome," Lucas said. "I don't know how I got here or why I did, but I'm glad *some* good may come from today."

The man smiled. "Me, too."

"Where are we going?" Lucas asked.

"I don't know," the man said. "Forward. I gave up on knowing my destination some time back."

"My name is Lucas Kane," Lucas said. "What's yours?"

"Wang Min," the man said. "Sorry, no. Min Wang. I sometimes forget that you Westerners reverse the two."

"Well, Min, I would have preferred to meet you under different circumstances," Lucas said.

Min laughed. "Likewise."

There was a light in the distance. It was very faint, and little more than a pinprick. But it was there. Lucas felt a small rise of hope. And that's when the images started swirling around them anew, the intensity far greater than that of the previous ethereal specters.

Lucas saw a temple. He saw monsters approaching. He saw… Wait.

"Min, that temple!" Lucas exclaimed. "I've dreamed of that! I've been in your memories!"

Min frowned. "You have?" he said. "I hardly remembered that before seeing it now. It would seem you may know me better than I know myself."

The two men had slowed. These fresh memories were starting to crowd in around them now, pressing in on them from every side. They were like a kaleidoscope of the past.

"I am reminded that memory can be a burden that one need not always carry," Min said. "We must continue, Lucas, or we will lose ourselves."

"Yes," Lucas said. "Yes, you're right." And that's when he saw Kadath's corridors. He saw the sphere. He saw – "Rachel!"

"It would seem your past is now mingling with my own," Min said. "Pay them no heed, Lucas. Onward, or we are done!"

Lucas squeezed his eyes shut. He couldn't look at her. If he did, he would follow her. And then Lucas would belong to this place. Letting out a yell, he charged forward. Lucas could feel Min do the same beside him. Through his eyelids, he could see the light growing. Growing –

He ran through the light and collapsed to the ground. Squinting, he looked at the world around him. Min was gone, as was the biomechanical labyrinth. Lucas was back in Kadath. Only… What had happened?

Blood painted the walls around him. Corpses lay sprawled periodically in either direction. Was this the same corridor he had just exited?

Lucas wandered down the halls. Part of him wanted to call out, to find the remaining residents, but another part of him thought that might be a very bad idea. So, instead, he simply walked along, searching for signs of human life – any signs at all.

"Lucas?"

Lucas turned. Ronald Myers was moving toward him, followed by about thirty people armed with whatever weapons they had scrounged together. Ronald had a strange frown on his face as if he couldn't quite believe what he was seeing.

"Ron?" Lucas said. "What're you doing here? We weren't supposed to meet for hours yet."

"Lucas, where have you been?" Ron asked. "I was sure they'd gotten you! Why – How –"

"How did you get here so fast?" Lucas said. "I couldn't have finished talking to you *that* long ago!"

Ronald stepped up to Lucas, the look of disbelief still etched into his face. "Lucas, it's been a *week*," he said. "We were supposed to meet seven days ago, and you never showed."

"That's not possible," Lucas said. "I was *just* talking to you. Maybe an hour has passed, at the *most*. No more than that."

"Well, possible or not, that's what happened," Ron said.

Lucas's heart was racing in his chest. He looked over all the people gathered with Ron. "What happened?" he asked. "Why are you here?"

"Things went to hell, that's what happened," Ron said. "The sphere's plague spread everywhere, Lucas. It's like it injected a virus into the air made from pure, undiluted fear, and everyone sucked it right down. And still, Wade and the others refuse to lift a frigging *finger!* If we wait any longer, we'll all be dead. So, we won't. We're going to blast that awful thing back into the ocean where it belongs."

"Ron, this is a bad idea," Lucas said. "You're going to get yourself killed, and everyone else with you. The sphere's not going to go easily. For that matter, did you ever stop to think that maybe it *wants* you to go to it? What if it's a trap?"

"It doesn't matter, Lucas," Ronald said. "This is our home, and this is our only chance. If we don't do something, then we're all dead anyway. I'd personally prefer to go out fighting."

Gerald White worked his way up to the front of the group to stand beside Ronald. "Seriously, where have you been, Lucas?" he asked. "You say you've lost a whole week? How do we know you haven't been sent by the sphere to stop us? It certainly wouldn't be the first trick we've seen it play."

"I get what you're saying, Gerald," Lucas said, "but when was the last time you saw the sphere try to reason with someone?"

"We're doing this, Lucas," Ronald said. "We have no choice. I've seen too many of my friends die to back off now. Either help us or get out of our way."

Lucas studied the desperate, resolute faces assembled before him. He sighed, then, nodding, stepped aside. Ron offered him a grim smile before leading the group forward. Lucas watched the people shuffle tensely past him and winced. He couldn't let them go. Not like this.

"Ron, wait," he said.

Ronald turned. "What, Lucas?"

"Do you have any other weapons?" Lucas asked. "They stole my scalpel."

TOWER WORLD

Sephora descended the wall of the labyrinth like a humanoid spider, her dark skin glistening with a sheen of sweat and slime. Her arms were bent backward at an unnatural angle, her chin jutting upward as her wide, ferocious mouth flexed, and her hair dangled pendulously from her scalp. She reached the ground at the same moment the kraken-centipede arrived at the edge of the labyrinth, its thick, vast tentacles drifting through the air as its human hands gripped and feet balanced along the lips of the walls. Beyond it, Connor could make out two other massive horrors clambering forward. He thought they might have been the two halves of the behemoth.

"Where are Min and Mitsuko now?" Sephora asked as she reached the ground. "Did they leave you again, Connor? My, aren't you disposable! Or did you maybe leave *them* this time? That's not very Christian of you if that's the case."

"Your timing is brutal, Sephora," Connor said. "Could you maybe come back in ten minutes?"

Sephora's laugh was as light and lilting as ever. "Oh, Connor, the day of judgment is *never* convenient. There was always one more thing to do. You above many others should understand that. Speaking of biblical things, my companions certainly seem like that to me. If the big one – or big ones, as the case currently stands – could be called the behemoth, then I think it's only fitting that the other would be the leviathan, don't you agree? That certainly adds a particular mythic gravitas to the whole situation, at least in my mind."

Connor looked back at Lucas's head. "Can you do anything about this, Lucas?" he asked. "Maybe fry them with eye fire?"

"I don't know *what* precisely I can do in this world," the head said. "It is all still strange to me."

Connor chuckled dryly. "The mammoth talking severed head says this is strange," he muttered. "Okay. Sure. Why not."

Rachel looked behind her at the descending terrors and shrieked. She tried to stand to her feet and fell back to her hands and knees.

"It's all right, I've got you," Connor said, wrapping his arms under her armpits and gently lifting her. At last, Rachel was standing, though her limbs were still trembling disconcertingly.

"Does anyone see a way out?" Connor asked, looking desperately around him. Try as he might, he couldn't find a way up to the tower's next level.

The kraken-centipede – or leviathan, as Sephora had termed it – used its tentacles to lower itself to the floor and then leisurely advanced beside Sephora. The other two nightmarish creatures leaped off the top of the wall and landed with matching thuds. Then one of the fiends climbed on top of the other, and the two began to merge back together into one giant grotesquerie. Connor felt a lump rising up his throat. There was nowhere to go. There was nothing to do. He couldn't foresee many scenarios in which he or Rachel lived through this.

"S-Sephora?" Rachel croaked. "Dr. Jenkins, is that *you?*"

Sephora paused with a frown, her gaze piercing into Rachel. Her long, pointed teeth gnashed together. "I think I know you," she said. "Yes. I'm almost certain of it. Was your name… Rachel? Rachel… Wilcox, maybe? Or Wilkins?" She skittered forward, seeming more intrigued than bloodthirsty at the moment. "You weren't assigned to this world. How did you get here?"

"What *happened* to you?" Rachel asked. "How did you become… *this?*"

"I evolved," Sephora said. "Now. Answer my question, girl."

"The subject, Dr. Jenkins," Rachel said. "He's just beginning to manifest, and already he's incredibly powerful. He has staked his claim in this world. This head is a piece of him. And he transported me here."

"Why?" Sephora asked. "Did he banish you?"

"No," Rachel said. "It's… all fuzzy. But I think I… died. And I don't think he wanted to lose me."

Sephora grinned, clucking her tongue in a chiding manner. Rotating over onto her stomach, she stood up like a human being.

The portal in her stomach looked disturbingly like a gaping mouth, drool seeping out of its vicious gash. Beyond its slithering tongue was a churning electric vortex to a place of utter eldritch madness. "It sounds like you became attached to the subject. That is a big no-no, Wilkins. He belongs to humanity, not you."

"Of course, I know that," Rachel said. "But you don't understand what he has come to be. He is good. And kind. And brave. Surprisingly so. He is… not what I anticipated. And he is *certainly* not the iron-fisted conqueror you intended."

"Rachel?" the Lucas head said, frowning. "What are you talking about? What do you mean, the subject?"

Rachel turned to look back at the head. "I'm sorry, Lucas. I haven't been honest with you about who I am, or about what *you* are."

"Well, this is all truly fascinating, and I wish we could explore it further," Sephora said, beginning to advance again. "But unfortunately, I'm short on time, and you have solidified my conviction that we must act quickly to avoid unmitigated disaster. These primaries must be culled before their influence overwhelms *everything* I've worked to achieve. Move aside, and I will spare you, Wilkins. Side with the primary, and your life is forfeit."

"No, Dr. Jenkins," Rachel said. "You don't understand. I haven't sided with the primaries. I've sided with the *subject*. And maybe you didn't hear me when I said he had taken authority over this world now. Whatever control you had no longer exists."

The leviathan and the behemoth had slowed, watching Sephora. It was almost like they were somehow taking orders from her currently, or at least suggestions. But they were growing impatient the longer this conversation took. They were creeping forward toward Connor and Rachel, their various limbs and tendrils reaching hungrily. Connor could tell they were going to give in to their urges at any moment and attack. He could hear his heart hammering in his chest. His mouth was so dry.

"This whole world is yours, Lucas," Rachel said, looking back at the head. "It is connected to you. It is a part of you. You can make it do what you want and reshape it as you will."

The Lucas head blinked, and then closed his eyes –

One of the labyrinth's doors dilated open, and Min tumbled out, sprawling onto the ground. He moaned, trying to push himself up on trembling arms and legs. The two gargantuan beasts snapped around to face Min, moving far quicker than their size should have allowed them.

"Min, no!" Connor cried. "Lucas, stop them! Please!"

"I found them," the head said.

The two giants stopped, their bodies trembling.

"There is one level above this one," the head said. "The path to it must be forged. It cannot be found. I will begin the process."

The Leviathan and the Behemoth both bellowed, and then they flung themselves at each other. Their limbs ripped at one another; their tentacles thrashed, crushed, and choked; their beaks and mouths bit and gnashed. Then their bodies began to warp, elongating and thinning as they intertwined. Sephora looked up at the two terrors, her jaw slack. They were melding together now, their flesh becoming one as they stretched farther and farther upward. They were angling to the side as they continued warping and changing and reaching toward the cathedral's ceiling. One of the Leviathan's tentacles whipped out of the mass as if seeking freedom. It touched the cathedral wall and adhered, fusing into the biomechanical material and becoming like a brace for the growing structure.

Connor watched, his jaw dangling, as the two monsters became something else. He thought he knew what that was, but it took a few seconds before his mind could grasp what his eyes were seeing. It was a stairway. A small oval split open in the cathedral ceiling, the stairwell rising steadily toward that one point of blackness in the ridge.

"No," Sephora groaned. "No, please!"

Connor looked down at Sephora and saw her body moving in strange, jerky movements like a poorly puppeteered marionette toward the fleshy staircase.

"This experiment is no longer under your control, Dr. Jenkins," the head said. "Nor are your services as a primary needed any longer. You have been superseded."

"Everything I did was for you!" Sephora yelled. She was stumbling up the stairs now, her feet consistently threatening to adhere to the flesh below them. "Please, you have to understand! You must believe me!"

"How many hundreds of lives did it take to make this place?" Lucas asked. "Or was it thousands? How many souls did you consign to this hell for my sake?"

"Without them, you would not exist!" Sephora cried. "We *made* you, Lucas! We forged you into a being with the potential to transcend mortality!"

"I am grateful to be alive," Lucas said. "But is my existence worth all of those that it took to bring me into being?"

"Yes!" Sephora said. "Unequivocally, yes! You are humanity's evolution!"

"And now it is time for you to put your beliefs to the test," Lucas said. "My life shall be built on the bones of one more."

Sephora was sobbing now as her body stumbled to the top of the staircase. Despite everything, Connor felt compassion for her welling up within him. There had to be another way.

"Lucas, you don't have to do this," Connor said. "She can

change. She can be saved."

"There is room for mercy only if there is also a place for justice, Connor," the head said. "And sometimes judgment must outweigh leniency. Besides. There is not enough material to finish the stairway without her."

Sephora moaned, her voice reverberating through the cathedral. Then she screamed as she reached the top of the stairs. Her body cracked, flowed, and elongated as she became the final piece between the entry up above and the structure Lucas had built from the beasts. With a wet gurgling and one last snap, her cries ceased.

Another of the exits from the labyrinth opened, and Mitsuko flopped out. She landed on the ground, groaning as she forced herself to turn over. Connor tore his gaze away from the stairwell's gruesome construction and hurried over to his friends. He could tell there was something wrong with Mitsuko as he drew closer to her. Her left arm was too long, her fingers elongated and grayer than the rest of her skin.

"Mitsuko?" Connor asked, kneeling beside her. "Are you all right?"

"I almost lost myself," she murmured. "The dark memories nearly consumed me, Connor." Her gaze cleared slightly, and she looked up at him with pain and tears in her eyes. "I had a family in Japan," she said. "A daughter. She was *beautiful*. I wish… I had loved her better when I had the chance."

"Oh, Mitsuko," Connor said softly. "I'm so sorry. But maybe you'll get another opportunity."

"I hope you're right," she replied.

"Can you move?" Connor asked. "Is anything broken?"

"I think I'll be fine," Mitsuko said. "Apart from the arm, I guess. Min, are you alright?"

Min crawled over to Connor and Mitsuko. "I will recover," he said. "I nearly wandered too deep as well, Mitsuko. The only reason I didn't was that I received some help from an unexpected source."

"What?" Connor said. "Someone got into your darkness? Who?"

"His name was Lucas," Min said. "I don't know how he got there, and frankly, I don't think *he* knew, either. When I passed through the exit, he vanished."

"You don't say," Connor said. "I've met Lucas as well. Or at least part of him."

"What on earth do you mean?" Min asked.

Connor pointed toward the front of the cathedral. "That giant head up there?" he said. "That belongs to Lucas."

"You had to ask, Min," Mitsuko muttered.

"It gets stranger," Connor said. "He made that staircase out of the monsters that were following us. Including Sephora."

"You're kidding," Mitsuko said.

"I bloody well am not," Connor said. "Come on. If you can get up, I'll introduce you two."

"Who's the woman?" Min asked.

"Her name's Rachel," Connor replied. "I pulled her out of the Lucas head's mouth."

"You *had* to ask, Min!" Mitsuko groaned.

"My apologies," Min said.

Connor helped his two friends up, and together they limped toward Rachel and the Lucas head.

"I hear we owe you our thanks," Min said when they neared the dais. "So, you have my gratitude for your help."

"You are welcome," the head said.

"Are you really Lucas Kane?" Min asked. "Do you remember meeting me a few minutes ago?"

"I am a part of Lucas Kane," the head said. "Since Lucas

planted me here, though, I have noticed myself to be more distanced from the total sum. I find my knowledge and recollections of things happening to the rest of us to be fuzzy and intangible. In short, I *seem* to remember you, but it is more like a ghost hidden behind gauze than a true recollection."

"Fascinating," Min said. "I am very much indebted to your other self as well, then."

The head smiled slightly. "I am sure it was their pleasure."

"What did you *do* to them?" Mitsuko said, her eyes glued to the staircase.

"I altered their function," the head said.

Mitsuko nodded slowly.

"I'm Rachel Wilkins," Rachel said, stepping toward them. Min bowed to her, then introduced himself and Mitsuko.

"I suppose I should be grateful," Mitsuko said. "But, to be honest, I hardly find them less frightening in this form."

"Ah, yes, I understand," the head said. "Their current configuration does raise the question, which is more terrifying? The ravening animal that acts chiefly from instinct, or the rational mind that can alter its reality based solely on its whim? The mindless monster, or the omnipotent power?"

Mitsuko nodded her head slowly and swallowed. "Yes," she said. "That about sums it up." Her gaze flicked down briefly to her newly mutated arm.

"I suppose one could say it comes down to if the rational mind intends you harm," the head said. "Or if it deems you too small to be worthy of consideration."

Mitsuko turned her gaze to the head, carefully appraising it.

"What's up there, Lucas?" Connor asked. "Do you know?"

"It is the end of the journey," the head replied. "The final attainable level of the tower. The place you will all fulfill your purpose here and shape the course of the future."

Min and Connor exchanged a glance. They liked the sound of this less and less every moment.

"Lucas, let me stay with you," Rachel said. "My place is at your side. Please, don't send me away."

"You are needed with them, Rachel," Lucas said. "There must be four. Don't worry. You will be with us again."

Rachel wiped tears from her eyes and nodded. Climbing back up onto the platform, she hugged the head's cheek. She kissed the grey surface.

"Okay," she said, turning to the others. "Let's go."

The four travelers gathered at the base of the stairwell and stared up it at the tiny dark opening so far above them.

Connor exhaled slowly. "Well," he said, "once more unto the breach."

They began their ascension.

KADATH FACILITY

A sledgehammer clutched in his hands, Lucas followed Ron and Gerald through Kadath's corridors back toward the sphere. At last, they came to the wide doors concealing the bay where the ghastly orb sat, awaiting them. Lucas recognized the guard who was still standing watch in front of the bay as one of the men who had driven him off previously. Regardless, this hardly looked like the same man. There was a sunken, haunted quality to his face. Lucas half-wondered where his fellow guard had gone.

"Let us through, Parks," Ronald said, stepping up to the guard. "You know this has to happen."

Sighing, Parks nodded. "Yeah. It does."

The ragtag band stepped to the doors, and Parks cycled them open. As they slid aside, Lucas saw it: the sphere, its surface alive with ravening, electric madness. It was oddly like looking into a whirling, soul-consuming, cosmic abyss, and coming home all at the same moment.

"Move, people!" Ronald bellowed. "Do whatever it takes! Get that thing out of Kadath!"

The men and women unleashed a battle cry of pure, feral desperation and charged into the bay. The sphere welcomed them. Unfathomable horrors pulled themselves out of the shadows pooled in the corners of the bay, coalesced out of the floor, or ripped free directly out of the sphere's roiling surface. Tentacles and barbed tendrils whipped and thrashed through the air before embedding in human skin. Teeth and claws slid out of fleshy sheaths just in time to bury their length in exposed muscle.

Lucas felt like he was swimming in a sea of panic. It was drowning his senses, muddling his mind. He stared, slack-jawed, as the brave, steadfast people he had entered the room with were picked off one by one – some by the waves of tangible fear, many by the monstrosities manifesting throughout the room, and even more by each other. He watched Gerald cave in the guard's – Parks's – skull with a fire extinguisher. Another man stabbed a woman in the eye with a screwdriver.

This attack was no longer a coordinated assault. This was pandemonium. It was chaos. It was a slaughter.

Ronald was faltering beside Lucas, clutching his head. Lucas realized how close they were to losing everything. They needed to act right now. Grabbing Ronald's arm, he tried to will him to be all right. To focus.

"Ron!" Lucas cried, though his voice was barely audible through the screams. Ronald looked at him, his gaze woozy. Lucas pointed at the control panel nestled near the sphere. Ronald's eyes seemed to clear, and he nodded. The two men dashed through the melee, their feet slipping over blood and slime. They were growing closer to the panel, and to the sphere itself. Lucas forced himself not to look at it. If he gave in, even for an instant, then he would have to stare at it. And if he stared at it, then he would be lost.

Energy arced out of the sphere like bolts of lightning. The discharges danced around the bay, striking men and monsters alike. They were almost like feelers, searching delicately for the succulent objects of their desires. Or a jellyfish's tendrils, floating through the water until they found their prey and struck –

The strange electric power hit Lucas in the chest. He watched it jump to Ronald, and then he felt his body lift off the ground as his perception erupted in a frenetic burst of nightmare and void. He felt the sphere, sensed its endless oceans spinning with universes within consciousnesses within oblivions. It was more than any psyche could hold. More than any collection of minds could fathom. Its sea of conscious Stygian terror was going to pour itself into him, and in so doing, it was both going to absorb him and utterly obliterate all that he believed himself to be. The sphere was a gateway, and the gate was opening.

Arms wrapped firmly around Lucas, pulling him back. He heard a voice screaming in his ears. They were hovering over the violent, hemorrhaging crowd, retreating toward the open bay doors. Lucas forced himself to look back and saw Regan, her eyes bottomless cesspools full of raging spectral fires. She was weeping black ichor.

They swept through the doorway and landed in the corridor beyond. Lucas saw that Ronald was already standing in the hall nearby, alternately weeping and laughing. He was crying blood, his body shaking uncontrollably. Ronald looked to his right toward Regan and Lucas.

"Ron?" Lucas managed. "Are you okay? How did you –"

Ronald began to scream. He scrambled away from Regan and Lucas, then, turning, he tore off down the corridor in hysterics, looking as if all the demons of Hell were right at his back. Lucas watched in shock as his friend ran. Then he looked back as he heard Regan shifting behind him.

The girl was as white as bleached bone, her hand trembling as she extended one finger and gently pressed the hatch control. The double doors swished closed, mercifully muting the slaughter still taking place within. "That was not advised, Lucas," she said, her voice quaking.

"It let him go," Lucas said quietly. "It let Ronald escape."

"Yes," Regan replied. Her eyes were slowly returning to normal, the color beginning to seep back into her skin. "He is a carrier for its madness now. The sphere's influence will spread even faster than it did before as he further contaminates Kadath's inhabitants."

"How do we stop it?" Lucas asked. "How can we possibly defeat something like that?"

"We can't," Regan said. "You glimpsed what it contains, did you not? We can do nothing against it. All we can do is escape.

"Kadath is already lost, Lucas. It always was. And now we must choose if we will be consumed with it."

TEN

SHATTERED

"I don't know how to explain what I've seen. Or what has happened. Kadath has returned. One moment the anomaly was there, fluctuating sporadically and emitting its unusual particle waves – just as it has since the facility was destroyed. And the next, the entire facility had reappeared, sending shockwaves through the ocean. This is not our facility, though. Repeat: this is not our facility. My readings are chaotic at best, but it almost seems like multiple dimensions have crashed into each other and fused together at this very point. At this time, I don't know if this nexus is going to spread or if it is self-contained. Oh, no, what's happening now –"
Phillip Reed – Leng Corp. Specialist

TOWER WORLD

Connor took a tentative step onto the quivering stairway, holding his breath as he heard it squelching beneath his feet.

Rachel and Min were behind him, while Mitsuko had insisted on going up first. Slowly, steadily, they traveled upward. Every so often, Connor spotted a talon or tooth jutting from a stair, each one serving as a reminder that Lucas had built this stairwell from living beings.

As Connor continued upward, he noticed that several of the stairs were staring at him. Connor couldn't help but shiver as he realized these things were still alive. Moving on, Connor came to several small tendrils waving slowly in the air. They brushed or stroked his feet as he passed them, almost like they were imploring his help.

There was no railing on the stairway and nothing to keep them from plummeting to the ground, which grew increasingly distant below them. Connor tried not to look down. In many ways, this was significantly better than the ladder they had climbed before, but, in other ways, it seemed much worse. Probably part of the problem was that he could so clearly see the ground here. And, also, he never knew if his feet were going to come down on something sticky or slick.

The stairs seemed to sway more the closer they grew to the top. They were all walking hunched over now, keeping as close as they could to the surface of each progressive step. The color had been a mottled swirl of shades the whole way up, but at the final few steps near the top, the pigment became a much more uniform chocolate brown. Connor felt his stomach seizing within him as they climbed up Sephora.

Mitsuko made it to the next level and gasped. Usually, Connor would have asked what she saw, but he couldn't take his mind off the fact that this had been a person just minutes ago. Someone he knew, if only briefly.

"C-Connor…" a voice choked.

Connor scanned the last few stairs until he saw her: Sephora's face had been stretched and fused to the edge of the hole as part of the binding between the two levels. He could still make out her features, but they were in nothing like a typical configuration.

"Sephora?" Connor said, kneeling before the altered face. "Can you hear me? I'm so sorry this happened to you. I…"

"It's… ter-rifying, Connor," she said. "I'm… s-so scared… Not even… what *dying* is-s… like…"

Extending his hand, Connor touched Sephora's eyebrow and said a prayer for her. Then Min put a hand on his shoulder, and he stood up. "Goodbye, Sephora," he said. "May your time in this hell be short." He walked on, as did Min and Rachel. Sephora tried to stop them, especially Rachel, but they didn't. Instead, they all climbed up onto the next level. They looked up at their new surroundings and gasped in almost perfect unison.

"What… is… this?" Min asked.

No one replied to him.

KADATH FACILITY

Lucas had thought he might never return to his lab again, and yet here he and Regan were. He couldn't seem to escape the place. But where else was there for them to go right now?

Regan peered around the laboratory with apparent interest, her eyes wide and curious. For just a moment, she appeared so young. Lucas wondered if perhaps this was what she would have looked like had she been allowed to be a typical teenager.

"So, this is where you made your scientific discoveries?" Regan asked.

"Yes," Lucas said. "This is where I doomed Kadath."

Regan shook her head. "You must not think of it that way, Lucas, even if it feels and looks like that," she said. "Kadath was doomed to fall from the moment they laid its foundations. It is in many realities, and in almost every one that I have glimpsed the sphere consumes it. *You*, however, are only in this one. In fact, Kadath was placed here by my so-called mother and others because I felt drawn to this location. Which means it is as much *my* fault as yours. Likely significantly more so."

"I don't know if that's a comfort or not," Lucas said. A few moments passed, then Lucas said, "So, what is your plan to escape Kadath? Steal a shuttle?"

Regan turned from her explorations to look at Lucas. "No," she said. "That won't be enough. It's not just Kadath that's in danger. I have traveled across dimensions, Lucas, and I have noticed several kinds of alternate realities. There are primary realities, which are the most stable, and there are secondary realities, which are like ripples on a pond. Then there are bubble realities. From what I've observed, those only seem to exist for a short time before they collapse on themselves.

"From everything I've seen, it seems extremely likely that we are in a bubble reality, and that we will still die even if we escape Kadath. Also, it is a fact that, in many realities, the sphere opens, releasing the things it contains out into the world. We need to try to create a primary reality where that doesn't happen. So, I intend to smash this existence into others. We will force them to fuse together until we reach our primary reality. And then we will be able to escape into it."

Lucas stared at Regan, his jaw hanging limp. "You want to… merge dimensions into each other? Flatten them into one? Regan, how would we ever do that? And even if we could, what happens to the people in them?"

"We will only meld a small part of each reality," Regan said. "No one else realizes it yet, but the sphere is already creating a field around Kadath, like a dome. We will simply use it as our guideline. The sphere has already pierced this dimension, too, which will make this easier. The most stable dimensions will survive and repair themselves. They may even end up safer because of this."

"And what about the less stable ones? Like this one?"

"It is going to be annihilated in any case, Lucas," Regan said. "It is inevitable."

"And the people in it…?"

"To my knowledge, the only novel person in this dimension is you," Regan said. "Every other person is present in many other varying versions of this world."

Lucas was silent for a moment. "So… everyone *dies* so that we can live?"

"They won't even know it happened," Regan said. "And it's *not* just so we can live. It's to maintain containment of the sphere. As I said, in most possibilities I've seen, the sphere cracks and lets the forces inside it out. We have to try to stop that if we can."

"Regan, I can't consciously destroy an *entire world!*" Lucas said. "I won't!"

"Yes, you will, Lucas," Regan said. "You're a scientist. Look at the data. Everyone in this bubble universe will be eliminated when it collapses, regardless of what we do. Everyone also likely has doppelgangers in any number of other universes. Perhaps they even share the same soul. They injected you into this universe, and you are the only person we know of with no other copies. Even *I* am less special than you in this regard."

"Regan, you're still talking about the conscious extermination of an entire planet! Maybe even *beyond* a planet! If it happens naturally, I suppose maybe that's one thing. But for us to do it for our own ends?"

"Don't think of it like that, Lucas," Regan said. "Think of it as forgetting a memory. The actions taken in this dimension cease to exist. But that doesn't mean those people do. And besides, you talk about natural processes, but there's nothing *natural* about this dimension. As near as I can tell, the Golden Dawn's and Leng's meddling created it with the powers beyond the sphere."

"Wait, what?" Lucas cried. Then he shook his head. "Never mind. It's too much all at once."

"Lucas, this world will end," Regan said, stepping up to him and looking him in the eyes. "The only question is, will you, too?"

Lucas tried to move his mouth, to make words come out, but he found that he couldn't. His mind had completely frozen, and he was utterly speechless.

TOWER WORLD

Connor was utterly speechless. He couldn't summon the words to speak about what he was seeing. Judging by the silence around him, the others felt the same.

The floor below their feet was almost like a shiny black marble. The angles and corners of the walls, meanwhile, could be seen if looked at from specific perspectives, but the walls themselves were transparent. It wasn't even like they were windows. Windows still had frames, but there were none here to mar the pure crystalline surface. What was floating through the air, though, was what truly captivated Connor and stole his breath.

They were like enormous shards of glass, some as big as a transport. Some of them were perfectly clear and mainly discernible by the light playing through them and glinting off their edges. But others were like glimpses into other worlds or peoples' lives. Some were clearly from a person's perspective, while others were like a flying or swimming creature traversing a land or seascape. Some shards were like an otherworldly paradise. Others seemed closer to a nightmarish hell.

All the shards drifted slowly around the room, anchored to a circular orbit around the space's center. A round marble platform nestled there, a black pole rising from its middle that pierced through the vaulted ceiling into the sky beyond, ending at a sharpened point amidst the clouds. Connor briefly noted there was something on the platform. Still, he was distracted by the realization that the clouds and the shards all rotated in perfect synchronization around the towering midnight needle.

Breaking her paralysis, Mitsuko slowly moved toward the shards' orbit. Her feet drifted across the ground as if she were in a dream. She moved toward one shard in particular: it featured someone running through the woods toward a laboratory as the sunlight was leached from the day, a small hand clutched in the person's grip. Reaching up, she stretched onto tiptoes and touched the shard. Nothing happened.

Groaning, she slumped. "I so hoped…" she said.

"Was that yours, Mitsuko?" Min asked, coming up and placing a hand on her shoulder. She nodded.

"I think so, yes," she replied.

Rachel gasped behind them. Everyone turned to face her. She had made her way over to the circular platform and was examining what was lying on it.

"What is it, Rachel?" Connor asked.

"I… I knew them!" Rachel exclaimed, looking up at Connor with wide, shocked eyes.

"Wait," Connor said. "What do you mean, 'them'?"

KADATH FACILITY

"I can't," Lucas said. "I can't do it."

"You *can't?*" Regan replied. "Lucas, you *must.* There is no other way."

"I was just fighting to save this world," Lucas said. "And now you want me to be part of its destruction? No."

"Look where those efforts *got* you, Lucas!" Regan said. "Look where it got your friends! You can't save them. *Any* of them. They are already dead, whether they still breathe or not."

"What happens to Kadath's people when we combine the realities? Do they die? Do they fuse with the other versions of themselves?"

"I don't know," Regan said. "They might meld with their other selves. They might go mad. Or they might be annihilated."

"How can you be *okay* with that?"

"This is the only way we have a chance of beating the sphere, Lucas! If we don't, then its victory will be absolute. There are no other options. If we give in, if we don't do this, then its influence will spread and eventually destroy all that there is of humanity. It *hungers* for humankind. For *all* conscious life. The forces it holds behind its surface are as old as time and as dark as the void. You haven't seen its full breadth. You don't know yet. It will not stop with Kadath: It will overwhelm everything and everyone. But if we do this, then some may be spared. Including you."

Squeezing his eyes shut, Lucas shook his head. "I need time, Regan," he said. "I need to think."

Regan sighed. "Time is something we are extremely short on, Lucas. But very well. I will leave you with your thoughts. Just, please, don't take long. Summon me when you are ready. I will come."

"What will you do?" Lucas asked.

"I will prepare myself for the merging," she replied. Then she turned and left the lab.

Lucas took a deep breath and exhaled it slowly. Then, turning, he strode over to his lab's bathroom. Turning on the sink, Lucas splashed water in his face, hoping the cold liquid would clear his thoughts. How could he do what Regan was asking? Would he ever be able to look at his own reflection again if he did?

Lucas peered up into the mirror mounted above the sink. His breath froze in his lungs. He didn't see himself at all. Instead, he saw four bedraggled people clustered together on a floor of black marble, their gazes turning one by one upward to stare at him. He gasped. "Rachel!" he cried. His hand reached out and touched the glass.

TOWER WORLD

Mitsuko, Connor, and Min approached the platform that Rachel was staring at intently. At last, they could make out what was on it: There were four seemingly fossilized corpses arranged around the black pole, their hands linked together for eternity. It almost appeared that their fingers were fused.

Connor felt his stomach drop. "The relic," he murmured.

"How is *this* the way out?" Min asked. "How can we escape through *them?*"

"I don't think they offer the escape we hoped for," Mitsuko said.

"The wayfinder said we wouldn't like the way when we found it," Connor added quietly.

"How do you know them, Rachel?" Min asked.

"They were scientists and research assistants," Rachel said, her voice distant. "Dr. Jenkins – Sephora – was one of the lead researchers on a project striving to evolve humanity beyond physical existence. It was one of several projects that sought to harness the strange energy waves radiating from the remains of a destroyed underwater facility called Kadath. They were working to perfect a two-centuries-old process called consciousness fusion, which, if it succeeded, would create someone beyond a mere human – a post-human, maybe – who could lead the rest of us into a new golden dawn for our species. These were four of the people on Dr. Jenkins's team."

"And you were as well," Mitsuko said flatly. Rachel nodded awkwardly.

"Would I be correct then in assuming you people had a hand in creating this hellhole island?" Connor asked. "What buggered bright idea could have *possibly* possessed you to do *that*?"

"I… We… It was for the good of our species," Rachel replied.

"Almost every despot in history has used a version of that excuse to commit their atrocities and genocides," Min said. "It is how you turn a people into sheep. Were you a sheep or a shepherd, Rachel?"

"I was… a sheep, I suppose," Rachel murmured, her gaze trained firmly on the dark marble floor.

"But it worked," Mitsuko said. "Didn't it? Or at least it was in the process of working. And that's why we're here, and why Lucas Kane exists."

Rachel nodded again.

"Bloody fecking *hell*," Connor growled.

"I didn't know what happened to them," she said, motioning to the four on the circular dais. "Many of us were handpicked from the team to watch over certain aspects of the subject's development, but I didn't know they became the *base* for this world. For... him."

"So, when Lucas's head said that he and this place were built from hundreds or thousands of lives, he was being literal," Connor said.

Rachel paused before nodding a third time.

"Which means we're just food, doesn't it?" Connor continued. "Actual bloody *brain food!*"

Rachel's gaze snapped up. "No," she said. "Not the three of you. Well, four now, including me. You rose past the rest of the people injected into this world, probably because of some triggering event that made you receptive to this place's power. But, whatever the reason, you have kept your own minds while strongly influencing Lucas's. You're much of the reason he is the way he is. We call you primaries. These were the first four, responsible for his lower thought. And… we're the next four, supplying the higher cognitive thinking. The memories. The personality. The conscience. Of course, *everyone* who came here affected him to one degree or another. But not like you three."

"There's no way out of here, is there?" Mitsuko asked. "Not alive, anyway."

Rachel swallowed. "I…"

Mitsuko closed her eyes and shook her head, tears spilling silently down her cheeks.

"Look," Min said. "Look! That's him!"

Everyone swiveled to stare at where Min was pointing. Connor saw a man gawking down at them from one of the shards. He looked uncannily like the head Connor had met before. The man pressed his hand against the glass dividing them. And then he pushed his palm through it.

The gargantuan hand flailed in midair, more of its arm pushing through the shard. Its fingers elongated, reaching for the ground, as the rest of the limb followed it. It almost seemed fluid as it flowed and reshaped and shrank. A body followed it, then a head, and legs, the whole being swirling downward. Lucas landed on the floor and reconstituted. He looked around, surprised, his eyes taking in the four people gathered near him.

"Rachel?" he said. "You're… you're alive?"

"Hi, Lucas," Rachel said, a smile flitting across her lips.

Rushing over to her, Lucas kissed her, wrapping his arms around her. "I thought I lost you forever," Lucas said. "How did you get *here?*"

"You sent me here," Rachel said. "You saved me."

"So, this is him," Mitsuko said, taking a step toward Lucas.

"Yes," Rachel said, looking at Lucas with something mixed between pride and devotion. "This is him."

"What happens if we kill him?" Mitsuko asked. "Right here and now. Do we get out then?"

All eyes turned to look at Mitsuko. Connor realized she had her sword in one hand and her machete in the other. Her gaze was desperate and hardening by the second.

"Mitsuko?" Connor said slowly. "Put them down."

"He's not our enemy, Mitsuko," Min said. "I wouldn't be alive right now if not for his help."

"You can all stay here and die for him if you want," Mitsuko said. "But I have a daughter who's waiting for me in Japan. I'm not going to let her down again." She took a step closer to Lucas. "Your other head and Rachel both made me think, Kane. Which is scarier: the mindless monster, or the omnipotent power? Personally, I currently find myself leaning toward the omnipotent power. After all, how can you know if the rational mind behind that power is even aware you exist? And if it does, how can you know it intends good for you? Maybe it's better to take matters into your own hands when you can."

"I don't want anyone to die for me," Lucas said.

"There is darkness in you, Kane," Mitsuko said. "We've been trying to survive in that darkness for what seems like eons. What will it take for that darkness to rule you?"

"You're right," Lucas replied. "There *is* darkness in me. I'm just beginning to wrap my head around even a glimmer of what I am, but I know that."

"So why?" Mitsuko asked. "Why should you get to live while we all die?"

"I don't *want* you to die," Lucas repeated. "And I honestly hardly know what's going on right now, or why you would even *need* to. But I do know this: there are far worse things than me at work. And if I don't act right now, then whole dimensions are probably going to be slaughtered. Help me stop them. And then we can figure out what happens after that."

Min and Connor had worked their way to either side of Mitsuko. Mitsuko didn't even notice them, her every sense focused on Lucas. Now she saw movement flicker in the corner of her eye, though, and she spun toward Connor.

"What if you kill him, Mitsuko?" Connor asked, his hands raised. "What then? Do you honestly think that will free you from this place? What if it just kills *us* at the same time?"

Min placed a hand on Mitsuko's shoulder, which made her flinch. "It's all right," he said. "He didn't have to save me, Mitsuko. He *chose* to. That has to count for something." Reaching his other hand out, Min placed it on Lucas's shoulder.

"We're going to figure this out," Connor added. Gingerly he brought his hand forward, placing it over hers to gently lower her sword.

Briefly, it registered with Connor that all of them were touching each other: Rachel and Min gripping Lucas, and then Min, Mitsuko, and Connor clutching one another. It also struck him that they were all standing in a haphazard circle of sorts, with Lucas in the center. Funny, they almost resembled the dead people clustered around the black pole on the platform –

The world lit up, electrified. Connor felt his mind melt and erupt and run into others. It began to solidify again, but as it did, it fused with those around him. The shards were becoming a whole. They all poured into each other, becoming one, their bodies jittering and shaking as they became the four around the pillar while Lucas became the pillar itself. Then they rocketed upward and outward, blowing through the top of the skyscraper, the circling clouds catching on them and leaving streaks of cumulus in their wake.

The five becoming one pierced the bubble of the tower world and burst free of its atmosphere. The malevolent gloom three of the five had tried so carefully to avoid swarmed them, pressed in on them. They could feel it intimately now, this conscious Otherworld of madness and hunger. It gnawed on their extremities and whispered unequaled terrors that slithered into their ears. Lightning that laughed in shrieks singed past their eyes in unnatural fluorescent bursts. Thunder that spat up galaxies and then swallowed them back down rolled ominously past.

Those same three conscious pieces of the Lucas-being cried out in alarmed horror as they looked down to see the tower world crumple below them, collapsing in on itself as the Stygian dimension finally moved to suck it dry and crunch up its corpse. The oceans poured over the beach and the forests, saturating the foundations of the tower as the red cobblestones were wrenched free of their carefully constructed patterns to whirl helter-skelter through the tidal currents. The skyscraper itself, meanwhile, was buckling, its black surface rippling and shattering as its realm folded inward around it. Trees were uprooted and sent sailing through windows, their branches stretching skyward like arms beseeching mercy; mutated beings were dashed helplessly against sharp corners and rent asunder by the thrashing waves.

"That island belongs to *us*, not this place. We need it."

"Yes. Move. Quickly."

The five-who-were-one swooped back toward the tower world, fighting against the pull of the limitless entity that sought to swallow them both. With intense concentration, the coalescing beings began to absorb the tower world's husk into themselves, making it a permanent part of their collective. The ocean full of hands, the forest of faces, the midnight skyscraper itself with all its hidden depths and unknown heights, the Lucas-being took them all into their conglomerate body and soul.

The Otherworld was not pleased with this development. Turning all its attention on the Lucas-being, it began to dissolve them, pulling them apart atom by atom and thought by thought. Its galactic tendrils lined with teeth like skeletal mountain peaks entwined around them, chewing and cutting and smothering as its oblivion whirlpool sucked them downward and outward, stretching them to their breaking point.

"Gah! It *burns!*"

"We must escape. We need to return to Kadath."

Images burst and bled behind their eyes. It was almost as if the place were trying to speak to them. To make them understand. Slowly the images became thoughts, the ideas mutating and thinning into whispers.

"How? We don't know the way!"

You are mine. I made you. I am in you. You cannot escape me now, or ever.

"Focus. If we don't try, we will die here!"

Little tenderling, why do you run? This is your fate. This is your destiny. Don't fight. Succumb.

"I feel it! *It's worming inside our minds!*"

It's all right. I will slurp down your souls like caviar and savor them one by one as they pop in the fathomless abyss of my mind. Do not fear; you will not be there when I hollow your vessel clean and fill your husk with my glory. The worlds beyond will rupture with truth. Consciousness will be cleansed of self.

Closing their eyes, they found the image in two sets of their memories and imagined –

KADATH FACILITY

The ground dissolved below Lucas as he fell, sealing up again once he passed through it. The voices in his head were screaming from terror, pain, and lingering trauma, the sounds ringing inside his skull. He realized their voices had joined his own.

Lucas hit the next level with a reverberating thud, bouncing slightly before finally settling on the grating. He groaned as he felt the harsh realities brought about by metal meeting flesh. Smoke was rising from his body – or were those the evaporating tendrils of a ravening cosmic horror?

Lucas lay there, recovering his breath, as the others inside his head tried to collect themselves and calm their nerves. He could feel them, moving behind his eyes. It wasn't really like they had physical forms anymore: *He* was their physical form. But somehow, they were simultaneously distinct and one mind. As they – as *he* – finally rallied, Lucas began to hear them speak with their own voices – which was strange, since they all used his mouth.

"Ouch," one of them said. Lucas thought it was the preacher. "That hurt like a bull tapdancing on a man's balls."

"Did we just make the level above us open up so we could pass through it?" another voice said. Lucas knew this was Rachel.

"That is the absolute *least* strange thing of everything we just went through," said a third voice. This was Min.

"What happened?" Lucas asked. "How did we become… this?"

"Let me out!" cried the fourth voice. This one had to be the woman who had tried to kill him. Mitsuko? Yes, that was it.

"Please! I can't be here! I have to get back to my daughter! How do I get out of this?"

"Take ease, Mitsuko," said Min. "Be calm. It's all right. We're all rather stuck at the moment. Panicking won't put a stop to that."

"We're here, Mitsuko," said the preacher. Lucas got the impression his name was Connor. He vaguely sensed that they had met before and that Connor had helped him. "We're alive. That means there's still hope. Now. We need you to take a breath, dear. Okay?"

"You're the strongest of us, Mitsuko," Min said. "We need you."

Mitsuko took a long, shuddering breath through Lucas's mouth, trying to calm herself. "I'm sorry," she said. "It's my fault we're in this position in the first place. If not for my rashness…"

"We understand," Connor said. "Sometimes, it's easier to remain collected when you don't know you have something big to lose."

"What's your daughter's name, Mitsuko?" Min asked. "Do you remember?"

Mitsuko was silent for a moment, then she spoke again. "Akari," she murmured. "Because she was my bright light."

"That's beautiful," Connor said. "Now. We need you to hold onto that bright light, all right? We'll either get out of here altogether or not at all."

"Of course," she said.

Slowly, gingerly, Lucas forced himself to stand up. The first thing he noticed was the pain radiating through his body. But the next was that he felt strangely full — as if the newcomers had packed the gaps inside him to overflowing. Memories were floating in his head now from multiple lives. They felt like an extension and culmination of the dreams he had experienced since his life began. He supposed it was a blessing that most of them only remembered a small fraction of their total experiences. If they recalled everything, he thought his head might burst.

"So, this is Kadath," Min said. "I recognize it from the nightmare memory tunnel."

"Where are we, Lucas?" Rachel asked.

"I don't know," Lucas said. "Not in the science wing. Maybe Dome One?" That was when Lucas heard the sobs. They were soft and quiet, but they were nearby.

"That could be dangerous," Mitsuko said.

"Yes, but it could also be someone who needs our help," Connor replied. "We can't leave whoever it is to suffer just on the *chance* it's an evil monstrosity."

"And how often in our travels has it been an innocent who needed our help, Connor?" Mitsuko asked.

"There was an entire *settlement* that needed our help, Mitsuko," Connor said. "We failed them all."

"We'll see who it is," Lucas murmured. "And we'll try to keep a safe distance, just in case."

Lucas advanced toward the crying until he came to an open hatchway. Focusing, he looked through the wall beside the door, being careful to stay out of sight. The room was empty. But how?

The beast leaped out of the opposing hatch behind Lucas, its barbed tentacles flailing. Lucas whirled around and gasped. The thing looked like it was straight out of a submariner's fever dream. It wasn't crying anymore but was instead now tittering incessantly, the sound becoming more of a non-stop chatter as it continued. The whipping group of tendrils crowning its body lashed out, the hooks at their ends embedding in Lucas's shoulder and arm. Then it yanked him off his feet, dragging him toward it.

Lucas's legs stumbled beneath him, but, at last, he was able to regain his footing. He braced himself on the ground, his arms shooting out to either side to grip the hatchway's frame. He looked up at the monster, his mouth twisted into a snarl.

"No," five different voices said.

The hatch in front of him slammed shut, shearing off the creature's tentacles. He heard it screeching on the far side of the door before it began laughing hysterically, a loud, keening noise. It hammered on the far side of the metal slab, but Lucas held the panel closed with his mind. Then he heard a sound like a chainsaw on the far side of the door, and the thing started bawling like a small child. It seemed a very long, excruciating time before the creature stopped. When it finally did, though, Lucas relaxed his control of the hatch, and it swished open again.

"Lucas?" Charles Ryan said, the industrial saw blades on his left arm slowing to a halt. The beast lay twitching at his thick metal feet.

"Charles?" Lucas replied, taken aback.

"Lucas, what's wrong with your eyes?" Charles asked.

Frowning, Lucas stepped closer to Charles and looked at his reflection in the glass viewport. Lucas's eyes were blazing like twin suns.

"They had me out on an extended dive," Charles said, sitting next to Lucas on a dense, welded bench. "I knew it would be a long one when I set out, but it ended up taking significantly more time than even their worst estimates. Then, when I get back, I find this place looking more like a charnel house than a research and mining facility."

"Is anyone still alive?" Lucas asked.

"Next to no one in *this* section. But I've heard chatter from other parts of the station. It sounds like Wade's trying to keep things together, and he's not doing a very good job of it. But why don't you know this, Lucas? I should be asking *you!*"

"Time doesn't seem to mean what it used to," Lucas replied.

"And how did you get over here, especially without having seen anything?"

"Space doesn't appear to count for much, either."

"You know, before I went out there, I heard a physicist talking about how the laws of physics are breaking down here," Charles said. "Maybe you know him. His name's Stephen Cooper. Anyway, he discovered that many things previously possible only on the quantum level were starting to happen on ours."

"That could definitely explain some of what's been happening," Lucas said.

Charles cleared his throat. "So, where's Rachel? And what's up with the eyes?"

"They're both… complicated."

"Try me."

Lucas swallowed. "Rachel was killed," he said.

"Wh-what?" Charles choked. "No. No, *no!* What *happened?*"

"William West, Cohen, and Summerisle were sent by Blake to investigate me, which was code for capture and conduct experiments on me. They caught Rachel first. And then, when they were trying to get me, West shot her. I tried to save her, but…"

"She… can't be gone," Charles said, shaking his head. "Not Rachel. She was… one of the best."

"I said she died," Lucas replied. "I didn't say she was gone."

Charles gave Lucas a strange look. "What do you mean, she's not gone?"

"Something happened to me, Charles," Lucas said. "I don't think I'm strictly human anymore. Honestly, I'm not sure I ever was. Which I think explains the eyes."

"And Rachel?"

"She's… a part of me now."

"Come again?"

"Hi, Charles," Rachel said.

"What the actual hell!" Charles cried, jumping to his feet. He shook his head again as if trying to clear the insanity away. "Rachel? That's not…"

"It's me, Charles," Rachel said. "I'm… a part of Lucas now."

"That's not possible," Charles said. "How did this happen?"

"It's a long story," Lucas said. "And an even stranger one. I don't think there's time for it now."

"You've got someplace better to be?" Charles asked.

"Yeah, actually," Lucas said, standing. "I think this whole dimension is about to end, Charles. And I have to decide if I want to help make that happen."

Charles's jaw dropped. "And… how does one make that kind of a decision?" he asked.

"Beats the hell out of me."

"So, we're in some sort of bubble that's about to pop?" Charles asked, walking down the corridor beside Lucas.

"That's what Regan tells me," Lucas said. "If I choose to trust her, then it's a surety. But if we merge this reality with others, then everything beyond Kadath in this dimension will end without question."

"But she says no one will actually die?" Charles said. "Because there are copies of everyone in other dimensions?"

"Once again, if I choose to believe her."

"And why am I getting the feeling you're beginning to?"

"Because I *saw* something, Charles," Lucas said. "I was in another existence or dimension or whatever, and it was *alive*. Not as in, it contained life. But *it* was alive. And it's insatiably hungry.

Before, I was in the bay with the sphere, and it felt like that same place was somehow *inside* it, almost like the sphere was a *gateway* to that realm. Regan said that in most dimensions, the sphere cracks open, letting that place out. And I'm beginning to think that, if that happens, it will be the end of humanity. Everywhere. Without exception."

"Whoa," Charles exhaled. "That's heavy." He paused for a moment. "So, what's the next step?"

"I'm going to talk to the only person I know who might be able to tell me how true this is," Lucas said. "I'm going to go to William West."

"You're going to talk to *West?*" Rachel cried. "Lucas, that is a *terrible* idea!"

"Who's West?" Connor asked. "Should we be worried?"

Charles gave Lucas a strange look. "Lucas, did you just talk in an Irish accent?"

Lucas smiled sheepishly. "I never said Rachel was the *only* voice inside my head."

"How many are in there?" Charles asked.

"There are five of us, including me," Lucas said. "I think."

"Okay," Charles said. "Good to know, I guess."

"First, let's find some weapons," Lucas said. "I won't be caught off-guard by that bastard again."

The security office was abandoned as well, the occasional streaks of blood and discarded personal effects serving as the only signs that people had ever been there. Charles and Lucas quietly, cautiously, worked their way back into the deeper rooms of the block, until, at last, they found what they were looking for: the armory.

"I thought maybe we'd find *someone* here," Lucas said quietly.

"Even just one or two people holed up."

"It's been like this everywhere I've gone thus far," Charles said. "This place is a tomb now."

Lucas found a scattergun and an SMG. Cradling the SMG in his arm, he slung the scattergun over his shoulder. Charles, meanwhile, contented himself with an assault rifle.

"You won't have to worry about Cohen or Blake, by the by," Charles said.

"Really? Why's that?" Lucas asked.

"They were two of the first corpses I found when I got back to Kadath," Charles replied. "Whatever got them, it was brutal."

Lucas nodded. "Let's go."

"Whoa, wait a minute," Charles said. "Do you see that?"

Lucas frowned. "Yeah. I do."

"It almost looks a bit like the shards from the top of the tower," Min said.

Charles cocked his head but didn't say anything further.

The corridor before them was shimmering, the air sliding like chunks of glass passing around each other. Lucas approached it cautiously, his brow furrowed. It almost seemed he could hear the shards singing low and soft as they glided over one another.

"What do you think will happen if we touch it?" Connor asked.

"When I touched the shard that reflected my life, nothing happened," Mitsuko said.

"Yes, but this is in the middle of a corridor in another dimension, and there's nothing unusual on the other side," Min said.

"Maybe we should find a way around," Rachel suggested.

"Do you think there's another path to the shuttle, Charles?" Lucas asked.

"Not that I'm aware of, Doc. But that doesn't mean there isn't."

Lucas looked around. Then he took a deep breath. "Ah, what the hell." Reaching out his hand, he touched the shifting, shimmering shards. The shards cracked, breaking apart as if he were punching his fist through glass in slow motion. Lucas pressed more of his arm through, up to his shoulder. Then, turning sideways, he sidled forward.

"Huh," he said as he reached the far side. "It doesn't seem to do anything at all." Then he looked back. Charles was gone. "Charles? Charles, where'd you go?"

A bulky metal hand pushed through the shards, followed by a hulking mechanized body. Seconds later, Charles was standing beside Lucas again. "When you disappeared, I figured I better follow before I lost you again," Charles said.

Lucas smiled. "I guess we're both crazy."

"The ghost in the machine and the scientist with multiple personalities?" Charles replied. "I think that goes without saying, Doc."

"So, what's different?" Lucas asked, turning forward again. "What changed?"

"It's cleaner," Charles said.

"Yeah," Lucas replied. "Not as many bloodstains."

"Lucas, you said not long ago that time didn't mean what it used to," Connor said. "Do you think we just jumped backward?"

"Makes as much sense as anything else right now, I suppose," Charles said, shrugging his massive shoulders.

"We need to keep moving," Mitsuko said. They did, cautiously advancing through Kadath's eerily quiet halls. It wasn't long, though, before the echoes of screams fractured the silence.

The shouts were coming from a four-way junction up ahead. Running forward, Lucas and Charles looked around the left corner to see a group of people racing toward them, pursued by a swarm of creatures that looked like cobras fashioned from raw meat, human skulls, and spinal columns. One by one, the squealing, hissing terrors lunged up, impaling their sharp tails into their victims' spines. Then their cowls enfolded around the tops of the people's heads, their mouths stretching wider and wider to engulf their targets' crowns, and the creatures – vanished. The men and women began jerking and spasming, agonized shrieks ripping free of their mouths as their limbs whipped and thrashed. It looked as if they had all gone hysterical with pain. One by one, they collapsed on the corridor's grating.

"They're already dead, Lucas," Charles said. "Come on."

Lucas was struck momentarily by how closely Charles's words echoed Regan's, but he couldn't argue. Nodding, he hurried on.

At last, they reached the shuttle station. Lucas was reminded briefly of his final look at Arkham Station. He wondered if that one had ended up blooming like this one.

The walls here crawled with obscene life. Tentacles slapped against the room's ceiling and floor, teeth chattered manically in jaws made from what seemed like a flexible coral, and eyes bulged as they grew out of the wet crimson fungal masses that spread like a disease across every surface. There were other things, too, that looked like bundles of tentacles clustered around a gently throbbing membrane. There was something cradled inside that translucent layer of flesh. It pushed against the diaphragm like an unborn baby stirring inside his mother. Whatever was in there, it would be born soon.

Carefully, quietly, Lucas and Charles picked their way to the shuttle platform. They had just about made it when they felt the station shake. Red warning lights began to flash overhead, followed by a deceptively calm emergency message: "Warning. Warning.

Decompression detected in Dome One. Flooding imminent. Please evacuate the area. Emergency containment procedures activated."

Over the voice and the klaxons, Lucas now heard something else: a roar. It was faint but growing louder every moment.

"We need to go," Min said. "Now!"

A shuttle sat docked and waiting on the platform. Charles opened the doors and gestured for Lucas to get in. Lucas did, and Charles followed just as the shuttle bay's hatches started closing on their own. Saltwater poured into the room, fighting against the closing panels. It almost looked like the water was going to break the hatch –

The shuttle shot off down its tube, leaving the flooding behind.

The shuttle began to decelerate as it reached Innsmouth Station in Dome Two. The doors opened, and Lucas started to step forward through the open portal. He paused. A second barrier of transparent fragments hung in the air before them, the pieces drifting through the air and ricocheting off each other as they collided.

"I think it's another time fracture," Lucas told Charles.

"Well, I don't know what other choices we have," Charles said. Lucas nodded and stepped through the shifting wall of crystal clear shards.

The platform was still deserted beyond the flowing wall of broken time, though now warning lights throbbed in the ceiling overhead. Lucas and Charles strode between the empty rows of seats and the abandoned waiting areas, then opened the hatch at the room's far side. A security guard snapped around, his eyes wide.

"How did *you* get in there?" he asked. "Dome Two is in lockdown!"

"Don't worry about it," Lucas said. "We're not in there

anymore." Lucas and Charles stepped into the corridor and paused.

"Do you hear that?" Mitsuko asked.

"Yeah," Charles said. "I do."

"Let's go left," Lucas said.

Lucas and Charles hurried down the corridor as unearthly, savage sounds seemed to close in around them from every direction. Their nerves sizzled with jittery energy; their senses heightened to notice every shifting shadow. Whatever was coming would find them soon. It was only a matter of time.

"This must be what the death of Kadath sounds like," Rachel murmured.

"Huh," Charles said, bending down.

"What is it, Charles?" Lucas asked.

"A present for you, Doc," he said, straightening. In his hand, he held a scalpel.

Lucas almost laughed. "I'll take it," he said. "Thanks."

They heard people scream through the wall to their left. Lucas swiveled and peered through the metal, then turned back to Charles. "I think we can save these," he said.

"But what's the point?" Mitsuko asked. "If they're all likely doomed anyway, aren't we just delaying the inevitable?"

"It's in our power to do something *now*," Connor replied. "*That's* what counts."

"It's your call, Doc," Charles said.

Lucas nodded. "Then let's do it." Turning back to the wall, he ripped it open just like he had the floor upon reentering Kadath.

There were three people curled up on the ground, covering their heads as if to shelter from the monstrosities descending upon them. One beast loomed in a hatchway, its large, leathery wings sprouting from a lumpy, almost cylindrical body bookended by clusters of undulating tentacles. Behind them, two creatures that seemed forged from liquid meat and twisted darkness poured forward, arms and mouths and eyes bubbling up to the surface before being reabsorbed into the boiling mass of their bodies. They were joined by two more of the deliriously thrashing beasts which mouthlessly babbled and laughed and moaned as they stuttered toward their victims.

Lucas unslung his SMG and opened fire, unleashing a battle cry that almost sounded like it was coming from five throats at once. He pumped one of the viscous, throbbing things full of projectiles, mercilessly pummeling the beast and driving it back into the second one. Momentarily redirecting his attention, Lucas turned to the open doorway where the flying creature was almost through and slammed the hatch closed with the flick of his wrist. Then he returned his attention to the immediate threats. The one Lucas had shot wasn't dead yet but instead seemed to be trying to reconstitute itself. He didn't want to give it a chance.

Charles ducked through the hatchway to Lucas's right and thundered into the room. He was shouting, too, as he engaged the industrial blades on his left arm and descended toward the vile terrors, the thick metal teeth churning into wet flesh as he also brought his assault rifle to bear. Lucas kept firing through the rift in the wall, covering Charles, until at last, the SMG stopped firing with a soft *thunk*. Unsure if it was jammed or out of ammunition, Lucas stowed it over his shoulder and pulled out the scalpel Charles had found for him. Allowing the hole to seal back up, Lucas followed Charles into the room.

One of the three huddled people realized what was happening and jumped to his feet, pulling his own scalpel into his hands. He joined Lucas and Charles as they beat and sliced and shot at the horrors, which blessedly fell one after the other. The room reverberated with a cacophony of shrieks and screeches, grinding and shouts, gunfire and squelching.

Lucas felt keenly the waves of other consciousnesses surging through his limbs as they all attacked as one body. First, Mitsuko would cut with the scalpel, then Connor would draw the scattergun off Lucas's shoulder and fire, then Min would dodge. They all flowed together in a ballet of mind, each one using their unique skills before backing away to let another implement theirs. Lucas had never experienced anything like it before. It was exhilarating.

When the last two beasts finally fell, Charles swiveled around. "Hey, Doc!" he said. "Tear open the hatch!"

Following Charles's gaze, Lucas opened a hole in the middle of the door, exposing the flying nightmare hovering on the far side. Charles nodded, then raised his assault rifle and pulled the trigger. The thing blew backward, squealing in pain until, at last, it collapsed in a heap on the corridor's floor.

"It's dead, right?" Charles asked as he struggled to reload his assault rifle.

"I think so," Lucas replied. "It's still twitching, but…" Lucas turned toward the three people who were now collecting themselves, allowing the hatch to seal back up as he did. He helped the two women to their feet. One of them, a lab tech, Lucas thought he might recognize from a lab near his – which was confirmed when she knew his name. "This place is about the farthest thing from safe there is right now," Lucas said. "Do you have someplace you can go?"

"We were heading to the evac bay," the man said.

Lucas nodded. "I guess that's as good a place as any," he replied. "Get there as fast as you can. But… try not to launch right away, okay?"

"Are you coming with us?" the man asked.

"No," Lucas said. "Charles and I have some things to finish

here. You go ahead. Just stay safe."

"Thank you," he said, extending his hand. "Dr. Kane, was it?"

"Lucas," Lucas replied, smiling and shaking the hand. "Now, move!" The three people nodded. They gripped each other, offered their thanks one more time, and then hurried through the hatch. The metal panel slid closed behind them.

"Well then," Charles said. "Shall we?"

Lucas and Charles continued toward West's lab.

"Lucas, what do you hope to find with West?" Charles asked. "What do you aim to achieve?"

"I don't know," Lucas replied. "An excuse, maybe. I want him to say that what Regan told me is impossible and that we don't have to do what she said. Or maybe he'll *agree* with her, and that will convince me there's another way."

"But why ask the man who may be the evilest person still alive in Kadath?" Charles asked.

"Because I don't know where else to go," Lucas murmured.

They were nearing the sphere's bay again, as well as closing in on Dr. West's lab. They had waded through bloodbaths and flooding, seen rooms devoured by the strange, maddening red fungus, and fought off horrific apparitions. Now they had nearly achieved their goal.

Turning down the corridor that led to West's laboratory, they saw another shifting time fracture filling the air before them. Lucas and Charles stepped through this one without a second thought. Instantly the chaotic cacophony was replaced by an eerie silence. The quiet was almost deafening. Perhaps it would have been if someone weren't waiting for them.

"You're stalling, Lucas," Regan said. "We are running out of time."

"Maybe you haven't noticed, Regan, but time is broken," Lucas replied as the girl advanced down the corridor toward them. "If we're running short of it, we can always go back to when there was more."

"Haven't you wondered why you're jumping back and forth between days and weeks?" Regan asked. "The edges of this dimension are cracking. The bubble is about to burst, and it frankly won't matter *when* you are as it does."

"I don't think we've met before," Charles said, stepping forward. "I'm Charles."

Regan glanced over Charles, then returned her gaze to Lucas. "We need to do this, Lucas. Before it's too late."

"I'm not ready yet," Lucas said. "I need to know for certain that there's no other way."

"And you hope to find your answer with that *hack?*"

"He's my last option," Lucas said. "Then, I'll do what you want."

Regan sighed. "Very well," she said. "But I'm going with you this time."

Lucas led them to West's laboratory and paused at the door. He hefted his scattergun while Charles readied his assault rifle. "You ready?" he asked.

Charles nodded, while Regan just looked annoyed. Lucas pushed the hatch control, and the door opened. They stepped inside. Lucas and Charles gasped.

"Why, Lucas!" West exclaimed, his voice weaker and hollower than the last time Lucas had heard it. "Do my eyes deceive me? I thought you had died *weeks* ago! This is indeed a monumental surprise. What brings you to darken my doorway today of all days?"

"West… what did you do?" Lucas asked.

West looked like a crippled husk of himself, his warped, hairless body enfolded in a metal wheelchair straight out of an old mad scientist's laboratory. His exposed skin was a feverish lattice of cuts, stitches, and ports, making him look almost more like Frankenstein's monster than Frankenstein himself. Lucas found him at once repulsive and horrifying, but also somehow tragic.

"Watch out, Lucas," Mitsuko said. "He's not alone."

"Oh, you have other voices conversing with you, too!" William exclaimed. "How wonderful! I have three of my own, you know, though I haven't heard much from them since I banished them to the mind-web. Every once in a while, though, I'll pull one of them up to have a chat. Dr. Branom is of particular merit, though his betrayal stung no less than Murdock's or Hannah's."

"What manner of monster *are* you?" Regan asked, cocking her head to the side. "You're *almost* like us now, but… not quite. Other minds are mixing with yours, but they're not truly *yours*, are they?"

"I don't believe I've had the pleasure of making your acquaintance, my dear," William said. "I'm Dr. William West. But, please, call me William." His wheelchair rolled toward her. "I have a feeling you are most *certainly* someone worth knowing. Are you, perhaps, like good old Lucas here?"

As West and Regan spoke, Lucas took Mitsuko's advice and surveyed the entire laboratory. The more he did, the tenser he grew. The room was enormous compared with most other locales in the science wing, including his own rather spacious lab. And nearly every available space in it contained some new terror. First, there were the people strapped down to examination tables throughout the lab or enfolded in odd chrysalises attached to bizarre machines. Most of these test subjects had tubes and wires running out of their necks or other parts of their bodies. Some were completely headless.

What was stranger, though, were those creatures who *weren't* strapped down. These misshapen things were almost unanimously decapitated and walked with halting, jerky movements like marionettes with a poor puppeteer. The most dangerous-looking creatures did still have heads, however – or at least likely did. One wore an old-fashioned diving helmet and carried an immense pair of shears (Lucas couldn't be sure if this one had a head, as he couldn't see anything through the helmet's dark glass), while the other looked like it had been torn apart and reassembled with old saw blades.

"Ah, I see you're admiring my handiwork!" West exclaimed, his attention once more turning to Lucas. "Marvelous, aren't they? They are mostly just worker bees, though. The true queens are those machines back there. Those magnificent engines toe the line between the scientific and the truly mystical. They will allow me to conquer the sphere, and to ascend above mere mortality. As well as allow me to escape this doomed plane before it truly and completely collapses."

"Does that answer your question, Lucas?" Regan asked. "Even the deluded lunatic knows what is happening."

"Oh, my dear!" William cried. "Your words sting! And here I had thought we were beginning to be *friends*."

"You're utterly mad, West," Lucas whispered. "What you've done here…"

"I have done what no one else dared to do, Lucas," West said, his breath wheezing in his lungs. "What no one else even had the *imagination* to *dream*. And I am now humanity's greatest hope for salvation from the sphere's glorious, conscious chaos." West rolled closer to Lucas. "What did you think to find here, Lucas? What were you trying to prove? Were you finally just giving in and offering yourself to me? Did you hope to join me in my estimable quest? Did you merely want to see a friendly face? In all honesty, my breath is bated, and I simply must know."

"I came here for hope," Lucas said. "To find a way to save this place and this dimension. Or to get confirmation that it truly is beyond rescue."

"Oh, this plane is doomed past any shadow of a doubt," West replied. "My research on the subject is nearly impermeable. The only question now is who escapes and who goes down with the station. Speaking of which…" With that, West rotated around to face his mangled creations. He squinted his eyes as if concentrating on some deep problem. Then his spastic headless victims turned from their tasks toward the three interlopers. At the same moment, the thing that was half-covered in a diving suit and half in surgical attire came to life, its massive shears dragging on the ground as it advanced.

"You caught me just as I was about to make history," West said. "On any other day I would have been entirely *overwhelmed* with curiosity about what makes you and your young friend tick, and I couldn't have focused on anything else until I had cut you apart to find out. But today is the day that I best the sphere at its own game, and even the tantalizing conundrum you represent cannot dissuade me. If you'll excuse me."

"West?" Lucas said. "West, what are you doing?"

"You know, it's funny, Lucas," West said. "In a way, I got the idea for this little experiment from *you*. How fitting that you would be here to see its culmination."

"Ah, to hell with this shite!" Connor snarled.

"Couldn't agree more," Charles replied.

Connor took over Lucas's arm and opened fire with the scattergun at the oncoming horrors. Charles leveled the assault rifle and joined him. As they were shooting desperately at West's creations, his most mangled construct – strangely, the only one that assuredly still had a head – lifted West out of his wheelchair and laid him gingerly on a specially augmented examination table.

"Don't you worry, Lucas," West called. "You'll still have your part to play in this. My children will ensure that your prodigious energies are put to use in this great conflict. You all are about to witness – and assist with – something that has never occurred in recorded history."

The dissected creature plugged several conduits into West's neck and body. West shivered before going still, his eyelids fluttering incessantly. The construct then shambled toward the far side of the lab. It tapped several controls on a console there, then the metal wall directly in front of it parted down the middle and slid open as sirens began blaring and lights strobed overhead.

Regan took Lucas's SMG and somehow fixed it just by looking at it intently. After that, she joined Lucas and Charles in mercilessly cutting down every moving thing. Despite their efforts, several of the creatures were getting too close for comfort. Charles engaged his thick blades again and stepped forward, cutting one of the headless things in two.

The mindless puppets seemed to be using their bodies as a living shield for the diver with the shears. It was nearly within reach now, and so it hefted its immense weapon in both hands. The blades started opening and closing with a terrible rusty squeal that sent shivers down Lucas's spine. Lucas saw an opening and fired the scattergun directly into the thing's diving helmet. The shot shattered the thick glass panel in the front while several pellets also blew out the back. Dark energy started seeping out of the hole, as well as something else: tiny flecks of light that whizzed off into the air and vanished. Still, it kept coming, raising the shears to the level of Lucas's neck.

Regan raised a hand and sent the thing flying backward, clattering on the steel floor. Aiming her SMG at it, she shot it until it stopped moving. The other monsters hesitated as if they suddenly weren't entirely sure what to do. Lucas and his compatriots exploited that opportunity with extreme prejudice.

At last, Lucas looked up to see what the dissected being's actions had wrought. The far wall had opened to expose a deep, empty area behind incredibly thick glass with an airlock set off to one side of it. On the far side of this space was another glass wall, and beyond that was a second set of metal blast shields. These panels were now sliding open, parting to reveal a cavernous storage bay. And sitting in the center of that storage bay was the sphere.

"Resonance chamber preparation complete," a calm voice said through the overhead speakers. "Commencing consciousness burst protocol."

"Um, should we leave?" Charles asked, his eyes widening at the sight of the sphere.

"Yes, I rather think we should," Min said.

Regan, however, was drifting toward the far end of the laboratory. Reaching the glass, she placed her hand flat against it, peering intently at the sphere. "It knows we're here," she murmured. "It sees us. It *feels* us." As if to prove this point, tendrils of energy began arcing off the sphere like coronal mass ejections, lashing out into the air in multicolored radiance.

"Get away from there!" Rachel cried. "We don't know what's about to happen!"

Lucas and Charles ran to grab Regan, while West and every other person hooked up to his equipment began a low escalating growl that developed into a guttural shout. Charles slowed and looked around the room as it filled with the droning din, his panting breath fogging up the inside of his viewport. Lucas's hand wrapped around Regan's arm, pulling her out of her reverie.

"Beginning process in 3... 2... 1," the soothing voice said above them. "Mark."

It was like a miniature supernova sparked behind the glass. The white-hot blaze surged through the room before slowly tightening inward, concentrating into a ball of roiling power. It was blinding. And it was conscious.

Lucas and Charles cried out, stumbling backward as they fumbled to shield their eyes. Regan just cocked her head to the side again, a smile spreading slowly across her lips. There was a look of almost childlike wonder on her face, mixed with something else, as well. "Yes," she said. "We can use this."

"Regan!" Lucas cried as his whole body vibrated from the chain reaction taking place on the other side of the glass. "We need to go!"

"You were *right* to come here, Lucas," Regan replied. "I thought it was folly, but obviously you were drawn to West for a reason. I think we can make this our catalyst."

"I can feel it," West and all of those linked to him droned. "Yes. *Yes!* It is *glorious!*"

The micro-supernova began to fluctuate, blazing white arms and legs and heads pressing out of its flashing brilliance before being reabsorbed into its core. The thing was growing in both size and intensity. A face materialized in the fluctuating blaze, its mouth opening wider and wider. It was West.

"I am," the West face said, its voice a chorused deluge of sound. "I am transcendent. I am free. I am all."

Regan chuckled. "You are even more delusional than before. But fascinating, nonetheless."

The West face sneered. "You think yourself to be some great thing, trapped in your little body of meat," it said to Regan. "I did not realize until now the true smallness of the human being, but now I see you for what you are. Pathetic."

"I am in this form because I choose to be," Regan said, her voice changing. It was doubling, tripling, becoming its own swarm of tones. "But make no mistake, West: We are more than you could *ever* grasp."

Lucas looked down at the ground. The shadow behind Regan was growing. It was no longer the shape of a teenage girl: it was becoming something else entirely, its waving tendrils squiggling upon the ground. The shadow's massive mouth yawned wide.

"But *I* am not your target, am I, West?" Regan said. "You did this to best the *sphere*, not me. I am small and inconsequential compared to the *sphere*. If you want to prove your true worth, you know what you have to do."

The West head laughed. "But of course, my dear!" it said. "Now, observe true conscious *might* at work!"

The sentient ball of energy exploded, once again filling the entire resonance chamber. Then it pushed through the glass on the far side, its sizzling being pressing toward the sphere. The sphere reached out in kind, its effervescent shoots blooming with rainbows of unhinged madness. The two forces touched and then entwined. They stayed like that for a moment, as if testing each other. Or maybe they were sampling one another. Then the sphere's abyss began to absorb the West being into itself.

"Wait," the West thing said. "No. No! No, no, no, *no*, it's too deep! It's too *deep* I can't see the *bottom what is happening to me?*" A maelstrom of colors and darkness and mouths were leeching into the brilliant white being. Its shape was twisting and malforming, bulging outward in places while curling inward in others. Its brightness was dulling, becoming darker and more muddied.

"It's sucking me down!" West's voice cried, both from the entity and all the people in West's lab. "I can't break free!" Then he screamed. *"BATHOPHOBIA!"*

The entity in the next room continued warping, adopting a new physicality. Its multitude of mouths pushed out from its body on thick little stalks, becoming almost like small tube-shaped legs filled with teeth. The West face's mouth elongated, becoming rounder as sharp fangs pushed out of its lips around the opening's circumference. Bulging bubbles of flesh formed over his eyes and nose.

"Lucas," that mouth and the mouths behind Lucas whispered. "Please, help me. I'm so afraid."

"Fail-safes engaged," the calm, soothing loudspeaker said. "Isolating anomaly."

"Oh no, you don't," Regan said, striding over to a terminal as the metal barriers started sliding back into place.

"Regan, what are you *doing!*" Charles cried.

"I'm using the resources available to me," she replied.

"Override initiated," the speaker's voice said. "Fail-safes disengaged." The panels reversed their course. Regan waited a moment as the sphere's tendrils pulled back, and then she advanced toward the airlock.

"Regan –" Lucas said with all five voices, starting after her. But he was cut off as the mammoth coalescing horror shrieked. Immediately the glass blew outward, knocking both Lucas and Charles off their feet as the piercing, high-pitched sound swept through the laboratory. Regan took shelter momentarily in the airlock's entrance; then, she levitated off the ground and through one of the gaping holes where once there had been protective glass.

"What the hell is she doing!" Connor cried. "Has she gone mad?"

Lucas stood, wiping the blood from his nostrils and ears while spitting it out of his mouth. Charles stood, too, his pistons and motors whining. Lucas noted that his faceplate had several small cracks now spiderwebbing across it. Charles nodded at him, and Lucas returned the gesture. Then they both sprinted toward the shattered display wall.

Regan was still hovering over the ground. She turned her head to look at Lucas as he reached the frame. Her eyes were once again like endless black shafts bored into her young face.

"Look behind you, Lucas," she said. Forcing his gaze away from her, Lucas complied. He saw the air cracking behind him, breaking off in chunks.

"This dimension is about to shatter," Regan said. "This is our last chance. Are you ready to do what must be done?"

Lucas couldn't deny what she said. He saw different timeframes intermixing, observed people vibrating faster and faster as the world around them became blurry and indistinct. Regardless of what he did now, it was all going to end. It was no longer a matter of time. Looking back up to Regan, he swallowed. "Yes."

Regan almost smiled. Raising her hand, she levitated Lucas into the air and positioned him on the far side of the throbbing, squirming beast that had been William.

"Lucas!" Charles cried. "Lucas, what are you doing! Stop!"

"Follow my lead," Regan said. "Act as it feels natural. You'll know what to do." Lucas nodded.

Regan extended her hands toward the creature, unleashing a feral roar that doubled, tripled, and quadrupled as each new voice joined it. Lucas did the same, his own five voices shouting with hers. He could feel himself siphoning away the beast's being, repurposing it, using it.

The bulbous creature shivered. And then it erupted into a whirling vortex of dark energy and viscous multicolored ectoplasm.

"Draw from its energies, Lucas!" Regan commanded. "Use it to unmoor Kadath!"

Lucas did. He located the boundaries of the field the sphere had established around the facility and used it as a pattern. He and Regan pulled and cut at the edges of that field, using the being's energy to rip it free of the dimension beyond. The area gave slightly, then tore. Then –

The sea beyond the field shattered. And with it, the bubble dimension it was contained in collapsed.

For a moment, Lucas could feel them: countless living beings eradicated in a single instant. He shrieked with them in all five of his voices, but it would never be enough. Nothing he did would ever undo the mass extermination in which he had just taken part. Regardless, they were far from done.

Their version of Kadath fell through the multiverse, colliding with and merging into another one. This one ripped free, too, and they slid into a third one. Then a fourth. And a fifth. Each time the tearing grew easier. He could still feel the damage done to the other realities, but he hoped they would recover as his dimension had not –

The sixth reality crumpled around them, simultaneously shattering and imploding similarly to how Lucas's own had. No. Please, no! *Not this one, too!* Once again, Lucas was awash in billions – no, *trillions* – of beings who no longer existed. It was too much. He couldn't take this anymore. The loss was simply too great.

"Don't falter now, Lucas!" Regan cried. "We're almost there!"

Lucas felt himself losing control. He was falling inward, folding into the flames within his own eyes. He was drifting inside himself, deeper, deeper –

"Lucas, what did we just do?" Connor asked.

Lucas shook his head. "I don't know," he said. "I think it was what we had to do. I *hope* it was."

"I – I didn't think… it would come to this," Rachel murmured.

"Lucas, I'm sorry." Walking over to him, she wrapped her arms around him.

"I can't stop hearing them," Min said. Tears were falling down his face. "All those lives, all those lights, snuffed out into darkness."

"Which is more terrifying?" Mitsuko muttered. "The ravening animal that acts chiefly from instinct, or the rational mind that can alter its reality based solely on its whim? The mindless monster, or the omnipotent power?" She had curled up into a ball, her knees pressed into her chest. "I suppose… the omnipotent power is *us* now, isn't it? *We* are the terror. *We* are the destroyer. *We* are the endless abyss."

"Do you think that makes us the Otherworld?" Min asked, his voice small. "The creator, and the devourer? Or are we just devastation?"

"What do we do now?" Lucas asked.

Connor looked up, his eyes like flint. Walking over to Lucas, he placed his hand on his shoulder. "We keep going," Connor replied. "We don't stop. And we seek to find repentance and redemption for the things we've done. We cannot undo what has happened, but we *can* protect what remains. We must. Because, if we don't, no one else will."

Lucas looked deep into Connor's eyes, feeling tears swimming in his own. He nodded. "Okay," he said.

Lucas pulled his consciousness out of himself and back into Kadath. As he did, they plunged into the seventh plane, and then – stopped.

"This is it!" Regan exclaimed. "We did it! We made it!" Regan pulled back from the power, and Lucas did the same. They both collapsed to the ground as the vortex of energy dissipated between them. Before long, it had evaporated completely.

"Regan…" Lucas said. "That…"

"Was an unmitigated success," Regan replied. She was beaming. The smile was incredibly discomforting when combined with the endless black pits which had replaced her eyes. "I feel them, Lucas. Six other versions of myself, slipping around beneath my skin. Together, we are even more powerful than we were apart."

"What happens now?" Lucas asked.

"We seal up Kadath so no one can enter it without our approval," she said. "And then we go outside."

Lucas and Regan slowly climbed to their feet. Through the shattered wall to Lucas's left, he saw the sphere still sitting there, its surface more subdued than it had been previously. It was almost as if it were resting, or biding its time. Or maybe it was just feeling satisfied with a long day's work. There was something different about it, too, but Lucas couldn't quite put his finger on what that was. Could it be that the air was fluctuating around it, like ripples radiating around a rock thrown in the ocean?

This time, Regan and Lucas stumbled through the resonance chamber's airlock rather than flying through its breaches. Charles lay sprawled on the ground with his metal arms splayed to either side.

"Charles!" Lucas cried. "Charles, can you hear me?"

Charles's faceplate was smashed, his face smeared in blood. Lucas reached inside and touched his friend's cheek. Charles stirred. "Doc?" he managed. "What… did you do?"

"It's a long story," Lucas said. "But the important thing is it's over now. And we're okay."

"Are we?" Charles said. "Was the sphere destroyed?"

"Well, no…" Lucas replied. "It's still here."

"Then how is everything okay?" Charles asked.

"It doesn't matter," Lucas said. "Right now, we just need to get out of here. Can you stand? Do you need help?"

"I got it," Charles said, slowly climbing to his feet. His body groaned and creaked as he ascended.

"Okay," Lucas said. "Now, we need to find a way out. Maybe a sub or…"

"I'll be fine, Lucas," Charles said. "You go on without me. I… don't think I need any more help from you."

"Charles, I…" Lucas trailed off. He nodded. "Okay. Goodbye, my friend."

"See you around, Doc," Charles said. "Take care of Rachel in there."

"I will," Lucas replied.

"Goodbye, Charles," Rachel said. "Thank you. For everything."

"Later, Rachel," Charles said, almost smiling.

Turning, Lucas followed Regan toward the door. At the hatch, he paused, though, looking back. "I'll come back, Charles. To make sure you get out all right."

"You've done enough, Lucas," Charles said. "Goodbye."

Swallowing hard, Lucas headed through the hatchway. "How do we get out of here?" he asked Regan.

"We find the nearest airlock," she said simply.

They wandered through Kadath's empty corridors until, at last, they reached an airlock.

"Don't we need suits or something?" Lucas asked.

Regan laughed. "Do you *think* you need a suit?"

Lucas shrugged. "I suppose not," he replied.

They both stepped into the airlock, and then Lucas cycled it.

"Warning," a calm speaker voice said. "Airlock cycling engaged. Decompression commencing."

Lucas found himself holding his breath, but he realized how silly that was. In a few seconds, he would either be alive or dead. In neither case did he have to hold his breath.

"It's fine, Lucas," Regan said. "Just imagine a protective bubble around yourself. Or see yourself breathing normally. Or, perhaps, you can finally breathe water like that sea life you love so much."

The airlock flooded, and then it opened into the ocean depths. Lucas and Regan flew out of the airlock and upward. In no time, Kadath lay below them. Turning around, Lucas and Regan paused. Lucas surveyed the underwater metropolis. As Charles had said, it was a sight. There was no doubt, even now.

Regan motioned with her arms, and together she and Lucas began fashioning a dome of sorts over Kadath. Finally, it completely encased the facility, and the two of them continued upward for the surface. They rose through the ocean depths, experiencing not a hint of bends or decompression sickness. But, of course, it would have been rather strange for them to have those issues while still being able to breathe in the water.

At last, they breached the surface, and Lucas took a deep breath of fresh, cold air. With a shock, he realized it may have been the first time he had ever actually done so. The sky was bright overhead, only a few clouds scudding in front of the sun. Lucas and Regan levitated over the waves, and there they stopped.

"Will that dome keep Charles from getting out?" Lucas asked.

"No," Regan replied. "It hasn't completely solidified yet. He will have time if he doesn't take too long."

"Did we honestly accomplish anything by bringing the sphere here?" Lucas asked.

"I don't know for sure," Regan said. "Perhaps. It was always a gamble, combining a closed sphere with an open gateway. Maybe we bought some time. It could even be we stopped it altogether. Or, conceivably, we mutated its signal and made it worse. Only time will tell."

"And then there's the matter of *us*," Lucas said.

"Yes," Regan replied. "There is that."

"It's already in us, isn't it?" Lucas said. "The Otherworld, I mean. The things contained within the sphere. We're already its conduits. We always were."

"Of course," Regan said. "We are children of the Otherworld. Its pull on us is undeniable, as are its fingerprints. We cannot *help* but disseminate its influence to some extent. But how much we spread it is up to us – or, at least, I *think* it is."

"Have we… have we made this world worse?" Lucas asked. "Have we doomed this dimension just like we destroyed those others? Was any of it for a purpose?"

"If this dimension is doomed now, then it was already," Regan said. "But, Lucas, we are as much products of humanity's desires as we are of the Otherworld's madness. *They* sought transcendence. They yearned for superhumans and something greater than themselves. They *wanted* us. Let's go show them what their search has wrought."

Lucas nodded. "All right."

"Where shall we go first?" Regan asked.

Lucas's answer was instantaneous. One good deed wouldn't be enough to find redemption, but perhaps it would be a start. "We're going to Japan."

OUTRO

BRIEFING OMEGA

For Golden Dawn-approved eyes only.

Following the reappearance of the Kadath facility and the emergence of the seemingly impenetrable field erected around it, we have received numerous reports of two entities emerging from the ocean near the station's relative position. These two beings were seen hovering above the waves before proceeding to travel across the ocean's surface at a staggering speed. While initial recordings were, unfortunately, lacking in quality, we can confirm that one of the entities does indeed appear to be Regan Waite, adopted daughter of former Leng Corporation CEO Meredith Waite. Regan Waite is also the only known success of our long-running consciousness fusion projects.

Further information has thus far been difficult to attain, though two breakthroughs have recently come to light. We have learned that a test subject injected into one of our most recent consciousness fusion tests has reappeared in her Japanese hometown. We have thus far been unable to apprehend this subject for questioning, but our top units are working to acquire her. More successful, though, was our detainment of a submersible escaping Kadath, containing a lone passenger: a heavy miner hybrid named Charles Ryan, previously thought deceased. He is currently being debriefed, with full results forthcoming. Of note, though, is his mention of a Doctor Lucas Kane – an individual for whom there are no known records. We think it is highly probable this Dr. Kane could be a *second* successful consciousness fusion product. Should this be the case, it is likely he was the one accompanying Regan Waite. We are combing our databases for every such experiment currently underway to ascertain from which one this Dr. Kane could have arisen.

While Kadath has returned, the particle waves the anomaly was previously producing have continued unabated – though in an altered state. It is not yet known what effect this alteration will have on the previously recorded rise worldwide of both receptors and apparitions. Initial findings seem to indicate that the rate of secondary anomalies occurring around the world has not declined. In actuality, it may even have increased.

Also unknown is the effect these two entities will have on our mission – and Earth overall – in the foreseeable future. We certainly *hope* they have come to usher the worthy enlightened into the transcendent golden dawn. However, should their aims prove less altruistic (or even hostile to our mission), measures are being implemented to nullify whatever threat they may ultimately pose.

Unfortunately, without further information, we are essentially running blind regarding these two beings. Only time will tell what they ultimately desire or how they will proceed. I fear we will simply have to bide our time until they finally make their move.

END COMMUNICATION

THE AUTHOR

Byron Leavitt lives with his wife and two daughters in a centennial Swiss-style house in Washington State. Many residents have come and gone throughout the years - carnivorous plants, jellyfish, a clowder of cats, and praying mantises, to name a few - but the ones who have always remained are Byron's gremlin, Brain, his butler, Egad, Headless Harvey, and the Gargoyle Baby (not to mention Grandma Phyllis in the basement.) Perhaps it's no surprise that Byron lives to revel in the weird and to cultivate wonder.

Byron is the author of the non-fiction book *Of Hope and Cancer*, as well as the forthcoming fantasy novels *The Fish in Jonah's Puddle (To Say Nothing of the Demon)* and *Alayaka*. He also wrote all of the story content for the hit board game *Deep Madness* and its accompanying book *The Art of Deep Madness*. Byron is currently working on the storybooks for the forthcoming *Deep Madness* prequel *Dawn of Madness*, a story-driven horror experience in a board game. He is very grateful to work at a company where he gets to play with monsters all day.

You can connect with Byron on Facebook at https://www.facebook.com/ByronCLeavitt. You can also learn more about him and his works on his website, which you can find at https://byronleavitt.com.

Diemension Games is an indie game studio and publisher founded by Roger Ho, Yichuan Wang, and Cherry Li. Diemension exists to create board games set in dark, wondrous, and immersive worlds with intense, pulse-pounding gameplay as well as art that is simultaneously gorgeous and gruesome. Diemension Games's first title, *Deep Madness*, raised over $4 million USD across two crowdfunding campaigns, releasing to very positive reviews. It has since developed a loyal fanbase of gamers located around the world. The company's second title, *Dawn of Madness*, raised over $2 million USD through a conjoined Kickstarter and preorder campaign, and is currently in development. Their next games, *Twisted Fables* and *Celestial*, will launch crowdfunding campaigns in 2020 and 2021, respectively.

For all the latest news and updates about Diemension Games's projects, be sure to visit https://diemensiongames.com and like the Diemension Games Facebook page at https://www.facebook.com/diemensiongames.

Descend through the ocean depths into unbridled madness.

Deep Madness is a cooperative board game of survival horror for 1-6 players. Journey with a team of investigators to the Kadath deep-sea mining facility, and discover the dark secrets lurking on the ocean floor. Something is down there, waiting for you: an ancient, incomprehensible power that channels your deepest fears and gives them flesh.

With each successive chapter, the nightmare unravels before you, ratcheting up the tension through fiendish gameplay and a progressively psychedelic story. Fight to stay alive as you hold your breath through flooded rooms while throbbing madness devours the station around you. Flee from the squirming hordes of monsters clambering down the corridors, and face off against the horrific Epic Monsters as each round brings you closer to certain doom. The question is not if you will discover the truth buried within Kadath's claustrophobic depths: it's if you will survive long enough to tell anyone about it.

Featuring 66 highly detailed plastic miniatures in the base

game alone (and over 259 across all of the expansions), *Deep Madness* is a tense, nail-biting experience you won't soon forget. Follow the latest about *Deep Madness* and the Deep Madness Universe at https://diemensiongames.com, and on Facebook at https://www.facebook.com/deepmadnessgame. Also, be sure to join the official Deep Madness Universe Facebook group at https://www.facebook.com/groups/DeepMadnessFans to interact with the fans of the Deep Madness Universe.

Before there was the deep, there was the dawn.

Dawn of Madness is a narrative-driven board game for 1-4 players that seeks not just to engross you, but actually to scare you. Dive into the psyches of the Wanderers, people transported to another dimension called the Otherworld that has eviscerated their minds and made their fragmented lives a part of its nightmarish hellscape. Learn the twisted secrets that led you to this strange place and confront your inner Terrors along the way. Fight the draw of your Malformations (the unnerving reflections of the darkest cesspools within your soul) and square off against the horrific Abominations: established denizens of the Otherworld out to devour you whole. Build up your Wanderer using fragments of the memories and situations you experience, and prepare yourself for a confrontation with one or more of your unique Final Bosses — gigantic, relentless horrors that hit uncomfortably close to home.

Each Wanderer features his or her own storybook chock-full of disturbing, surreal tales that change and shift depending on how you play the game, as well as four different endings you obtain through the choices you make. Available in both a standee version and one with 54 intricately detailed, decidedly unsettling miniatures (each one a unique sculpt, with approximately 116 miniatures available across all expansions), *Dawn of Madness* is the true horror experience you've been waiting for in a board game.

Learn more about *Dawn of Madness* by visiting https://diemensiongames.com or visiting the Deep Madness Universe Facebook page at https://www.facebook.com/deepmadnessgame. Also, be sure to join the official Deep Madness Universe Facebook group at https://www.facebook.com/groups/DeepMadnessFans to interact with the fans of the Deep Madness Universe.

Twisted Fables is a high-octane fairytale smackdown for 2-4 players. Inspired by 2D sidescrolling fighting games, *Twisted Fables* brings together some of the most cherished heroines from myth, history, and story and thrusts them into a fractured universe steeped in science fiction, steampunk, and magic. Join Red Riding Hood the cybernetic assassin, Sleeping Beauty the asylum patient,

Mulan the interstellar shock trooper, and Snow White the poisonous queen as their worlds collide, thrusting them into a no-holds-barred battle for survival and domination.

Featuring a unique spin on deck-building and fast, frantic gameplay that is both highly customizable and strategic, *Twisted Fables* is coming soon from Diemension Games. Follow *Twisted Fables* at https://www.facebook. com/TwistedFablesGame.

CELESTIAL

Long before the days of man, one of the Nine Dawn named PanGu created a race of beings that were both beautiful and mighty. He called this race the Celestials. Time passed, and PanGu was all but forgotten – as were the terrors from which he sought to shelter his creations. But now a crack has formed in the world's façade, allowing the dark sea roiling behind it to seep through. Death no longer means what it used to, and forces across the Four Dimensions are stirring to life. Strange, warped reanimated warriors are arising in the East. The scholar G'gong is leading a pilgrimage to the Void of Kun'Lun in the West, with the intent of razing PanGu's dominion to the ground. And in the South, the remaining Guardians of the Four Dimensions gather at Buzhou Mountain to prepare for war.

Celestial is a 1-2 player story-driven skirmish game unlike any other. Part Chinese mythology, part Lovecraftian horror, and part brutal epic fantasy, *Celestial* will be a board gaming experience you won't soon forget. Follow *Celestial* at https://www.facebook.com/celestialminiature.

Thank you for reading.

And thank you, once again, to all of our Kickstarter backers.

You are the reason this book and our company exist.

For all of your support (whether financially, verbally, or otherwise), we are unendingly grateful.